She was turned on

Not once in her life had Anna locked eyes with a strange man and felt the tingle of desire that was now vibrating its way through her body.

She flicked her eyes to the rearview mirror, trying to catch another glimpse of Marc the hottie in the backseat. His gaze was fixed on something in the front of the car. Perhaps she had just imagined that moment of heat when their eyes had locked?

Then she followed his eye line, and saw that her skirt had ridden up and that he was focused on the lacy top of her stocking, visible through the side slit. Her skin tingled as if he'd actually touched her. When she lifted her gaze to the mirror, he was watching her, his expression knowing. He looked as if he knew his way around the bedroom. In fact, he looked as if he'd written the book on passion, then banged out a couple of sequels for good measure.

No doubt about it. Anna wanted him…and she was definitely going to get him.

Dear Reader,

I've always been fascinated by the idea of a female chauffeur, ever since I saw *Sabrina* and wondered, what if *she* was the chauffeur, and not her father? Many years later Anna Jackson popped out of my laptop and onto the page.

The really fun part about this book was going to Bali for research. The sacrifices a girl has to make... I managed to squeeze five massages and two facials into ten days, a triumph of scheduling. And without giving too much away, yes, Anna's massage experience borrowed heavily from my own. Enough said.

I really enjoyed hearing from readers after my first Harlequin Blaze novel, *Can't Get Enough,* was published last year. Thank you! Writing is a lonely sport, and it's nice to know when something has struck a chord with people, so I'd love to hear from you either via e-mail to sarahjmayberry@hotmail.com, or in care of Harlequin Books, 225 Duncan Mill Road, Don Mills, Ontario M3B 3K9, Canada.

Cheers for now,

Sarah Mayberry

CRUISE CONTROL
Sarah Mayberry

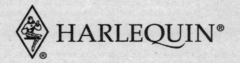

HARLEQUIN®

TORONTO • NEW YORK • LONDON
AMSTERDAM • PARIS • SYDNEY • HAMBURG
STOCKHOLM • ATHENS • TOKYO • MILAN • MADRID
PRAGUE • WARSAW • BUDAPEST • AUCKLAND

ISBN 0-373-79255-7

CRUISE CONTROL

Copyright © 2006 by Small Cow Productions PTY Ltd.

All rights reserved. Except for use in any review, the reproduction or utilization of this work in whole or in part in any form by any electronic, mechanical or other means, now known or hereafter invented, including xerography, photocopying and recording, or in any information storage or retrieval system, is forbidden without the written permission of the publisher, Harlequin Enterprises Limited, 225 Duncan Mill Road, Don Mills, Ontario, Canada M3B 3K9.

All characters in this book have no existence outside the imagination of the author and have no relation whatsoever to anyone bearing the same name or names. They are not even distantly inspired by any individual known or unknown to the author, and all incidents are pure invention.

This edition published by arrangement with Harlequin Books S.A.

® and TM are trademarks of the publisher. Trademarks indicated with ® are registered in the United States Patent and Trademark Office, the Canadian Trade Marks Office and in other countries.

www.eHarlequin.com

Printed in U.S.A.

ABOUT THE AUTHOR

Sarah Mayberry is an Australian currently living in New Zealand. She lives very happily with her partner of many years, Chris, who is also a writer. Before writing for Harlequin, she worked in publishing and as a scriptwriter/story person on television drama. Like her characters, Sarah has a "thing" for cars and romance, and she firmly contends that if everyone drove a Mini Cooper, there would be world peace.

Books by Sarah Mayberry

HARLEQUIN BLAZE

Don't miss any of our special offers. Write to us at the following address for information on our newest releases.

Harlequin Reader Service
U.S.: 3010 Walden Ave., P.O. Box 1325, Buffalo, NY 14269
Canadian: P.O. Box 609, Fort Erie, Ont. L2A 5X3

A special thanks to my father and brother for letting me "be inspired" by their lives for this book, and to my stepmum, Moira.

Thanks also to Caz, La-La, Satan, Hanky Panky and Emms for their support, and to Wanda for making me better. And of course, Chris. Where would I be without you?

1

"ANNA JACKSON?"

Anna swiveled on her heel, turning toward the voice. The woman standing in front of her on the busy Sydney street was dressed in a neat navy suit, her hair perfectly coiffed, her face stretched into an expression of incredulity.

"It *is* you!"

Anna smiled. She still got a buzz out of people's reactions to the new her. Especially her old law colleagues.

"Hey, Mary. How are things?"

"You look so different!" Mary said, shaking her head. "I would have walked right past you. I mean, I nearly did."

"It was time for a change. You know how it is." Anna shrugged.

Mary's hand strayed to her own sensible brown bob as she eyed Anna's new short and spiky platinum blond haircut. "I haven't seen you around for ages," Mary said, fishing for information.

"I quit," Anna said simply.

"Oh. Wow. I didn't hear. So which firm did you go to? I know Sullivan and Makepeace were looking for someone in corporate governance…."

"Actually, I've started up my own business," Anna said lightly. She glanced toward the gleaming black Mercedes sedan parked behind her. Mary followed her gaze, frowning as she took in the car's license plates: Lady Driver.

"It's a luxury car service," Anna explained. "High-end business, that kind of thing."

"You mean you've quit law?" Mary said. She sounded scandalized, as though Anna had just confessed to running a string of hookers.

"Yep."

Mary shook her head. "Why on earth would you do that? You're such a great lawyer, Anna. One of the best. God, I used to sweat buckets when I knew I was coming up against you."

Anna had gotten used to people not understanding why she'd tossed in her career, but she was surprised at the tug of pride she felt at the other woman's compliment. "Really?" It was hard not to feel flattered.

"Hell, yeah. Formidable—that's how my senior partner once described you," Mary said admiringly.

The buzz of pride faded. *Formidable.* Great. Just how she wanted to be remembered.

"I guess I decided that there was more to life than work," Anna said.

Mary opened her mouth to argue, but maybe she saw something in Anna's face because she shut it again without saying a word. The look she shot Anna was equal parts confusion and concern.

Anna knew what she was thinking—Mary simply couldn't understand how anyone could turn her back on a prestigious, lucrative career to become a glorified taxi driver. For a split second Anna considered telling her. But it was her business, her very private business. Anyway, it wouldn't take the other woman long to find out why Anna had quit her job and turned her life around. The Sydney law community was big, but not that big. Mary would go back to the oak-lined offices of her firm and ask the right people the right questions, and within an hour she'd know.

"Breast cancer," someone would tell Mary in a hushed tone. *"Went off the rails, threw it all in."*

"Well. I wish you the best of luck," Mary finally said. "If I know you, you'll have a fleet of cars within a year."

Anna just smiled. She couldn't think of anything she wanted less, but Mary was being kind.

"Thanks. Look after yourself," Anna said.

Giving her one last, uncertain glance, Mary strode briskly away. No doubt she was heading off to wage a war of words with a sharp-witted foe, Anna guessed. Precedents would be cited, clauses referred to. Veiled threats would be tossed back and forth as the lawyers circled one another. It would be tense and exciting and challenging.

Anna narrowed her eyes to follow Mary's retreating figure. There had been times in the past five weeks since Lady Driver had gotten off the ground when she'd been assailed with doubts about what she'd done. It was all so new, so different, so scary. But watching Mary walk away, Anna realized that if ever she'd had any doubts about giving up her law career, they'd just evaporated completely. She wouldn't trade places with the other woman for anything—not even her own string of hookers.

She was still smiling when she turned back to the car. The dark tinted windows reflected her image back at her, and her smile broadened as she took in the striking-looking woman she'd become. First, there was the hair. Annie Lennox, eat your heart out. Then there was the hot pink curve of her lips and the smoky kohl of her eyes—gone were the somber, conservative browns and grays of her old makeup palette, never to be seen again. And instead of the severe, staid style of her previous suits, she now wore a figure-hugging, sexy skirt suit in dark charcoal with a hot pink pinstripe running through it.

There was hardly a trace of the old Anna Jackson left, she assured herself. That was why she liked it so much when people from her former life like Mary barely recognized her.

Sliding into the driver's seat, Anna put her chauffeur's cap on.

Knowing she still had ten minutes to kill until her next client, she eased her small leather-bound notebook from the side pocket of the car door and flipped it open to a well-thumbed page. She couldn't look at the words inscribed there without remembering the setting she'd written them in—the sterile whiteness of the hospital, the muffled clatter of nurses doing their rounds, the all-pervading smell of antiseptic. As always, a wave of fear gripped her as she recalled the hours of waiting and wondering.

But she needed the fear. It kept her honest, kept her nose to the grindstone as she worked to change her life around. Because she'd promised herself that she'd change if she got a second chance. And it was tempting to let things slide, to go easy on herself now that the fear was receding.

She read over the list, even though she didn't really need prompting to remember the pledges she'd made to herself. *Change job*—crossed out now. *Make over me,* also crossed out. The rest of the list was still intact, waiting to be tackled.

She frowned down at the page as she ran her eye over point number two again. It wasn't entirely true, was it? She wasn't really *made over.* Not when she considered that she'd barely addressed all the other things on her list. *Be more impulsive* still challenged her. Along with *be adventurous.* There was a sublist of things she wanted to try under that one—scuba diving, skydiving, bungee jumping, motorbike riding, snowboarding. And she hadn't done a thing about tackling any of them. But nothing on her wish list caused her to swallow nervously and twitch in her seat quite so much as item number five: *Need more passion in my life.* She'd even underlined it several times, just to highlight to herself how important it was.

And she'd done absolutely nothing about it. It had been a year, and she'd changed her hair, her wardrobe, her makeup, her job. But she kept shying away from the hard stuff. The really life-changing stuff.

The sound of the back passenger door opening interrupted her musings and she twitched the rearview mirror into place just in time to make eye contact with the man who was ducking his head into her car.

"You here to pick up the Lewis party? Sorry, we're a bit early," he said. He had a round, friendly face, and Anna found herself smiling at him.

"Not a problem," she said. Sliding the notebook back into the side pocket, she reached for the door, preparing to usher her clients into the back of the car.

"It's fine, stay where you are," the man assured her.

He turned away to talk to someone outside, then slid into the backseat. A second man followed, but Anna was too busy starting the car to register him immediately.

Then she flicked her eyes up to the rearview mirror, and found herself gazing into eyes so dark they were almost black. No, not black, she swiftly corrected herself—a very dark brown, like rich, bittersweet chocolate. Thick, dark lashes and a strong, straight nose added determination to a face that Anna quickly saw was dangerously attractive. Black hair, high cheekbones, olive skin and the shadow of stubble on his jaw completed the picture. And his mouth—she'd thought the eyes were killer, but the mouth was something else altogether. A chiseled curve, the top lip slightly thinner than the luscious, provocative bottom lip, with the corners turned up as though its owner was always on the verge of laughter.

There was something smoldering and intent and hungry about his gaze as he locked eyes with her in the mirror. A shiver ran down her spine, and she stirred in her seat, suddenly unable to keep still.

"You've got the address, right?" the first man asked, and Anna blinked.

"Yes," she said, wrenching her eyes forward.

She concentrated on her driving, smoothly pulling out into the traffic.

But as she wove her way confidently through the lunchtime rush, a frown creased her forehead as she registered that her heart was beating a little faster. And her palms were damp on the steering wheel. And her breasts felt heavy and full in her bra. It took her a moment to identify the feeling.

She was turned on.

As revelations went, it was a biggy. She only just stopped herself from planting a foot on the brake and bringing the car to a screeching halt. It had been a long time—a *looonnngggg* time—since she'd felt anything like desire. But surely it took more than a look—a few seconds of eye contact, if she was getting specific—to switch that part of herself back on?

Not once in her life had she ever locked eyes with a strange man and felt the tingle of desire that was even now vibrating its way through her body. This sort of thing didn't happen to her. All her past relationships had grown out of mutual respect and affection.

She was thrown, completely thrown. She felt oddly vulnerable and exposed, too. She flicked her eyes back up to the rearview mirror, trying to make sense of this phenomenon. She felt a strange relief when she saw his dark gaze was fixed intently on something in the front of the car now. Perhaps she had just imagined that moment of heat when their eyes had locked?

Then she followed his sight line, and saw that her pencil-slim skirt had ridden up and that he was fixated on the lacy top of her stay-up stocking—visible through the side slit of her skirt—along with a good expanse of thigh.

She couldn't help herself—she pushed her skirt down instantly. When she lifted her gaze to the mirror again, he was watching her, his eyes knowing.

She riveted her attention on the road ahead, swallowing nervously. Oh, boy. She had no idea how to handle this situation. He was obviously interested. What if he asked her out? How would she say no without offending him? How awkward. God, she was hopeless in these kinds of scenarios. This was why she'd always turned to work instead of putting herself out there more.

Tension tightening her belly, Anna glanced at the clock in the dash. Five more minutes, and they'd be at their destination and he'd be gone. She just had to endure five more minutes….

Then she remembered her list.

Hadn't she just been sitting here, worrying over how to get more passion into her life? And wasn't there a bona fide sex god in the back of her car right now—*and she was worrying over how to get rid of him?* She took a deep, unsettled breath. This was what she'd just admitted to herself, wasn't it—she'd changed the easy stuff, but now that the going was getting tough, she was balking.

She snuck another peek at him. He was the kind of man she'd only ever stared at in expensive restaurants—sexy, powerful, confident. He looked as though he knew his way around the bedroom. In fact, he looked as though he'd written the book on passion, then banged out a couple of sequels for good measure.

Her mind began to race. If she was being true to her undertaking to change her world around, she would do something about this. She'd ask him out. Or do whatever it was that women did to get men to ask them out.

She felt like a born-again virgin, uncertain and awkward and completely clueless. And, if she were being completely honest with herself, excited. Because he was hot. He was definitely hot.

Oh-boy-oh-boy. Could she do this? Could she really do this? She felt as though she was standing on the edge of a precipice, preparing to take a dive into the unknown.

The ring of a phone broke into her hectic thoughts. She watched in the mirror as Mr. Sexy flipped his cell phone open with a smooth wrist action. He had nice hands, she noted, with long, strong-looking fingers. Her stomach clenched as she imagined him touching her. Stroking her hot skin. Tracing the curve of her—

She shook her head, amazed at how quickly her thoughts had gotten out of control. She'd never responded to a man like this. Ever.

"Yes, Sally?" he said into the phone.

It was the first time he'd spoken. His voice was deep and low, a perfect match for the rest of him. Something else to add to the erotic fantasy that was rapidly taking shape in her subconscious.

"I'm sorry, but it's out of the question," he said into the phone. She saw that he was frowning, his gaze focused on the paperwork he'd pulled out of his briefcase. "I need you to help with the bid presentations."

There was an implacable note to his voice that caught her attention. Eyes fixed on the road ahead, she frowned.

He sighed heavily, obviously frustrated with what he was hearing from his caller.

"Let me ask you one question, Sally—are you committed to this job or not? Because we discussed the issue of work hours before you started, if I remember correctly," he said.

His tone was hard and cold, and Anna felt her lip curling into an instinctive snarl. *What a jerk.*

Instantly she remembered the difficult weeks when she'd first gotten home from the hospital. She'd been wrestling with so many things during that time and the senior partners at her law firm had called her, one after the other, to consult on cases. And one after the other, they'd all hedged their way around to asking her to cut short her sick leave and return to work. She'd come back—but only to wind up her most pressing cases and hand in her resignation. It had taken several months to extract herself from her partnership and prepare the groundwork for Lady Driver, but finally she'd walked away from it all. Now the memory of their lack of consideration—their lack of humanity—

lit a renewed fire of anger in her belly. They'd been so callous, so unfeeling. And she'd almost wasted her life working alongside them.

And now this…*jerk* in the back of her car was bullying one of his employees in much the same way. She had to bite her tongue to stop herself from saying something. Instead, she ground her teeth together and settled for braking late at a red light, bringing the car to an abrupt halt and jostling her passengers. He glanced up, annoyed at the less-than-smooth ride. Anna eyed him coldly in the rearview mirror.

"Sorry," she said, her tone implying she was anything but.

He ended his call, and she studied his face briefly before accelerating away from the intersection. Not by the flicker of an eyelid did he look remotely guilty or uncomfortable about what he'd just done.

The initial desire she'd felt when she looked at him curdled into disdain now that she saw him for the arrogant business bully he was. So what if he had broad shoulders and bedroom eyes? He had no soul, and he was happy to suck the joy out of other people's lives. Her world had once been filled with people like him. But not anymore.

Her hands firmed on the steering wheel. The sooner this trip was over, the better, list or no list. For a few crazy moments there she'd let herself get swept up in Mr. Arrogant's superficial charm, but now she saw him for what he was. Once he was gone, she would wind down the windows and clear his woody aftershave from her car, and just as easily flush away her body's aberrant reaction to him.

Relief washed through her, and she told herself it was because she'd soon be rid of a man she'd swiftly decided she didn't like. But then her innate self-honesty kicked in and she admitted to herself that maybe some of her relief was because she didn't have to push herself out of her sexual comfort zone and acknowledge the zing of attraction between the two of them. It was all so much easier and more manageable now she knew he was a jerk.

She should probably be disappointed in herself, she knew. But he'd taken the pressure off with his boorish behavior. Another day, with another man, she'd be braver, bolder, she promised herself.

For now, she just wanted to get the slave driver out of her car. Her lips pressed into a determined line, she eased her foot down on the accelerator.

IN THE BACK OF THE CAR, Marc stared absently at the blur of traffic and buildings rushing by outside, wishing he could dismiss his niece's phone call from his mind as easily as he'd extracted himself from the call itself. Sally was just eighteen, and supposedly keen to find a place in his business and start her working life, rather than slog her way through three years of university doing a commerce degree. He wasn't opposed to her ambition—in fact, he admired it—but he expected her to earn her place on his team. He'd built his computer solutions business up from nothing, and he'd never let anyone take a free ride. The truth was, he was disappointed that Sally thought she could skip out early from work to go skiing for the weekend just because she was related to the boss. She was a good kid, but they were in for a bumpy ride if this was a sign of things to come.

Without him consciously willing it, his gaze wandered back to the front of the car. More specifically, to the legs of the woman behind the wheel. Clearly, despite the fact that he'd already told himself he wasn't interested, subconsciously he was hoping for another glimpse of the expanse of lace and leg that had been so abruptly withdrawn from display. He frowned, wrenching his eyes away. Tara's betrayal had burned him badly, and the last thing he needed or wanted was to be attracted to someone.

Ten years of marriage, flushed away. He couldn't think about it without feeling a surge of bitterness. He'd been so determined to make his marriage work. He'd dedicated his life to building the security they needed before they started a family. And just when everything had come to fruition, he'd walked in on Tara and John.... More fool him for catching an early flight home to spend more time with his wife.

But despite his best intentions, despite having every reason in the world not to, his gaze kept creeping toward the front of the car.

She was focused on the road, and he studied her face in profile. Her hair was hidden beneath a traditional chauffeur's hat, but she had a small, straight nose, sloping cheekbones and a full, hot pink mouth that promised almost as much as those legs. Her driver ID was displayed on the dashboard, and he saw her name was Anna Jackson.

I wonder if you're as hot as that look you gave me, Anna?

Then he remembered the way she'd pulled her skirt down, and how her eyes had reprimanded him for looking in the first place.

He wasn't in the mood to play games. If she hoped to intrigue him or excite him with a pretense at being coy, she could think again—he wasn't in the market.

Registering the tightness in his trousers, he corrected himself—okay, maybe he was in the market, but not for the sort of cat-and-mouse courtship Anna-the-chauffeur seemed to be offering with her come-hither eyes and her stay-away skirt tweak. Now, if she was to offer him one hot night, no holds barred, no strings attached... That was about his speed right now.

"Marc, have you been listening to a word I've said?" Gary said beside him, and Marc realized that the background drone he'd been tuning out had been his friend debriefing after their recent meeting.

"I'm with you," he said, tearing his eyes away from her.

"So are we still going ahead with the offer?" Gary asked.

"Yep," Marc said.

Gary looked baffled. "Even after all the stuff they just revealed about their expected losses for this financial year?"

Marc smiled, his razor-sharp mind winging back to that
meeting. The executives of Sum Systems had given every appear-
ance of being frank and earnest when they revealed the perilous
state of the company's finances. Apparently their little routine
had even been good enough to convince Gary.

"Have you ever walked into a business and been granted full
access to the books like that?" Marc asked, idly smoothing a hand
over the car's supple leather upholstery.

Gary opened his mouth to speak, paused, then suddenly broke
into a smile.

"Right. I see." He nodded. "They're trying to put us off."

"Oh, yeah. Just a little," Marc agreed.

"But we're not going to be put off," Gary said.

"Correct," Marc confirmed.

Gary nodded again, then fell into silence. Marc used the opportunity to glance at the driver. Despite himself, he was intrigued. She kept her gaze firmly pinned on the road, but he
could tell she was aware of him. A sudden urge gripped him, and
he leaned forward in his seat.

"It's okay, I'm not going to take you up on your offer," he said
in her ear.

He watched in the rearview mirror as her toffee brown eyes
widened with shock.

"I beg your pardon?" she asked, her tone chilly.

"You heard me. You're off the hook," he said, enjoying the
flush of color that ran up her cheeks.

Her eyes flashed, and he was aware of Gary staring at him,
mouth agape.

Her mouth firmed, and he saw a muscle pulse in her jaw. Then
she flicked the indicator on, and pulled the car over. For a second
he thought she was about to kick him out of the car—then he saw
that they'd arrived at his company headquarters. He checked his
watch, impressed. She'd gotten him from downtown George

Street, across the Sydney Harbour Bridge and into the north shore in under ten minutes.

"Nice timing," he said drily.

"I thought so," she said before opening her door and sliding out of the car.

Gary shifted uncomfortably beside him. "Do you know her?" he whispered furtively.

Marc didn't bother responding; his attention was all on the woman who was even now moving to open Gary's door. She was dressed in a charcoal gray pinstripe skirt, slim-line, with a matching fitted jacket. The fabric clung to her curves as she walked, and he saw that the rest of her body more than lived up to the promise made by that flash of thigh earlier. She was a very sexy woman. Full-breasted, if he was any judge, with real curves, not all ribs and hips like the half-starved women in his social circle.

Feeling his body tightening once more, Marc realized that he was fixating on Anna Jackson again. Hadn't he just decided he wasn't in the market for anything? It disturbed him that in the space of a ten-minute car ride, their driver had managed to almost completely dominate his thoughts.

This is not going to happen, he decided abruptly. He didn't need this kind of complication in his life, no matter how hot the package it came wrapped in. Wanting someone, desiring them, was dangerously close to needing them. Depending on them. And he'd learned the hard way that there was no such thing as loyalty, trust or honor between men and women. He wasn't prepared to make the same mistake twice. There were plenty of other women out there who could scratch a physical itch, all of them much safer bets than a woman who, for whatever reason, seemed to hold some fascination for him.

Fascination he did not need. His life, his world, was all about control. And he wasn't about to change it for a luscious mouth and sexy thighs.

Despite the fact that she was circling around to open his door, he beat her to it, pushing it open and surging out of the car. Not bothering to look at her—proving to himself that he didn't need to, or even want to—Marc strode toward the entrance of his company headquarters.

And that, he thought to himself, *is the end of that.*

IT WAS ALMOST FOUR O'CLOCK before Anna found the wallet. Many of her passengers brought newspapers or magazines with them, along with takeaway coffees, and the odds were good that they would leave their castoffs behind when they exited at the end of their trip. In the five weeks she'd been in business, Anna had formed the habit of checking on the rear of the car after each client to ensure it was at its best for her next passengers. But the wallet had wedged itself between the door and the seat cushion, which explained why she hadn't spotted it earlier.

Made from the softest black leather, the wallet was slim and very expensive looking. Just holding it in her hand gave her an odd feeling of prescience, and when she opened it to check for ID she wasn't really surprised to learn that it belonged to Marc Lewis, he of the slave-driving ethos and burning bedroom eyes.

"Wouldn't you know it," she muttered to herself, studying his driver's license photo. She looked like a surprised frog in hers; he, of course, looked sleek and sexy. Typical.

Sighing, Anna checked her job sheet for contact details, and pulled out her mobile phone. A feminine voice answered on the second ring.

"Lewis Technologies."

"This is Anna Jackson calling from the car service that Mr. Lewis booked this afternoon. I'm ringing to let you know he left his wallet in my car," Anna said briskly.

She opened her mouth to explain that she would drop it off when she was scheduled to be on the north shore again on her next job, but after a second she became aware that she was talking to thin air. She was about to redial when a male voice sounded in her ear.

"I understand you have my wallet."

It was him. The deep husk of his voice made her shiver. What was it about this man that got to her so badly? She cleared her throat.

"Yes, that's right. I'll be on the north shore again this afternoon—" she said, but he cut her off impatiently.

"No good. I'm heading out to Manly now," he said, naming a suburb way across town.

"Well, I'll just leave it at reception in your building for you," she said tartly, her hackles rising all over again at his high-handed attitude.

"I need it this evening, I've got an important dinner at the opera house," he said. He was clearly annoyed. Which made two of them.

"Don't you have a lackey who can run your wallet to you, Mr. Lewis? I really don't have the time to be chasing you across town," she said coolly. Ten years of practicing law had given her a killer business voice, and she used it to full effect.

"My lackeys, as you call them, are all busy doing their jobs. Your job, I understand, is to drive people places. What would it take for you to bring my wallet to me at the opera house at seven this evening?"

Her first impulse was to name a ridiculous sum to penalize him for his unending egotism. But then she remembered that she was the owner of a fledgling small business.

Sighing, she slid her cap off and ran her hand through her hair.

"What's on at the opera?" she asked.

"I beg your pardon?"

"Are they still performing *Carmen?*"

There was long silence, then she heard him talking to someone else. "*Carmen's* still running," he finally confirmed.

"I'll meet you on the steps at seven," she said crisply, making a snap decision.

Carmen was one of her favorite operas, and part of her promise to herself in her new life was to be more spontaneous.

"Bill the company for your time," he said dismissively.

"Steps at seven," she repeated, then ended the call before she was tempted to tell him she'd thrown his wallet in the harbor.

Why did he annoy her so much? He was just a typical, run-of-the-mill successful businessman—used to getting what he wanted, when he wanted it. She bet he was rude to waitresses, and that he treated his staff like disposable machines.

But you still think he's sexy, the honest little voice in her head chimed in. She shied away from the thought, not wanting to go there.

Determined to distract herself, she spent the time before she had to pick up her last client indulging in some window-shopping. As soon as she saw the dress she knew she had to have it. It was in the window of an upscale boutique in the heart of the city, and she knew without checking that it would be insanely expensive. Old habits of thrift and self-control held her frozen in front of the window for a heartbeat, but then Anna reminded herself that life was now. And she had a mandate to be more impulsive. She'd spent her last thirty-two years planning for some ineffable, unknowable time in the future when she could sit back and enjoy herself. But she'd learned the hard way that life could be snatched from her hands in the blink of an eye.

Within three minutes she was shimmying into the fitted black washed silk dress. The halter neck draped low over her breasts; the waist cinched in tight, accentuating her hips and bust; and the skirt kicked out again at knee length. It was impossible to wear with a bra, and she slid hers off with a definite feeling of decadence. It was the sexiest dress she'd ever seen, let alone worn, and it looked great with the high stilettos the saleswoman recommended. Suppressing the stern voice in the back of her head telling her she couldn't possibly go out in public without a bra, Anna smoothed a hand down the suedelike softness of the skirt. She wanted this dress. She wanted to be the sort of woman who owned a dress like this. She'd overhauled her entire wardrobe since she'd left the law firm, but if she was honest with herself, she'd admit that she'd still played it pretty safe in her choices. A suit was still a suit, even it was more fitted or made from a sexier fabric. But this dress…this dress was a commitment to the new her. Biting her lip, she reached for her credit card.

She was back in her car with the shoes and dress in a bag beside her in under ten minutes. A pleasant expectation warmed her as she dropped off her last client for the day. She was going to the opera to see *Carmen*, and she had a sexy new dress.

Suddenly she realized that there was only one thing missing to make it a perfect evening of impulse and pleasure.

Slotting her phone into the hands-free cradle, Anna turned the Mercedes toward the city. She hit the speed-dial for her brother's mobile phone as she tossed a coin into the toll-booth basket on the way across the Harbour Bridge.

"Danny speaking," her brother said, his voice bright.

"Hey, it's me—what are you up to tonight?" she asked.

"Anna Banana. Is this a trick question?"

"Just answer it," she said, laughing at her brother's mock suspicion.

"I'm as free as a bird," he said instantly.

"Great. Meet me at the opera house. We're going to *Carmen*, my treat," she said.

"Whoa! The lady's going crazy!"

"Dress nice, and get your skates on—the show starts at seven-thirty," she warned him, ending the call before her brother could make any more cracks about her unusual behavior.

Traffic was slow funneling toward the harbor, and she pulled into the underground parking garage at the opera house with just five minutes to spare until her appointment to return Marc Lewis's wallet. Staring at her watch, she reluctantly abandoned her original idea of changing in the ladies' room, then returning her work clothes to the car. Instead, she found a corner parking space and reversed her car into it. Sliding out of the car, she glanced around the deserted, dimly lit garage. There was no one here, and in this dark corner she was virtually assured of privacy. Twenty seconds, thirty seconds maximum, she'd be changed and ready for a glamorous night out. She reached for the buttons on her work shirt, but her fingers staunchly refused to go to work.

Oh, yeah, she was *such* a changed woman.

She gritted her teeth. As much as she wanted to be a wild and crazy femme fatale, she had years of being a good girl to overcome. Crawling into the backseat of her car, she hunched behind the driver's seat and began unbuttoning her blouse. Her elbow connected with the side window as she slid one arm free, then she knocked her head on the roof as she tried to give herself more room. When her watch got caught on the cuff of her shirt, she sighed with frustration and closed her eyes.

Okay, so this wasn't going so well. Untangling her shirt from her watch, she checked the time. She'd chewed up three minutes being Little Miss Prim in the backseat of her car.

"You're such a pussy," she goaded herself. "Who cares if anybody sees? At the end of the day, what does it matter?"

For a moment she had a memory flash of those long hours in hospital, the endless bouts of nausea and the hushed sympathy of her friends and family.

"To hell with it," she muttered under her breath as she stepped out of the car. "What's the worst thing that can happen?"

MARC SLID HIS CAR into a parking space and pulled on the hand brake. Turning off the ignition on his Jaguar convertible, he hit the button to bring the roof up and unfolded himself from the deep bucket seat. He had a few minutes until he was supposed to meet the chauffeur to get his wallet back, and he calmly pulled his suit jacket on. He kept aftershave in the glove compartment for work-to-evening gigs like this, and he sprayed himself perfunctorily before locking the car up and heading for the exit. The underground parking lot smelled of damp and concrete, and he frowned at the dim lighting—it was a thief's wet dream down here.

He was almost at the entrance to the exit stairwell when he saw the woman. At first he just glimpsed a flash of movement out of the corner of his eye, but when he frowned into the dark corner he saw it was a woman standing behind her car door—a half-naked woman. She was down to her bra and skirt, and her back was to him as she slid the catch at the back of her bra loose.

He couldn't quite believe what he was seeing. He froze, completely captivated by the impromptu strip show. As he watched, the woman turned slightly, offering a glimpse of firm, full breasts and a trim torso. Her face was in shadow, but he could see that her hair was short and spiky, accentuating her long neck. Then she was pulling a black dress over her head, shimmying into it. Once the dress reached her waist, she slid down the zipper on her skirt and he caught his breath as the skirt fell to the ground to reveal lacy black bikini panties, a full peach of a butt and lacy stay-up stockings. He was hard in an instant, and he almost called out an objection as the dress was pulled down, masking all that curvy womanhood from his view.

God, maybe he did need a woman. It had been six months since he'd left Tara, after all. If his little encounter with the lady chauffeur today and his current state of arousal were anything to go by, parts of him were obviously missing the joys of feminine companionship.

The woman was ducking down now, doing something with

her shoes. Realizing he was about to get caught ogling like a teenage boy, Marc tore his gaze away and continued crossing to the stairwell.

He took the steps up to ground level two at a time—anything to kill the erection that was straining at his trouser zipper. *Stop thinking about her,* he ordered himself. He had an important business meeting tonight; he couldn't afford to be distracted like this.

The smell of the ocean hit him as he stepped out into the night air. Above him, the stylized white sails of the opera house roof curved up into the darkened sky. Marc sucked in a deep breath and let it out in a rush. Slowly the desire bubbling through his blood dissipated, and as his need faded, his sense of humor returned. He grinned. It wasn't every day that a man got treated to a real live illicit sex fantasy. He should just chalk it up to experience, rather than feel frustrated and vaguely angry that he had so little control over his own desires.

Hell, he could even tell the guys about it over dinner. It'd make a great icebreaker.

The click of high heels on concrete sounded behind him, and he tensed. There was every chance it was the woman from below, coming up the stairs behind him. He couldn't help himself. Despite his resolve not to be captive to his own desire, he had to look, had to confirm the sensual impression he'd received in the shadows underground.

He swiveled on his heel. And froze.

She stood poised at the top of the stairs, her head angled away from him as she scanned the broad steps to the opera house. Her dress—*the* dress—dipped low in the front and clung lovingly to the curves of her hips and thighs, the darkness of the fabric a perfect foil for the smooth creaminess of her skin. She wore dainty high heels, with the barest suggestion of a strap around her ankle. And she was unmistakably the woman who had driven him across town that morning—and, incidentally, driven him crazy with a flash of her lacy black stockings. *Anna Jackson.*

He hadn't seen her hair before, because she'd been wearing a chauffeur's cap. The short white-blond spikes were a surprise, not what he'd expected at all. It suited her, however, the severe hairstyle setting off the planes of her face, highlighting her large eyes and wide mouth.

Her head turned, and he locked eyes with her across the ten feet or so that separated them. He was close enough to see her pupils widen minutely as she met his gaze. And to note the pulse point flickering on her long, elegant neck.

He remembered the voluptuous curve of her breast, glimpsed for just the fraction of a second, and the way she'd smoothed the skirt down over her hips and butt.

He wanted her. He wanted her more than he'd wanted anything in a long time. The realization shook him. Suddenly she'd assumed far too much importance and stature in his world. He didn't want to feel this way about a woman he'd just met for a brief few seconds. He didn't want to feel this way about anyone.

"Mr. Lewis," she said, closing the space between them. The movement caused her breasts to sway subtly. His eyes dropped to follow the movement, then he caught himself and wrenched his attention back to her face.

He clenched his jaw. *This is not going to happen,* he told himself.

"Ms. Jackson," he said.

She held his wallet out. "There you go—signed, sealed and delivered," she said.

He reached for it, determined to avoid the temptation of touching her in any way, no matter how insignificant or incidental. But somehow he overshot the mark, and his fingers brushed hers as he took the wallet from her grasp.

She flinched, almost snatching her hand back. Which meant

she'd felt it, too—the unmistakable rush of electricity as desire met desire.

"Thank you. As I said earlier, bill the company for your time," he said, unable to stop himself from studying the smooth tilt of her cheekbones and the lushness of her mouth.

She shook her head. "It was no bother. I decided to see *Carmen,*" she explained.

"All the same," he said.

"It's fine, Mr. Lewis. I haven't been inconvenienced. It's no big deal." She shrugged.

The movement made her breasts jiggle ever so slightly. When he lifted his eyes back to her face he saw she was blushing, and guessed she'd caught him looking.

"I really have to go," she said, turning away.

Marc reached out on impulse. His fingers wrapped around the soft skin of her forearm just below her elbow, his thumb grazing the tender flesh of her inner arm.

"Wait," he heard himself say.

She froze, her body angled slightly away as if she was afraid to look him in the face.

Marc knew what she'd see there—desire.

"I want—" he said before he caught himself. "Perhaps I could take you out for dinner sometime as a thank-you?"

She tugged gently on her arm, and he released her.

"I don't think that would be a good idea, Mr. Lewis," she said.

"Why not?" he asked. His hunting instincts were aroused now. He hated to lose. In anything—business or pleasure. And he didn't want her to walk away. Suddenly that seemed important.

"Because you're one of my clients, for starters," she said.

"Anna! There you are. I've been looking everywhere."

Marc glanced up to see a tall, ruggedly handsome man bearing down on them. Dressed in a designer suit, he appeared as if he'd just stepped out of the pages of a fashion magazine.

"Danny," she said. She stood on tiptoes to kiss him on the cheek.

Marc took a step back. She had a boyfriend. Or a husband, for all he knew. He felt his lip curl as the old, too familiar bitterness swamped him. He wondered if her husband knew she made a habit of changing in public places. Or that she looked at men with so much heat in her eyes that it was more blatant than any verbal invitation.

"Excuse me. I won't keep you any longer," he said crisply.

Abruptly, he turned on his heel and walked away. He should have trusted his instincts where she was concerned. He wouldn't make the same mistake twice.

2

"HEL-LO! Who on earth is the horn-dog?" Danny asked as Anna watched Marc walk away.

Suddenly she felt as though she could breathe again. She took in a deep, greedy lungful of air, let it out, then turned her attention to her brother.

"Just a client. No one we need to worry about," she said.

She slipped her arm through his and started walking.

"I'm thinking a glass of champagne in the bar, then the show, and supper afterward. Sound good?" she said breezily.

Her pulse was still pounding in her ears after the look Marc had given her as he asked her out for dinner. Although she'd gotten the definite sense that he'd wanted to ask for something else. Something a lot more private than a meal.

Just thinking about it made her breathing go crazy again. Anna closed her eyes and pressed a hand to her stomach—although the part of her that was begging for attention was a lot lower than that.

"That dress is fabulous, by the way," Danny said as they climbed the broad steps to the opera house.

She couldn't help smiling as her brother automatically slipped into the campy drawl he used with his close friends. In the business world, and when he was visiting their father, Danny came across as the straightest of straight men. He called it his great gift—the ability to glide, chameleonlike, through the heterosexual world, with no one the wiser to his sexual orientation. But in his private life, he allowed his true self to show.

"Do you have any idea how Liberace you sound when you say *faaaa*bulous like that?" she asked.

"Yes. It's a very deliberate, much-rehearsed affectation that I've spent hours perfecting," Danny quipped. "So, you want to tell me what this impulse trip to the opera is all about? Are we celebrating something?"

Anna shrugged. "Just having fun, that's all."

Danny did an exaggerated double take. "Ex-*squeeze* me? Anna Jackson having fun? Something is definitely up."

Even though it was true, it made her feel defensive. She stiffened.

"What's wrong with me having a little bit of fun? Is the world going to stop? You have fun all the time, and no one says anything," she said.

Danny blinked, and she knew she had overreacted. Or simply reacted, perhaps. Danny was so used to seeing the cool lawyer's exterior she'd shown the world for so long that any display of feeling was probably a shock. "Sorry. But is it such a big deal that I want to go to the opera? And that I want to wear a nice dress?"

He slid his arm around her shoulder and she felt him press a kiss onto the crown of her head.

"You can take up the bagpipes and run around with your underpants on your head for all I care. You know that."

As they moved toward the door to the exclusive Opera Bar, she could tell he wanted to ask more questions. But they didn't have that kind of relationship. She was the one Danny turned to when he was in a fix and needed advice, not the other way around.

That was the way it had always been. She'd long ago settled into the post of replacement mother-figure for her brother. But the whole situation with Marc had really thrown her tonight. That, and the fact that her to-do list was still woefully short on being complete.

Suddenly she stopped in her tracks. "Danny, if someone asked you to describe me, what would you say?" she asked him abruptly.

Danny looked a little taken aback, but he quickly regained his composure.

"I'd say that you're an attractive, incredibly driven, organized, successful, focused woman," he said, obviously believing that he was serving up what she wanted to hear.

Anna winced. She knew that what he was saying was true, no matter how much she wanted to rail against it. She *had* only changed the easy stuff on her list. It was time to get serious if she really wanted to turn her life around.

She stared at her brother. He was gorgeous—tall, handsome, funny and charming. He always seemed happy, and she gathered from hints that he dropped that he had an active, satisfying love life. In short, he seemed to have it all together.

"I think I need your help," she said decisively, grabbing his arm and dragging him inside the bar.

"Okay," Danny said, looking completely baffled.

"Sit there. I'll get the champagne," she said, indicating a secluded corner where two bar stools were arranged around a high cocktail table.

Danny followed her instructions dutifully while she ordered two flutes of French champagne and quickly joined him.

Sliding onto the stool, Anna bit her lip a little nervously. It wasn't easy to overcome the habits of a lifetime and suddenly open up about her most personal thoughts.

"Anna—have you had some bad news?" her brother asked, his face carefully blank.

She grabbed his hand and gave it a squeeze. "No! No, of course not. All clear on my last scan," she assured him hastily. "Sorry, I was just trying to get my thoughts together. I guess I don't really know where to start."

Danny nodded. "Maybe I can help. Doe this have anything to do with the new hair and the new job and the new clothes?"

"Am I that transparent?"

"Well, I might be a raving queer, but I do notice when my sister has had a makeover," Danny said.

Anna took a big gulp of champagne, then nodded her head firmly. Okay, she was going to do this.

"When I was in hospital, after the operation, I made a list," she said boldly. "I was still waiting for the test results to come back, to find out if the breast cancer had spread into my lymph nodes, and I started thinking about the things I wanted to change in my life. It was a long list, Danny. Really long. Do you know why?"

She paused to take another big swallow of champagne. Danny was watching her intently, a frown puckering his brow. She answered her own question.

"Because I never do what *I* want to do. I'm always worrying about the future, and what I should do next to achieve this or get that. I'm always doing the *right* thing—not the thing that I really want to do. Do you know what I mean?"

Danny slowly nodded. "I think so. It's something I used to think about, when we were younger. You always put me and Dad first, and I used to worry that you didn't leave anything for yourself. But then you made partner at the law firm, and everything seemed rosy."

"It was. Well, to a certain extent it was. But when I made that list and saw how long it was, I realized how much of my life I'd spent doing what I thought other people expected me to do. Being good. And solid. And responsible. It made me sick. It honestly did. I had to call the nurse for a basin."

Suddenly she suspected that Danny might think she was talking about him, about the way she'd had to step up after their mother had died when Anna was just thirteen.

"I'm not talking about you here, Danny, okay? Or any of that stuff. I did that because I wanted to, because I love you and Dad. Please believe me," she said earnestly.

"It's okay. No offense. You had to grow up too fast, Anna Banana. I've always thought so."

Anna shook her head. She couldn't regret stepping into her mother's shoes. Someone had had to take care of what was left of their family, and her father had been so grief-stricken....

Still, there was no contesting the fact that it had set the pattern for her adult life. She stared at the straw-colored bubbles beading her glass, trying to pull her thoughts together.

"I knew that if I died, that was it, you know? I'd had my chance—and I'd played it safe. So I made myself a promise that if I got the chance, I was going to work my way down the list and start changing my life around."

"Ah," Danny said as though he was suddenly starting to see where she was going with this. "The hair, the job, et cetera, et cetera."

Anna leaned forward, grabbing one of her brother's hands.

"I want to have more fun, Danny. I want to laugh more, and worry less, and live my life instead of just watching it slip away while I save for my retirement."

He gripped her hand tightly. "Love you, Anna Banana."

"Love you, too," she said.

They smiled at each other for a long, emotion-filled moment.

"So, which bit do you need my help for?" Danny asked, signaling for the waiter to bring them another round of champagne. "I am totally and completely at your service, your own personal fairy godmother."

Anna smiled nervously. If she was going to do this, now was the time.

"Well, I've been working my way through my list, crossing things off. But I think I've stalled," she admitted. "I think I need some expert guidance."

"Right," Danny said, still looking confused.

"How many people have you slept with?" she asked abruptly.

Danny flinched. "Whoa, that came out of left field," he said.

"Could you just humor me for a moment? I swear this has a point," Anna said.

"Hey, I don't mind sharing. Somewhere between 'lots' and 'heaps' would be a good estimate." He shrugged. "Too many to count."

Anna tried not to stare. Could she and her brother be more different?

"I've only slept with three men," she blurted, getting the foul deed over and done with. "And I've never had sex outside of a bedroom."

It was Danny's turn to stare. "Anna, you're thirty-two years old. That's barely one man per decade of your life. And it's not like you've been married or anything. What have you been *doing?*" he asked.

She could feel embarrassed heat climbing into her face. "Okay, I'm a freak. I was a late bloomer. I didn't lose my virginity until I was almost out of law school. And I always used to think that there was plenty of time to catch up. Work seemed more important. And saving for the future. And lots of other stupid, nonfun stuff. That's why I need your help now," she said.

"Is this about to get really weird?" Danny joked.

Anna nudged him with her elbow. "Not funny."

She was beginning to regret having said anything. How pathetic she must look, sitting here asking her gay younger brother for advice on how to get laid. There was something to be said for keeping your own counsel—no one ever had to know how stupid your thoughts and feelings were.

"I'm sorry. It was a bad joke. And I think it's great that you want to get some more action. I'm all for the pleasures of the flesh. Hedonism is my middle name," Danny said.

"It's not that I don't like sex—I like it a lot!" Anna asserted, worried her brother now thought she was some kind of prude. "Once I get in the bedroom, everything's fine. I mean, it all works, if you know what I mean."

"I'm pleased to hear it," Danny said drily.

Anna swallowed a healthy mouthful of champagne in a big, stinging gulp. A warm buzz spread through her body—alcohol, and the seductive desire to bare all to her brother. She leaned urgently across the table.

"I want the kind of sex you see in the movies. I want someone to want me so badly he almost tears my clothes off. I'm sick of being colorless and boring and good," she said in a rush. "I want to feel alive, to really know that I'm still here."

To her surprise, she felt a tear roll down her cheek. Danny wiped it off with his thumb, then he reached for her hand and squeezed it again.

"It's okay, you are still here, and you will be for a long time to come," he said reassuringly.

She shook her head. "There are no guarantees, Danny." She sniffed inelegantly.

Danny passed her a freshly laundered handkerchief and began drumming his hands on the tabletop, deep in thought.

"Okay, okay. Sex. *Sexxxxx,*" he mused, as though he was trying to come up with an idea for one of his advertising campaigns. "What we need to do is hook you up with a hot guy. Let me think. There's Ned in accounting. He's cute and single and straight, from what I hear. I could have him over for dinner at my place, set you guys up."

Anna felt a dart of apprehension at the thought of a dinner date and all that it might lead to. "I'm not interested in getting into a relationship with anyone, Danny," she said hastily.

"But I thought that's what you were just saying?" he asked,

clearly baffled. "Did we or did we not just have an entire conversation about you improving your love life?"

"Yes. But I don't want to be tied down. I've just quit the law firm, I've got this new life. I don't want to feel trapped right now," she said, feeling pressured just at the thought of it. She wanted to be free. That was why she'd started up the limo service. She loved driving, and it meant she was outside all day. She was her own boss, and she was beholden to no one for anything. After carrying so much responsibility for so long, she didn't want anyone relying on her, expecting anything of her. The very thought of it made her feel claustrophobic.

"Okay," Danny said slowly. "Then I guess we need to get you a lover. Some red-hot stud who just wants you for your body. A couple of months of dirty-dog shagging and you'll be all caught up."

Anna sighed heavily. "See, this is the problem. I have no idea how to pick up a man, let alone a hot stud. My God, I wouldn't know where to begin," she said glumly. "You know that guy you saw me with before? This thing happened in the car between us earlier today, this eye thing. And there was a moment when I knew it was all on. And I let it go. I simply couldn't go there."

Maybe I am a prude, Anna thought wistfully. *Maybe I should just resign myself to reading about other people's passion in the pages of romance novels.*

"Do you think I've had too many years of coloring in between the lines?" she asked. "Maybe I'm too rigid and stuck in my ways to change. I don't think I've ever done anything in my life that I didn't consider from every angle."

"Anna, you've survived a major life crisis. Just because you didn't throw yourself at the first decent-looking guy who came along doesn't mean you're frigid," Danny reassured her.

"Marc Lewis is not 'decent looking,'" Anna said. "He's… molten. Pure sex. And I spent the whole time he was in the car coming up with excuses for why I couldn't possibly hook up with him, if by some miracle he actually propositioned me. And then, when he did…I chickened out."

Anna stared miserably at her empty champagne glass. Danny looked thoughtful for a moment.

"That's very interesting," he said.

"This is my tragic love life we're talking about here, not some special on the *National Geographic* channel," she moaned.

Danny just smiled smugly at her. "I want you to turn around in your seat and pretend you're looking at that lamp over your left shoulder," he said.

Perplexed, Anna stared at her brother but he just indicated that she should do as he'd instructed. Swiveling in her seat, she looked for the lamp shade Danny had mentioned. A dart of excitement raced through her belly when she saw Marc sitting beneath it, talking to a group of business-suited men at his table. She snatched her gaze away and twisted back to face her brother before Marc could notice her looking.

"Oh, boy," she said breathlessly. "How long has he been here for?"

"A while. Boring holes in your back with those big bad eyes of his," Danny admitted.

"Really? He's been looking at me?" she squeaked.

"Only a lot. So here's what we're going to do—a little seduction 101. I want you to go to the bathroom, and on the way back you're going to try and catch his eye. As soon as you've got his attention, give him a little smile, then come straight over and join me. I'll tell you what he does."

Anna flinched and shook her head. "I can't do that."

"Why not?" Danny asked.

"Because. Then he'd know how I felt."

Danny stared at her. "I think I'm beginning to see the problem," he said.

"And he's a client," Anna said defensively. "And he's an arrogant pig, too. I could never have sex with a man I didn't like."

"Arrogant pigs are great in bed. Trust me."

"Danny, all he's after is sex."

"Which is *so* offensive when all you want to do is play tic-tac-toe with him," Danny said wryly. "Just think about it for a second, Anna. Let yourself go there. You're an adult, he's an adult. You both want the same thing. What's stopping you?"

Anna tried to do what Danny was suggesting, tried to push aside a lifetime's conditioning to open herself up to a new experience.

Problem was, all her life she'd believed that the only thing that made it okay to want to sleep with a man was the fact that you were lining him up for the long haul—sex came with commitment in her book, always had. But she'd just ruled out a relationship, hadn't she?

The leaden weight returned to her belly as she considered the possibility of entering into a long-term relationship. No, definitely no commitment. So it was an affair or nothing. The question was, could she go there?

Having a relationship with someone just for sex—it was such a revolutionary, decadent, amazing concept. She couldn't quite get her head around it. No strings. No thoughts of tomorrow. No commitment. Just sex. Lots of it. In interesting positions, and exotic places. With a man like Marc, who oozed arrogance and power and heat.

Thinking about it made her squirm in her seat.

"I'm a gay man, and not completely tuned into Radio Woman, but I'm going to read that little wriggle as a good sign," Danny said.

For a second Anna allowed herself to indulge the fantasy that she could be the kind of woman who would take what Marc was offering and make hay while the sun shone. She could just stand up, sashay across to his table, then lean down and whisper in his ear. Something like, "Let's skip dinner, and go straight to dessert."

And then he would—

But her brain refused to go there. She couldn't imagine what he would do next, because she'd never been in a situation like that in her life. She'd never said anything so blatant to a man, let alone a man as experienced and knowing as Marc so obviously was.

Sighing heavily, she shook her head. "It's a great theory, Danny, but not for me. I'm just not cut out for that kind of thing," she said. "I think I should concentrate on the skydiving and the motorbike riding."

"Let me get this straight—you'd rather throw yourself out of a plane than let a man know you want to have sex with him?" Danny asked lightly.

"That seems to sum it up," Anna said. She felt a little sick inside. She was disappointed in herself, she realized. Checking her watch, she pushed back her chair and stood. "We'd better go in."

Danny followed her as she headed for the door. Drawing alongside her and taking her arm, he leaned across to whisper in her ear.

"Can't take his eyes off you, darling. Think about it, at least."

And despite everything that she'd just said, Anna felt an illicit thrill race up her spine.

SHE SHOULD HAVE KNOWN that once she'd involved Danny he wouldn't take no for an answer. He let her stew until the following Thursday, then turned up on her doorstep just after nine o'clock.

She was in her pyjamas, and she stared at him and then double-checked the time.

"Don't you normally go to the movies with Dad on Thursdays?" she asked, stepping aside to let him into her apartment.

"Early show," Danny said dismissively as he breezed past her. "I've brought you some inspiration."

He held up a shopping bag and moved to her kitchen table. "You're my new project," he said as he unpacked the bag. "I'm going to turn you into a vixen if it kills me."

"What if I don't want to be a vixen?" Anna challenged,

wrapping her arms around her torso. She'd had plenty of time to fully and completely regret being so frank with her brother that night. What mad impulse had made her bare her soul to him? Like he needed to know his sister was a hard-up, sex-starved neurotic on a self-help mission.

"Too late, you already wrote it on your 'things to do before I die' list. You're committed."

He held up a DVD. "*Top Gun.* Tom Cruise with his shirt off. Val Kilmer with his shirt off. Anthony Edwards with his shirt off. If that's not enough to get you going, I don't know what is. Plus there's that great love scene with Tom and Kelly McGillis."

"You are the straightest gay man I know," she said as she accepted the proffered DVD.

"I can appreciate good work. I'm a connoisseur." He held up a blank-labeled CD. "Music to inspire and motivate. Danny's special mix—Nina Simone, Sade, Tone-Loc—"

"Tone-Loc? How is a rapper supposed to inspire me?"

"'Wild Thing.' Tone-Loc has some very wise things to say about doing the wild thing." He slapped the CD into her hand.

"This is all really lovely, Danny, but it doesn't change anything. Except perhaps for making me even more frustrated than I already am," she said, eyeing the pictures of buff bodies on the back of the *Top Gun* DVD.

"Exactly. Frustration leads to desperation. Desperation leads to desperate measures…like calling Marc Lewis up and asking him out."

She rolled her eyes. "Never going to happen. The man would eat me alive."

"With a bit of luck," Danny said, winking.

Even though she was a grown, adult woman, Anna blushed from the tips of her toes to the roots of her hair. "Danny!"

"Yes?" he responded, the picture of innocence.

She shook her head. "You're hopeless."

Danny spent the rest of the evening expounding on his theory on casual sex.

"If you had a sore shoulder, you'd get a massage, right?"

"Sure."

"And if you had a toothache you'd go to the dentist, yeah?"

"I have a bad feeling about where this is going."

"I'm just saying that if you have an itch, and you're not in a relationship, what's wrong with finding someone to scratch it? It's just human nature to want to have sex. What's the big deal?"

She didn't have a ready answer for him. She'd been thinking about this a lot since their conversation in the bar. She didn't object to casual sex on moral grounds. If two consenting adults wanted to go for it, who was she to have an opinion? But she struggled to imagine herself being that intimate with a complete stranger, then getting up, putting her clothes on and walking out the door to never see them again.

When she said as much to Danny, he slapped his palm to his forehead.

"D'oh! I'm not suggesting you suddenly turn into *Looking for Mr. Goodbar.* Just live a little. Have a fling with an unsuitable man. You'll love it!"

Then Danny slid a manila folder across the table toward her.

"He's thirty-five, separated from his wife of ten years just six months ago. Mover and shaker in the IT industry thanks to some ground-breaking software he launched ten years ago, millionaire at thirty, hot, hot for you and just waiting for your phone call."

She stared at a newspaper photograph of Marc leaving a charity movie premiere on the weekend. He was wearing a dark suit, and he looked tall and powerful and predatory.

"I can't believe you researched him," she said lamely. He'd been married. Technically, was still married. But in her experience, people who'd been separated for six months had no intention of getting back together. She wondered if that accounted for the cynical gleam in his eye.

"You're a novice. I'm just doing the groundwork so you know what you're getting into."

"I'm not getting into anything. Good God, Danny—I feel like you're trying to pimp me out!"

As soon as she said it, she knew she'd hurt him. His face went blank and he reached for the folder.

"Sorry. I didn't realize. I thought this was what you wanted, that all you needed was a little push."

She watched as he stacked all his offerings together, ready to put them back into the carrier bag. What was she really afraid of here? Rejection? Getting in over her head? Her own desires? What did she have to lose, after all?

Nothing. She had absolutely nothing to lose—except her inhibitions and her stodgy old viewpoint. What it came down to was one thing: did she really want to change her life or not?

She squeezed her eyes shut tight. Brutal honesty time—she found Marc Lewis sensationally attractive. There, it was out. She'd thought it, even if she hadn't said it out loud.

"Maybe you could leave the DVD. And the CD. And…the folder," she said slowly.

Danny flashed her a big smile. "I knew it!"

"It doesn't mean anything, Danny. Except that I'll be climbing the walls if I actually watch this DVD."

He laughed at her lame joke, and later, after he'd left, she stared at the photograph of Marc for a good five minutes.

What would he be like in bed? There was so much heat in those dark eyes of his, so much strength coiled in his lean body. She wondered if he put as much focus and attention into making love as he did into his business. What would it be like to have his body poised above hers, all his hardness pressed against her softness?

Belatedly she became aware that she was panting. Sitting

alone in her kitchen on a Thursday night, panting over a black-and-white picture of an arrogant entrepreneur. She took a cold shower, put on another pair of freshly laundered cotton pyjamas and finally fell asleep, no thanks to Danny's bag of *inspiration*.

The next day, she stared at Marc's name on her daily call sheet. It was almost as if she'd conjured him out of the ether with her X-rated fantasies. And now she was going to come face-to-face with him again this afternoon.

It doesn't mean anything, her lawyer self rationalized. *He's a client. He gets in the car, you drive him to wherever he wants to go, he gets out, it's over. No biggie.*

Except that she knew that the whole trip she'd be thinking about what Danny had said to her, and about those moments of forbidden fantasy when she'd imagined what it would be like to make love to a man like Marc, and whether she had the courage to do anything about it now that she was being given a second chance.

IN BUSINESS, there were bad days, and then there were Bad Days. At around four o'clock Marc decided he was definitely having one of the latter. Nothing had gone to plan. Important contracts had gone missing with a courier, he couldn't get his U.S. manager on the phone, the accountants had turned up more irregularities while going through due diligence on the Sum Systems accounts and an unavoidable holdup at his lunchtime meeting meant he'd been running half an hour behind time for the rest of the day.

Now he felt the dull throb of a headache starting as he and Gary exited his corporate headquarters and headed for the waiting car.

"…I think we should drop it. That's my advice," Gary said as they slid into the back of the black Mercedes.

"I'm not backing off from this deal, Gary," he said, frustration making the words clipped and terse.

Veteran campaigner that he was, Gary didn't bat an eyelid at Marc's tone.

"That audit is pulling up big black holes at Sum. Has it ever occurred to you that the reason they were so keen to share the obvious bad stuff was to stop you from finding the really, really bad stuff that they'd hidden?"

"Read my lips—I am not backing off. I want that new data platform," Marc said. "It'll save us twelve months of development, and we can get our new database software out before Christmas."

"But at what price?" Gary asked bluntly.

"That's my decision, not yours," Marc said, irritation getting the better of him.

Gary sank back into his seat, lips firmly pressed together, and Marc felt a stab of guilt. He hadn't been the easiest man to manage since Tara's betrayal. He sighed heavily and glanced out the window as the car raced past the thick steel crossbeams of the Harbour Bridge. He didn't like being the kind of boss that everyone tiptoed around, but there was no doubting the fact that that was the man he'd become recently. He had to get a grip on the frustration and anger that seemed to be growing inside him day by day. He wasn't an angry man, usually. In fact, he used to be kind of a fun guy. His firm had the reputation of being a good employer, a great place to work. He prided himself on his corporate culture.

The truth was, he was letting his disappointment and hurt over the breakdown of his marriage leak into the other parts of his life. He knew it, but he just couldn't seem to control it. He felt so baffled and ripped off and angry. Hadn't he been a good husband? Hadn't he given Tara everything she ever wanted? Hadn't he been loyal and faithful?

His lips twisted as he thought of the shambles his parents had called a marriage—his father in and out as though the house had a revolving door, the other women, the backbreaking work his mother had had to undertake to keep him and his sister, Alison, clothed and fed. And still there had been times of extreme poverty, weeks of breakfast cereal for dinner, of living with candles for light because the electricity had been cut off.

He'd ensured he didn't make the same mistakes as his father. He'd done everything, damn it. And still his marriage had exploded in his face. The realization left him feeling lost, adrift, confused. And very bloody determined to never let it happen again.

The sudden screech of tires drew his attention to the front windshield and he saw that the car in front of them was braking and fishtailing wildly. Even as his own muscles tensed, instinctively wanting to do something to avert what looked like imminent disaster, their driver smoothly changed lanes with a practiced flick of the wrists. For the first time since he got in the car, Marc glanced toward the driver's seat.

His pulse immediately kicked up a notch. Warm brown eyes met his in the rearview mirror—déjà vu of the best kind. Anna Jackson, she of the sexy dress and the full breasts. He'd been thinking about her off and on all week. The one who got away. Or, more accurately, the one he'd decided he didn't want.

Yet he hadn't told his secretary to use a different car service.

She cut her eyes away from his, returning her attention to the road. He stared at her profile, remembering the man who'd kissed her on the opera house steps. His jaw hardened. He would not participate in the kind of betrayal that had destroyed his own marriage, no matter what the temptation.

"Okay, how about this? Let me handle the Sum audit personally," Gary said with the air of a man who had been doing some fast thinking. "Give me a week, and I'll go through the company like a dose of the salts. If I still think it won't work, you listen to me. If there's nothing too sinister, we close the sale. What do you think?"

Marc deliberately cleared his mind of the platinum-blond distraction in the front seat.

"What about the McPherson project? Can you hand it over at this stage?"

Gary shrugged. "I'll palm some of it off, and keep the hard stuff. A couple of weeks of late nights won't kill me."

For some reason, Marc found himself glancing toward the rearview mirror again. She was watching him intently, a small frown pleating the skin between her eyebrows.

"If you want it, it's yours," he said, shrugging. Beside him, he felt Gary relax. It was one of the reasons why Gary made such a good wingman—he was a worrier, a real perfectionist, with great instincts and a healthy dose of caution. A good foil for Marc's own sometimes reckless risk-taking.

Reaching for his briefcase, he pulled some papers out and shuffled through them until he found what he was looking for.

"I'll need you to get onto legal about these contracts, too, get them to extend the due diligence period. Sum put a clause in limiting our audit period to just two weeks, but we're going to need longer."

Gary nodded and pulled out his mobile phone, speed dialing through to the office. Marc leafed through the papers in his case, running his eye over the figures for his next meeting as Gary wrangled with legal. After five minutes, Gary ended the call and sighed heavily.

"They're saying they can try, but that Sum are within their rights to insist on the time limit. That way we have to make our decision at the end of next week, or we walk. You gotta admit, there's no reason for them to agree to the extension unless they're suicidal."

"I don't care what it takes, we need that time. These bastards are not going to slip through our fingers. Tell legal to do whatever it takes."

Gary rubbed his eyes wearily and pulled out his phone again. "We could always go public with some of the audit stuff, smoke them out."

Marc nodded slowly. "Not bad. Give them no choice but to deal with us. Play them at their own game."

"And leave yourselves open to a suit for breach of confidentiality," a cool voice interjected.

He shot his gaze to the front seat, capturing Anna's toffee eyes in the mirror.

"I beg your pardon?" he asked.

"You can't use information uncovered during due diligence to leverage a company into a sale. It's against the law, and would be immediate grounds for investigation under the Australian Security Commission's charter," she said.

"Who the hell are you, Perry Mason?" he asked, astounded that the chauffeur was sticking her oar into his business.

"Until recently, I was a lawyer," she said crisply.

"Then you'll understand what the word *private* means," he said tersely.

She didn't say another word, simply focused on the road, but a flush rose into her cheeks.

Gary was watching him, waiting for his decision. Irritated beyond words to have to give credence to her unlooked-for advice, Marc shook his head.

"Check with legal, but we'll have to assume we've got no more time. Hand the McPherson project over to one of the others, all of it, and concentrate on Sum until the end of the week. We'll review things then."

Gary nodded, and started dialing on his phone again.

Marc sat back in his seat, his whole body tense with frustration. Irrationally, most of it was directed at the ex-lawyer-turned-chauffeur sitting not four feet away. She didn't write the laws, or enforce them, but it didn't stop him from wanting to place the blame for this latest setback on her shoulders.

It didn't help that her skirt had ridden up once more, and a swath of black lace was again on show. His body quickened in response to the sensual display, but he very deliberately angled himself so that he couldn't see her, even in his peripheral vision. Pushing all other thought away, he concentrated on work.

3

WAY TO GO, ANNA, she berated herself as she skillfully turned a corner in the Mercedes. She still couldn't believe that she'd broken in on a client's private business conversation to offer a legal opinion. No, not just a legal opinion, she ruthlessly corrected herself. A legal reprimand. A schoolteacherly rap over the knuckles.

And to think, Danny had advised her to seduce the man! She could only imagine what he'd say if she told him that not only had she not asked Marc out, but she'd also given him a lecture on the Australian Securities Act.

And he hadn't liked it one little bit. Was, in fact, quietly seething if she was any judge of the matter.

The worst of it was that she'd been anticipating seeing him again all day. The moment he slid into the backseat she'd felt her heartbeat kick up, and her body tighten with expectation. Despite everything she'd said to Danny and to herself about him being arrogant and no better than her former bosses and her being totally not up to the task of seducing him, there was no denying the powerful sexual attraction of the man.

She'd been unable to stop herself from watching him in the rearview mirror and playing a game of what-ifs with herself. What if he asked her out again? Would she say yes? What if he looked at her the way he had at the opera house? Would *she* have the courage to ask *him* out?

She studied him; he looked tired. A small frown creased the skin between his eyebrows, and occasionally he rubbed a finger against his temple. She guessed he had a headache. By the sound of things, he was having trouble with one of his many business deals. She could remember days like this—the highly pressured cut and thrust of the corporate world. And then, before she knew it, the stuff about breach of confidence was flying out of her mouth.

What had she been thinking?

A mortified flush spread up her neck as she realized exactly what had been behind her impromptu legal advice. She'd wanted him to look at her! She'd wanted to get his attention, and the only way she knew how was to offer an unsolicited legal opinion.

If she could have, she would have banged her head against the steering wheel. Here was proof absolute that she was not cut out for the world of seduction and lust. Legal advice as a pickup line—it was so pathetic she could almost cry.

The worst thing was that she'd left herself open to a rebuke from a man who she'd already decided she didn't particularly like. But, as Danny had advised her recently, liking had very little to do with lust.

After that, the trip couldn't end fast enough as far as she was concerned. She saw the double doors of the Stock Exchange coming up on her right with a sense of relief, and pulled smoothly over to the curb. Pasting on a pleasant smile, she slid out of the car and held the door open for Marc's colleague, and then for Marc himself.

He loomed over her for a heartbeat as he unfolded himself from the car. It was just like the previous week at the opera house—suddenly she was unable to breathe as she stared at the strong column of his throat, swamped by the sharp, woody tang of his aftershave.

He didn't look at her, and she didn't try to make eye contact with him. God forbid he ever have an inkling of the thoughts she'd been entertaining before she'd blundered into his conversation. She was shutting the rear door when Marc's offsider spoke up.

"We should be about an hour. I'll call for you," he said politely before turning and disappearing into the building.

Startled, Anna reached for the day's call sheet. Sure enough, she saw that the Lewis job was a drop and wait. Her services would be required again in another hour, when she would have to take Mr. Lewis and his hardworking friend back to their headquarters.

Great.

She spent the next hour going over and over the fatal five minutes when she'd stuck her nose into Marc's business. It didn't get any better in the rehashing. The lawyer in her cringed when she remembered butting in on his conversation, thrusting her opinion onto him. Just as well she'd never had any serious intention of trying her hand with the man. Any chance she might have had was long gone now, that was for sure.

It was well after six by the time she got the call to pick them up. She'd been flicking through holiday brochures, trying to find an international resort that offered scuba diving courses as well as parasailing. She might be giving up on one thing on her list, but she was not walking away from the others. If it killed her, she was going to be more adventurous.

"Sorry we were so over time," the nice man said as he slid into the car.

"It's fine. All part of the service," she said cheerily, determined to be professional this time round at least.

The car dipped as Marc slid into his side and pulled the door shut, but she didn't so much as glance his way.

"Jacqui's going to kill me," the nice man said as he checked his watch.

"Have you got something on?" Marc asked.

"Dinner. Her sister's birthday. We're throwing her a big party at Catalina."

She was pulling out into the traffic when a masculine hand

grabbed the edge of the front passenger seat and Marc leaned forward.

"Change of plans. We're taking Mr. Newton to Catalina in Rose Bay. Do you know it?"

She nodded. Situated on the waterfront, the restaurant had been the site of many business dinners when she'd been a player in the corporate world. Not to mention the fact that she lived just five minutes' walk around the corner.

"Not a problem. You're my last job for the day."

All the fine hairs on her arms were standing on end by the time he released his grip and subsided into the backseat.

The two men talked quietly as she tooled the Mercedes through rush-hour traffic. She had to exercise real effort not to keep glancing in the mirror this time. Why did she find him so compelling? It wasn't just that he was a physically attractive man—she saw dozens of good-looking men every day.

He exited the car with his friend at the restaurant, and she waited patiently as the two men talked briefly. After a few minutes, Marc clapped the other man on the shoulder, and climbed back in.

"I need to drop past the office, then you can take me home," he said coolly as she shut the door.

She was acutely aware that they were alone for the first time as she pulled out into the busy traffic.

The silence seemed to take on a life of its own as she smoothly powered back through the city toward the Harbour Bridge, but after a few minutes the sound of his phone ringing shattered the tension.

"Marc speaking," he said, his tone brisk. "Alison. What's up? How's Frank?"

It was impossible not to overhear his conversation in such a small space, but Anna kept her eyes strictly on the road ahead. She wasn't going to risk stepping over the line again, not with this man.

"Whoa there! You want to slow down a little?" he said into the phone. "Just what exactly is it that I'm supposed to have done?"

Anna could hear the chipmunk chatter that indicated his caller was responding to his question.

"Well, I'm sorry that Sally feels that way. But we talked about this before she came onboard. Taking on a job as a management trainee in my business was not going to be a cakewalk. I expect her to put in as much effort as any other junior, even if she is my niece."

Anna couldn't stop herself from looking at him in the mirror then. *Sally.* Wasn't that the name of the employee he'd bullied last week? The one she'd got her back up over, because it had fired her own memories of being ill-used when she was recovering from surgery?

"And did she tell you what she wanted the time off for, Alison? Skiing. Hardly an emergency, I think you'd agree?" His tone was dry, even faintly amused.

Anna's hands tightened on the steering wheel. Sally was his niece. And he'd been perfectly justified in rebuffing her request for time off last week. Which meant he wasn't the corporate bully or slave driver that she'd judged him.

For some reason she felt absurdly relieved. It didn't make an ounce of difference to anything, but all of a sudden she didn't feel quite so...torn about being attracted to him. She knew her brother would roll his eyes, but liking had always been a part of lust for her, no matter what she tried to tell herself.

The click of him ending the call drew her eyes to the rearview mirror again. He was rubbing his jaw, his face closed and introspective. Now that she knew he wasn't a tyrant, his physical appeal seemed magnified. She found herself staring at the small triangle of chest that was revealed where he'd pulled his tie loose. She wondered what his chest would be like—hairy or smooth—and whether it was as strong and well-muscled as his athletic walk promised.

He glanced up, and their glances clashed. She fought a

battle against the flush of embarrassment that rushed to her cheeks, and lost.

"Would you like some music? Or perhaps the news?" she asked quickly, hoping to cover her reaction.

"Suit yourself," he said.

He flicked open his briefcase and drew out some papers. Did he ever stop working? Even when she'd seen him last week at the opera house he'd been having a business dinner. Perhaps he was one of those men who lived for work. Then she remembered that he was a self-made millionaire. Of course he lived for work—people didn't get that rich by not trying.

Deciding to take him at his word, she turned the CD player on. The smooth, honeyed tones of Nina Simone filled the car.

Determined not to give in to her preoccupation with her passenger again, she resolutely concentrated on the evening ahead. She had no idea where Marc lived, but she would probably be finished with him by eight-thirty at the latest. Maybe she could take in a movie, or rent a DVD to take home and watch. The more she thought about it, the more the DVD appealed. A good comedy, and a long bath with a nice glass of wine.

"Is this Nina Simone?"

She almost started at the sound of his voice, the silence had stretched for so long.

"Yes. It's a remix, which is why it sounds a little different," she explained.

The song ended, and the soulful husk of Sade's voice filled the car, sexy and smooth. God, why had she left Danny's inspiration CD in her car stereo? And why had she chosen to turn it on when Marc was her passenger? The last thing she wanted was to be surrounded by sensual smoky music with him sitting behind her.

Even as she was wondering if it would look too obvious if she switched over to the news, the Sade track finished and the funky sounds of Tone-Loc filled the car. She closed her eyes for a brief moment of humiliation as the rapper began bragging about how much his girl liked to do the wild thing.

She ventured a glance toward the rearview mirror. The light was dying, and his features were deeply shadowed in the back of the car. Nonetheless, she could feel him watching her. She was almost tempted to explain about the CD, that it was a gift from her brother. But she rationalized that he was probably more preoccupied with his business and the evening ahead than the music playing in her car. It was only in her world that it loomed important.

The streetlights were flickering on one by one as she turned off the bridge and into north Sydney.

"Go down the ramp to the left of the building," he instructed as she approached his corporate headquarters.

She followed instructions, coming to a halt when a security grill barred the way into the underground parking lot.

"Here."

He passed her a swipe card, and she slid the window down and ran it through the machine. The grill began to slide up with smooth precision.

She handed the card back to him and drove under the still-retracting grill.

The garage was empty. Her surprise must have shown.

"It *is* Friday night. I encourage my people to have lives of their own," he said.

"What about your life?" she said, and could have bitten her tongue off. What kind of a question was that to ask a man who'd just told her to mind her own business?

His face was unreadable in the darkness of the backseat.

"My life is just fine," he said after a long silence.

The sound of the car door opening echoed in the empty car park.

"I'll be ten minutes or so. Then we'll be going to Point Piper."

The door clicked shut, and she watched him walk toward the

lift. His stride was confident, as though he owned the world. Again she wondered what his body was like beneath his superbly cut suit. Not that she was ever likely to find out, but she had ten minutes to kill….

Deciding the frustration wasn't worth it, she slid her hat off and ran her hands through her hair. The great thing about her new cut was that it was incredibly easy to recover from hat hair. A couple of passes with her fingers, and the spikes were rejuvenated. Checking in the driver's vanity mirror, she confirmed that her Passion Pink lipstick was holding up okay, too. Pity there was no one to appreciate the fact. Pity, also, that Passion Pink was as close as she was going to get to bringing real passion into her life, the way she was going. Legal advice as a pickup line! Who was she kidding? Even if she could get past her self-consciousness and preconceptions, she was going to have an uphill battle on her hands landing any man with such puny weapons in her arsenal.

She was about to flick the mirror back up when she saw that one of her silver hoop earrings was missing. Discreet and stylish, they had been her mother's and held great sentimental value. She frowned in annoyance. Where could the earring have gone missing?

Perhaps it had fallen in the car? She patted the seat around herself, easing her hips from side to side to see if she could catch sight of anything silver. Nothing.

Not prepared to give up, she released her seat belt and got out of the car. Her seat was empty, however, and she slid a hand down the side of it. Again, zilch. Given that she'd done nothing but drive all day, the earring had to be in here somewhere, or back at her apartment. Turning on the car's interior light, she set to the search with a purpose.

MARC UNDOCKED HIS LAPTOP from his desk, slid it into its bag and slung the strap over his shoulder. His secretary had left a file on his desk with important papers for him to go over, and he added it to the papers in his briefcase.

Somewhere between leaving the Stock Exchange and arriving here his headache had burned itself out, and he pulled his tie off and slid it into his pocket as he headed back to the elevator. Vaguely he wondered what his housekeeper would have left him for dinner. On Fridays it was usually fish, and he hoped she'd managed to procure more of the excellent salmon she'd prepared for him last week.

As the lift doors closed on him and he began the descent to the basement, he allowed his thoughts to return to the subject that was occupying center stage in his mind.

The chauffeur, Anna Jackson. He'd been incredibly angry with her earlier, but his frustration had dissipated during his last meeting. She was obviously a clever woman. It was there in her eyes, in the comprehension and perception behind each glance. He wondered why she'd given up law to drive people like him around all day.

And he wondered whether he could resist the urge to ask her out for dinner again. Not that he particularly wanted to exchange small talk with her over a meal. If he had his way, if he could be bluntly honest and lay his cards on the table, he'd just take her back to his place and bury himself inside her until the itch that was his desire for her was gone.

He reminded himself again of the man at the opera house. He would not destroy a relationship. It would make him the worst kind of hypocrite.

Maybe he should have dismissed her and called a cab to take him home. Remove himself from temptation, as it were. Even as he thought it, his pride reared up inside him. Was he in high school, unable to control his libido all of a sudden? It was no big deal. She'd drive him home, and he'd get out of the car without asking her out—or in—and that would be that. And on Monday he'd tell his secretary to change car services.

Then he walked out of the elevator in the garage and saw her. All four doors of the Mercedes were open, and she was leaning across the backseat, one knee on the cushions, the other leg on the ground outside the car as she searched for something. The fabric of her skirt was stretched tight across her butt, and her hips swayed from side to side provocatively as she leaned farther into the car.

He was instantly aroused, hard as a rock. He clenched his jaw. He wanted nothing more than to walk over there and have his way with her. In fact, he was a little afraid of how strong the impulse was to take what he wanted.

He didn't like being out of control. It was one thing he knew about himself absolutely—he liked to be the one calling the shots, making the running. Even more so after Tara. Never again would he give another person so much power over his world.

So regardless of desire or lust or whatever this was, he was going to ignore it, and stick to his game plan. Anything or anyone that could inspire this much fascination in him was dangerous.

Resolute, he moved toward the car. He was just a handful of steps away when he became aware that she was completely oblivious to his approach. He cleared his throat, not wanting to be closer to her than he needed to be.

"Miss Jackson," he said.

Her head came up, and she glanced over her shoulder.

"Sorry, I didn't hear you," she said. "I was looking for my earring."

Then she scooted backward, enticing butt first. Too late he realized he was standing too close—or had he intended it to be that way? She stepped backward, head ducked to avoid the door frame, and backed straight into him. The full curve of her butt connected firmly with his groin, and the exquisite sensation of her pressing up against his already-aching erection was too much for his self-control. His free hand found her hip, and when she made to move away, he curved his fingers into her flesh and held her steady. She froze and for a heartbeat there was nothing but the sound of their breathing in the dim underground space.

ANNA'S BLOOD FELT like treacle as it pumped thick and hot through her veins. She'd barely registered that she'd backed into him when his hand clamped down on her hip. Then she felt the unmistakable ridge of his erection pressing against the curve of her butt. She froze, a thousand thoughts and feelings skittering across her mind. Then he shifted, just an infinitesimal tilt of his hips as he brought himself more firmly against her. It was an invitation, a question. Instinctively she rocked back, giving him the only answer she could.

The hand on her hip tensed, and she heard the sound of his briefcase and laptop bag hitting the concrete. Then his other hand was on her thigh, sliding down the fabric of her skirt as he reached for the hem. She shuddered as his fingers found the silk-covered skin of her leg and began a slow sweep up under her skirt. Heat pooled in her thighs and she rocked back into his hardness again. Then his hand slid from stocking-silk to bare flesh and she gasped at the feel of his skin against hers. He stilled, and the hand on her thigh tensed.

"The man at the opera house?" he asked, and she knew exactly what he wanted to know.

"My brother," she said. He gusted out a lungful of air, and then the hand completed its journey, sliding over her hip, and around to reach between her legs and cup the moist heat of her mound. He pressed his palm hard against her, grinding his hips against her from behind, and she groaned with the pleasure of it.

"Yes!" she gasped as his other hand raced up her ribs and closed unerringly over her breast.

For a second it was enough, his hands on her heat and her breast, but she knew there was more, so much more.

As though he could read her mind, he slid a finger beneath

the elastic of her panties and into the damp curls surrounding her clitoris. One brush, two, three over the highly sensitized nub, and then his knowing hands dipped farther still, seeking the slick wetness between her thighs. Automatically she widened her stance, allowing him fuller access. A finger slid inside her, and she gasped, her muscles tightening around him, clinging to his invasion. But too quickly he was gone, sliding back up to her clitoris, slicking his finger over and over the stiff little bead. She shuddered and writhed, awash with desire. His erection was still pushed hard against her butt, and she snaked a hand between their bodies to massage the length of him. He felt hard and long and she bit her lip, thinking about him inside her, filling her....

Then suddenly the delicious pressure between her thighs stopped and he withdrew his hand.

"Take your shirt off," he ordered in a rasping undertone.

She didn't hesitate. He remained pressed against her backside, his hardness urging her on as she slid her jacket off, then ripped at the buttons of her shirt. He helped her pull the cuffs over her wrists, and when she was down to her bra he spun her around in his arms and she looked into his face for the first time.

His eyes were dark and hooded, his cheekbones flushed. His mouth was slightly open, and she fixated on the glinting wetness of his tongue. His gaze dropped to rake her breasts, and when it rose again to meet hers she saw pure animal desire in him.

"So much better than I imagined," he said huskily, and then he leaned forward and took possession of her mouth. His tongue swept along the tender skin inside her lips even as both his hands came up to cup her breasts. Her nipples were already straining at the lace of her bra, and he rubbed his thumbs across them, then squeezed them gently but firmly between thumb and forefinger. She moaned and pressed her body against his. His lips left her mouth and blazed a trail across her cheek and down her neck. Her head dropped back like a too-heavy flower as he slid her bra straps off her shoulders and pushed the fabric of the cups away from her breasts.

She groaned as his mouth closed over a straining nipple at last. The wet heat of his mouth, the flick of his tongue across her nipple—it was almost too much, and she reached for his belt with shaking hands.

"Now," she demanded.

She slid his buckle loose, and undid his button and fly. His erection pushed proudly at the fabric of his boxers, and she at last closed her hand around the length of him. He inhaled sharply as she ran her hand down his shaft, then slid her thumb over the velvety head of his penis.

In response, he suckled harder on her breasts, the pleasure so intense it was almost pain. They were both breathing heavily, clutching at each other, desperate for completion. As she slicked her hand up and down his shaft, he swept her skirt up around her waist and tugged at her panties. She helped him pull them off, and then he picked her up, walked a few steps, and placed her on the trunk of the car.

She was literally mindless with desire. All she wanted was satisfaction, and the only way to achieve it was to have him inside her. She hauled him toward her, her hips rising up to meet his.

"Just a moment," he murmured, and she heard the crinkle of a foil packet being opened.

A second later, and a delicious anticipation stole over her as his penis probed her, and then he was sliding into her, filling her, going as deep as he could, the base of his shaft grinding into her.

"Oh, yes!" she cried, clutching at his hips and dragging him closer still.

She was panting, out of control. He pulled back, then plunged into her again. She felt as though she could scream with the pleasure of it. Never in her life had she been so aroused, so greedy, so determined to have it all.

Firming her grip on his hips, she matched his rhythm, riding with him as the sensations inside her tightened toward the inevitable conclusion. Her back arched as she stiffened in anticipation, and he took advantage of the action to tongue her nipples, sucking one into his mouth and pulling on it so firmly that she bucked.

The movement slid her off the trunk of the car, and he clutched at her hips, taking both their weights before spinning and pinning her against the concrete wall beside the car. She crossed her ankles behind his back, and he thrust into her again and again as she writhed against the wall.

And then she was coming, pulsating around him, her head thrown back, her fingers digging into his shoulders as she cried out. A breath later, she felt him tense as he followed her, his body shuddering as he came, too.

A heartbeat, two, three. She felt the tension slide out of him. The sound of their harsh breathing echoed back at them. He withdrew from her, releasing his grip on her hips. She slid down the wall, the heels of her shoes making a faint click as they connected with the ground. Her knees felt weak, rubbery, and she put out a hand to steady herself. He caught the movement, and reached out to support her.

"You okay?"

She nodded, lifting dazed eyes to his face. He looked just as blown away, she saw. Then his eyes raked down over her body and she felt a pulse of tension between her thighs.

Straight after the most mind-blowing sex she'd ever had, and all the man had to do was look at her and she was ready for round two!

She glanced across at him and saw that he was dressing, pulling up his pants, tucking his shirt in. She looked down at herself, saw her breasts straining upward, supported by her pulled-down bra. Her skirt was rucked up around her waist, her panties abandoned somewhere near the car.

Reality crashed in like an avalanche.

She was in a parking lot, for Pete's sake! She'd just had knock-down, drag-out sex with an almost-stranger in a parking lot! No, not just a stranger—a client! She might be new to the business, but she was pretty damned sure that having sex with the clients was not high on the agenda for self-employed limo services.

Her hands were trembling as she dragged her skirt down and her bra up. Her shirt was crumpled on the ground beside the car, and she crossed to pick it up. One of the buttons was missing. She tugged it on and did up as many as she could, but her bra now showed clearly in the deep V created by the absent button. She located her panties, simultaneously becoming aware that he had finished dressing and was now standing watching her. She couldn't bring herself to pull her panties on while he watched. Instead, she stuffed them into the side pocket of the open car door.

Smoothing a hand through her hair, she took a deep breath, then let it out again. Then she crossed to the open rear door of the car, and indicated for him to get in. He stared at her for a beat, and she kept her face as calm as she could. Inside, she was reeling, unable to comprehend what had just happened, her blood still fizzing with the excitement of it all. But she didn't want him to know that. If she was going to pull this off, she had to appear cool and calm.

Finally he picked up his briefcase and laptop bag and slid them into the car. She waited, her hand on the door handle, ready to shut him in. He paused on the verge of stepping into the car.

"What just happened..." he said, but she shook her head.

"I know exactly what it was, don't worry," she said hastily.

"Do you? You're doing better than me, then," he said harshly.

Her eyes flew to his face. "I didn't mean... I've never done anything like this before," she stumbled.

"That makes two of us."

A long, tense silence stretched between them. She knew her face was crimson with embarrassment, could feel the heat of it. Could this get any worse?

Finally he moved, sliding into the backseat. She shut the door on him with a heartfelt sigh of relief. Now she just had to get him home, and out of her car. Then she could tell the dispatch company she subscribed to that she was no longer taking jobs for Lewis Technologies, and she'd never have to see him again. She could pretend the whole thing had never happened.

Because even though she was managing to maintain a cool, calm facade, inside she was freaking out badly. What had she just done? With a client? In a public place? She couldn't believe that she'd gone from only done it in a bed to wild parking garage sex in the space of a few minutes. She'd practically torn the poor guy's clothes off. She could only imagine what he was thinking of her.

Silence sat thick and heavy between them as she drove up the exit ramp and waited for the security grill to rise. When she was confident the car would clear it, she eased her foot down on the accelerator.

"Wait a minute."

She braked instantly, then swung around in her seat when she heard the click of the car door opening. A second later he was getting into the passenger seat next to her, pulling on his seat belt.

He gave her a rueful look, and she guessed that he felt uncomfortable having her chauffeur him home after they'd all but devoured each other in his company parking lot.

Not that having him sitting next to her improved the situation from her point of view.

Why had this happened? And why did it have to be this particular man who'd pressed all her latent sex-vixen buttons? She slid a sideways look at him, but he was gazing out the side window, his face turned away. The silence tightened between them. Finally it became so unbearable that she stabbed a hand at the car stereo.

The funky sounds of Tone-Loc filled the car as he sang about doing the wild thing. *Dear God.* Instantly she stabbed the off button on the stereo.

They completed the rest of the drive to Point Piper in excruciating, tense silence.

He began offering her directions when she pulled off the main road and into the residential streets of Sydney's most expensive and exclusive suburb.

"Left here, then the second on the right," he said, his voice devoid of all emotion.

She followed instructions, and finally pulled up beside a high wall, broken only by a single gate and a double garage door. She knew enough about Sydney real estate to understand that the low-key street appeal signaled that behind the wall was a world of privilege and wealth that she could only dream of. Which made what had just happened between them even more surreal.

She got out of the car, but before she could even think about opening his door, he was already standing on the sidewalk. Stiff-shouldered, she collected his briefcase and laptop instead.

"Thank you," he said brusquely as she awkwardly handed the two bags over. Then he just stood there.

It struck her for the first time that for a man she'd mentally categorized as an experienced and knowledgeable player, he was about as handy with this one-night-stand business as she was. That awareness eased the tension banding her chest just a little.

"Look," she said suddenly, "don't worry. I'm not going to turn into a stalker or anything. It just happened, right? For some reason. But it's done now. No regrets."

She stuck her hand out, all business. He hesitated, then a wry smile curved his mouth as he shook hands with her. It was the first time she'd seen him smile, and it was enough to make her blink. The man was a knockout in the sex-appeal stakes, that was for sure.

"No regrets," he said, echoing her words. For a second they held eye contact, and heat sizzled between them again.

Wow.

Anna swallowed and dragged her hand from his grip. "Good night then, Mr. Lewis."

He nodded, and swiveled on his heel. She watched him unlock the gate, and then he was gone and she was left standing alone on the darkened street.

She sagged against her car and closed her eyes. Bad move, she realized as soon as selected highlights from her recent encounter with Marc flashed across her mind's eye. She could feel her nipples harden against the lace of her bra just from the memory of the man.

She knew suddenly that she'd meant what she said—no regrets. She'd just experienced the kind of mindless passion and desire that she'd previously only read about in the pages of a steamy novel. Her body still throbbed with aftershocks from his masterful lovemaking. Her breasts felt sensitized and tender and if she squeezed her thighs together she could invoke a faint memory of what it was like to have him inside her.

So, no regrets. Definitely no regrets.

In fact, she was even beginning to feel vaguely pleased with how she'd managed the whole awkward post-coital situation. She tilted her chin. Maybe the idea of bringing more passion into her life wasn't so crazy after all. Maybe she wasn't as uptight and straitlaced as she'd imagined. Head high, she circled around the car to the driver's side.

The streetlight caught the black paintwork on her car, and as she passed the trunk she stopped in her tracks and sucked in a breath of air. Outlined clearly on the shiny surface of the trunk were two round globes—a perfect impression of her bare butt.

She blinked and gasped, but the butt-print remained the same—highly visible, and eminently recognizable for what it was.

Exactly how many people would have seen her butt-print as she drove across town? Thousands. Literally thousands. She glanced down at her personalized number plates. Lady Driver. The butt-print gave the plates a whole new connotation.

Embarrassed heat flooding her body, she clicked open the trunk and reached for her polishing cloth. Somehow, during the drive over here, she'd managed to minimize the impact of what she'd just done. Maybe she'd had to do that so she could keep functioning and get Marc home. But now there was no holding back the full horror of what she'd allowed to happen.

She'd had sex with a client. Not just any client, either—an influential, high-profile millionaire client. And not just sex, either. They'd *consumed* each other in the not very salubrious surrounds of an underground parking garage.

Peachy. Just peachy.

She rubbed furiously at the mark. She had been way off beam when she'd fantasized about being a freewheeling sex vixen— she could fool herself for a few minutes of decadent excess, but she just wasn't up to the consequences.

Elbow pumping vigorously, she put everything she had into removing the evidence of her lapse from the trunk of her car. Pity she couldn't wipe the incident from her memory as easily. One thing was for sure—it was never going to happen again.

4

THE NEXT DAY, Anna woke to a few seconds of blissful ignorance before memory descended in vivid detail. She rolled her face into the pillow and groaned loudly. Her whole body flushed with mortification as she remembered the way she'd urged Marc to have sex with her, the way she'd writhed against him and grabbed greedily at his hard male body.

She had never, ever, ever behaved so…wantonly in her entire life. She pressed her hands over her eyes, wanting to block out the images that kept popping up in her mind's eye.

Kicking off the bedcovers, she strode into the bathroom and turned the water on as hot as she could stand it. Stripping off the T-shirt she'd worn to bed, she stepped into the steamy shower cubicle. And froze as she caught a glimpse of her back in the vanity mirror. A rash stood out redly across her shoulders. She frowned, then her eyebrows shot toward her hairline as she remembered Marc thrusting her against the wall last night when she'd slid off the trunk of her car.

Her mouth pressed into a tight line, Anna stuck her head under the shower jet and wished that she could just wash away the last twenty-four hours. Reaching for the soap, she worked up a lather and ran perfunctory hands over her breasts and belly. Deep between her legs, her muscles contracted pleasurably as her slick hands slid over her nipples. Anna gasped, earning herself a mouthful of water.

How could part of her still be turned on by what had happened between her and her client when most of her was mortified? It made no sense to her whatsoever. But, sure enough, no matter how perfunctory her washing technique, her body kept sending out definite signals that it was hot and ready for round two with Marc.

Switching the water abruptly to cold, Anna gritted her teeth as the icy jets pummeled her. Shivering, she climbed out of the shower and roughly toweled herself dry. Any gains made by the cold dousing quickly went by the wayside, and she stared down at her perkily erect nipples. What on earth was wrong with her? She'd just broken all the tenets and values she'd lived by her entire life. Shouldn't that mean something?

Thoroughly confused, she dressed in a pair of jeans and a T-shirt, then made a small choking noise as she caught sight of the neatly wrapped present on the kitchen bench. She'd almost forgotten! They were having a barbecue at her father's place today for his birthday. For a few wild seconds she considered canceling, but she would never do that to her dad. And Danny would be there, and she needed advice, stat.

Taking the portable telephone through into the living room, she perched on her armchair and squinted out into the bright morning sunlight. Her flat was on the third floor, with an excellent view of her neighbor's swimming pool and multicar garage. One of the privileges of living in Rose Bay—getting to see how the other half lived up close. She watched stray leaves drift down into the aqua water as the phone rang. Just as she was about to give up, Danny answered.

"What?" he growled, clearly grumpy at having been woken.

"I need you," she said, chewing anxiously on a thumbnail. "I'm having a vixen crisis."

"Really?" Danny sounded instantly alert.

"Can you come to Dad's early?" she asked.

"Give me an hour."

"Half an hour. I'm going crazy here, Danny."

"Okay. But no cracks about my bed-head."

Smiling faintly at her brother's vanity, she ended the call. For a few moments she remained curled on the armchair, knees pulled in tightly to her chest. She could hear the ticking of the clock on the mantelpiece, and the faint scuffle of people moving around in the flat upstairs. Then she realized she was frowning, and a deluge of confusing thoughts and feelings swamped her. Shaking her head, she pushed herself up and out of the chair. No. She was not going to sit here and send herself around the bend trying to sort out the confusing mix of regret and desire that had her in its grasp. That was Danny's job. She just had to get her ass down to her father's so Danny could minister to her.

Stuffing her feet into slip-on sandals, she grabbed her car keys and sunglasses and scooped up her father's present. She'd buy a cake on the way, along with some other premade salads. Her whole family happily acknowledged that she'd never mastered the art of cooking, and she was the queen of gourmet takeaway.

She made two stops on the way to her father's house in the suburb of Chatswood on the north shore. Her father's favorite cheesecake and a selection of gourmet salads in the trunk, she pulled up outside his neatly kept brick veneer house within half an hour. The fabric of her T-shirt pulled across her sensitive shoulders as she exited the car, and Anna slid her sunglasses on with a firm hand. She pushed all thoughts of having dirty under-ground-parking-lot sex with Marc out of her mind and reached into the trunk. She refused to think about it until she had Danny on hand to help straighten her out.

He was helping her father set up folding chairs in the backyard when she exited the kitchen.

"Anna Banana," her father said affectionately, pulling her in for a big bear hug. Stepping back, he surveyed her from head to toe. "You're looking beautiful, as always. Although I'm still not one hundred percent on this hair," he said, ruffling her blond spikes gently.

"It's fun," she said, having had this discussion before. "I felt like a change."

"I guess I should just thank my lucky stars you're both here in time to help set things up. Never seen either of you up and about so early."

Anna smiled a little guiltily, and Danny caught her eye. "Hey, Anna, you want to come help me with the big table in the shed?" he said meaningfully.

She smiled gratefully and followed him into the musty-smelling shade of her father's work shed. Eyeing a dangling spiderweb cautiously, she laid a hand on Danny's arm.

"Thank you so much for coming early. I just have to tell someone, get it off my chest."

"What on earth have you done?" Danny asked, the picture of urbane cool with his slickly styled hair and designer sunglasses.

"Last night, I had a job with Marc Lewis again," she said.

Danny's eyes sparkled and he rubbed his hands together. "*Ooooh*, I just know I am going to love this."

"I need you to be serious, Danny. I can't believe what I did. I honestly can't."

"Okay, unless you swung naked from a chandelier in Parliament, I think you might be overreacting a little."

"We had sex on the back of my car in the deserted underground parking lot of his building," Anna stated boldly.

To his credit, Danny only blinked once before pursing his lips thoughtfully.

"Okay, I'll admit I'm a little surprised—but also very, very impressed. You're a fast learner."

"Danny!"

"Anna!" Danny mocked her. He perched his sunglasses on top

of his head and pulled hers off her face so that they could make proper eye contact.

"Listen to me. You had sex with a consenting adult. That's it."

"In public. On a car."

"Whoop-dee-do. And it wasn't in public, it was in a private garage. You need to chill out a little."

Anna put her head in her hands. "You don't understand. He was a client. You'll note I use the past tense. And I just don't do things like this."

"No—the old Anna didn't do things like this. New Anna seizes life by the balls and gives them a bloody good squeeze."

Anna surprised herself by laughing at Danny's crude analogy. "I did a bit more than that last night, let me tell you."

"I wish you would. So…are we talking washboard abs? Tight little butt? Is he cut or uncut? Spill, lady."

Anna shifted uncomfortably. She could barely meet her brother's eyes as it was—she wasn't about to give him a blow by blow.

"I don't even know what cut means," she said evasively.

Danny sighed theatrically. "The Education of Anna. Is he circumcized or not?"

Anna could feel the heat staining her cheeks. *"Danny!"*

"Boy, this guy must have the smoothest charm in the world to get past this Miss Prim thing of yours and talk you into doing it in a garage."

"He didn't say anything. We kind of bumped into each other and then before I knew it we were having sex."

Danny grinned. "At the risk of repeating myself, I am *so* impressed. Wait until I tell Ryan and Scott."

"You cannot tell anyone! Don't you understand that I am freaking out here? I have no idea how to handle this situation."

"This is what you wanted, remember? *I want more passion in my life. I want the kind of sex you see in the movies. I want someone to want me so much he almost tears my clothes off.* Ring any bells?"

Anna stared at him. "Yes," she admitted slowly.

"And? Did last night not meet all of the above criteria? Were clothes torn? Did music swell, among other things? Were there impossible sexual acrobatics?"

"Yes. Well, apart from the music thing."

Suddenly Anna was back in her hospital bed, staring at her notebook and the too-long list she'd made, a testament to how cheated and scared she'd felt as she waited for her results. She'd seen her mother die from breast cancer. She knew what awaited her if she was unlucky. Had there ever been a more honest, soul-searching moment in her life? She didn't think so. And she'd made herself a promise that things would be different if she got a second chance.

And here she was, alive and well. A living, breathing, walking, talking second chance.

Danny was right. She hadn't done anything to be ashamed of last night. She remembered the high she'd felt as she'd exchanged polite handshakes with Marc after their encounter. She'd felt euphoric. Free. Sophisticated. In charge. And then she'd seen that stupid butt-print on her car trunk and been sucked down a sinkhole of regret and self-recrimination.

"You're right," she said, recognizing all her guilt and remorse for what it was—the old Anna trying to push the new Anna back into a nice, tidy, controlled little box. She was changing her life, and part of her was scared to do that.

"Of course I'm right. Get used to it," Danny said smugly.

Recognizing her reaction for what it was didn't necessarily make it go away—but suddenly it had assumed manageable proportions. The tight knot of tension in her stomach eased, and she stuffed her sunglasses into her back pocket and grabbed one end of the big picnic table.

"Where is this going?" she asked.

Danny groaned. "You know I hate physical labor." But he grabbed the other end of the table anyway.

They had the yard set up and the barbecue going by the time the bulk of her father's friends and family arrived for lunch. Danny captained the grill, decked out in a novelty apron, a beer in his hand as he traded cracks with their first cousin's husband, Mike.

She watched him, slightly bemused by how well he could play it straight. Brow puckering, she wondered if he found it a chore. What must it be like to play a part so much of the time? To be so worried that you wouldn't be accepted by your loved ones and work colleagues that you hid your true self from them?

"Get that serious look off your face, sweetheart. No frowning on my birthday," her father said as he drew up alongside her. He slid his arm around her waist and pulled her tightly to his side.

"I was just thinking that Danny's been slaving over the barbecue for hours," she improvised.

"You're right." Her dad cupped his hands to call across the yard. "Hey, Mike—want to give Danny a break for a bit, mate?"

Mike nodded agreeably and Danny handed over the apron and barbecue tongs.

"Good work, Dad. Make the guests earn their keep," he joked as he joined them.

Her dad winked at Danny, then nodded toward a woman standing near the back fence, talking to another guest. "I've been meaning to tell you—that's Larry from next door's girl. Bit of a looker, eh?" he said.

Anna bit her lip. It was no secret that her father was looking forward to both his children settling down. She'd had a break from his matchmaking since she'd been sick, but Danny was the constant recipient of their father's hints. The two of them had a permanent arrangement to go to the movies every Thursday night, and Danny had told her that their father was always pointing out good-looking women in the theater for Danny to notice. She'd advised him again and again that there was one foolproof way of ending the campaign—tell their father the truth. But Danny simply refused.

Seeing the loving light in their father's eye as he listened to Danny tell an anecdote from the office, Anna didn't think any less of her brother for holding on to his secret. No child ever wanted to disappoint a parent, and there was no denying that their father appeared to be looking forward to seeing Danny with a family of his own one day. It was a tough situation—and at the end of the day it was her brother's decision to make.

"You want another beer, Dad?" Danny asked as he drained the last of his own.

"Better not. You know what your mother always used to say— I make a sad and pathetic drunk. Even more so these days," her dad said, smiling lopsidedly.

"What about you, Anna?" Danny asked, about to head inside to the fridge.

"I'll come with you," she said.

It was much cooler inside out of the midday sun, and she ran a hand through her hair.

"Whew, it's hot out there," she said as Danny handed her a glass of juice.

"Try standing in front of the grill for a century or two. I swear my nipples are medium to well-done," Danny said.

"Ew, I don't want to think about your nipples!" Anna said, pretending disgust.

"Which reminds me—Mr. Stud last night. Without going into too much detail, I take it a good time was had by all?" Danny waggled his eyebrows suggestively.

"Without going into too much detail…yes," Anna said.

Danny spread his hands wide, obviously expecting more. "That's it? Not even a single adjective for Uncle Danny? Just one word to describe your first out-of-bedroom sexual experience…?"

"Okay. Spectacular," she said, deadpan.

Danny laughed. "You're not even going to tell me if his body lived up to the promise delivered by that suit of his, are you?"

"Nope."

"If you were gay, we'd have a ruler out right now, and I'd know everything about the man."

"Sorry." She shrugged.

"So, any chance of a rematch?"

Anna blinked. "Oh, no!"

"But if it was that hot…"

"No way. Marc Lewis and I were strangers in the night. No phone numbers were exchanged, not even a 'see you around.' I might be a babe in the woods when it comes to this stuff, but I know a one-night stand when I have one."

"You could still call him, see if he's up for round two," Danny suggested.

A wave of mortification raced through her at the very thought. Probably after the evening she'd had, she should be feeling a little more liberated about her sexual needs, but old habits died hard. There was no way she could be that blatant about what she wanted.

She tried to articulate her feelings.

"You know, Danny, I think I've kind of gone from zero to a hundred here pretty quickly, and it wouldn't hurt for me to slow down a little. Yes, I had a good time last night. No, I am not going to go home and put my hair shirt on and kneel on a bed of nails. But I think some baby steps might be called for from now on. Maybe I should just go out more, socialize with my friends a bit. Meet some new people. *Then* I can find someone to have some fun with. When I'm ready."

"Why can't you have fun with Marc Lewis?" Danny asked stubbornly.

"No," she said very firmly, flashing back to the out-of-control, can't-get-enough greediness of last night. "No. Marc is out of my league."

"But—"

"Danny—baby steps," she said over the top of him. "I've got my training wheels on, remember?"

That seemed to get through. "You're right. Sorry. I should pull back on making you my new hobby, eh?" He slung his arm around her shoulders, and she winced.

"Don't tell me you're sunburned already?" he asked as he peeled his arm off her.

"No. Last night…we might have moved venue from the trunk of the car to the wall at some stage. There's this rash on my back…."

"Ah," Danny said, nodding sagely. "Concrete burn. Bit of vitamin E cream and a couple of days will clear it up."

She stared at him. "Is there anything you don't know?"

"I'm not real good on where the female G-spot is."

She laughed. "And long may it be so."

She raised her glass, and he clinked his beer against it. "Amen."

A WARM BREEZE WAS BLOWING across the harbor as Marc padded down the steps toward the pool. Ripples raced each other across the pool's surface, and he executed a perfect jackknife dive, slicing right to the bottom. The water's chill embrace banished the last traces of sleep from his system, and he began powering along with his economical but effective freestyle stroke. Ten laps, fifteen, twenty. At lap forty he switched to an energy-consuming butterfly stroke, racing up and down the pool until his arms were leaden and his lungs on fire.

By the time he dragged himself from the pool he was breathing heavily, but he felt great. Relaxed for the first time in ages. He toweled himself down, gazing out across the ocean toward the Harbour Bridge. He couldn't quite see the opera house from his terrace—the promontory off Double Bay blocked his view— but the sweep of harbor and bridge that met his gaze was stunning enough to satisfy any man's lust for the picturesque. For a second he allowed himself a small fillip of satisfaction at how far he'd come. From a state-provided house in the hot and dusty outer suburbs of Sydney to one of the most desirable pieces of real estate in the world.

A bitter smile twisted his lips. Tara would have loved this view. She would have invited every single person she had ever met to the house, ensured they'd taken in every one of the five bathrooms and four living areas, then casually led them down through the garden to this pool terrace. She would have fed off their gasps of amazement and delight, just as she had always fed off others' envy and jealousy.

Marc turned abruptly away from the view. Deep inside, he knew that there had been much more to his wife than the pleasure she took in his achievements. Was he any different, standing here gloating over what was now his?

He was in no mood to be generous toward Tara, however, even if it was only in thought. Slinging the towel around his neck, he strode up to the house. Showering quickly, he pulled on jeans and a polo shirt, then padded barefoot across to his study. His laptop glowed welcomingly from his desk, and he sank into his office chair with an absurd feeling of relief. Work had been his one solace over the past six months, accepting all his focus and energy with open arms.

As he flipped the screen up, his gaze was drawn to his knuckles. He'd grazed them last night, he saw, and suddenly a hot flash of memory surged over him: Anna Jackson, her head thrown back as he pounded into her, holding her braced against the wall. She'd been so tight and wet, so responsive. The way her nipples had puckered under his fingers and tongue. The way she'd tensed her thighs around him and groaned deep in her throat as she came….

He shook his head to clear the memory. But it was too late. The loose, relaxed feeling he'd gained in the pool was suddenly gone; he had a raging hard-on, and a taste for Anna in his mouth.

He frowned. It was one thing to be haunted by fantasies about a woman that he'd seen half-naked in a dark corner of the world, but he'd had her. He'd touched her and filled her and spent himself inside her. The fascination should be over. He wanted it to be over.

All his life he'd prided himself on being a man in control of his more basic desires. He ate well, he exercised, he didn't indulge his temper. And he'd been faithful for the ten years that his marriage had lasted. It wasn't that he hadn't been tempted. There had been times. There had definitely been times. But after what his father had done to his mother, he'd never found it hard to push desire away and remember what he stood to lose if he gave in to his baser needs.

Yet here he was, Anna Jackson still holding center stage in his mind. Having her last night was supposed to have scratched the itch, purged the urge, as it were. But his body remembered the feel of hers. The heat of her skin. The fullness of her breasts. The curving slope of her belly. The long length of her legs clenched tightly around him, mimicking the action of her more intimate muscles as she held him inside her.

He didn't understand it. He didn't want to understand it. He just wanted her gone.

Resolute, he pulled up a new window on the computer. Gradually, thoughts of Anna Jackson slipped away as he lost himself in concentration. The tension eased out of his body, and the dull throb of desire tapered off as he held himself to the discipline of work. When he next looked up from the screen, two hours had passed, and he saved his notes and flicked the computer off hastily. Distracting himself with work had been so effective that now he was late for lunch with his sister.

Not many minutes later, he was tooling along the leafy streets of Point Piper in his Jag convertible. Traffic was light, and it didn't take long to make his way to the Woolloomooloo wharves.

Tossing the keys to the parking attendant at the W Hotel, he strode inside, blinking in the relative darkness of the foyer.

He spotted his sister reading a newspaper on a bank of couches to his left. She didn't look up from the article she was reading, and he walked across to stand in front of her.

"Sorry I'm late. Although it doesn't look like you were exactly champing at the bit."

"Can you believe the rubbish they put in the social pages? This Katie Menski woman is a poisonous viper, if you ask me. The things she writes about people!"

"Good afternoon to you, too."

"I just don't understand why it's allowed," Alison said as she allowed him to lead her out onto the promenade, where there was a range of restaurants for them to choose from. "Why doesn't someone just sue the newspaper? That'd put a stop to the viciousness."

"Mmm. What do you feel like? Italian? Seafood?" Marc asked, mildly amused by his sister's rant.

"I want pastries after reading that stupid article. Some nice calming saturated fats."

Marc let out a bark of laughter and led her into a wood-paneled patisserie. They found a seat by the window, and both pulled out their sunglasses to tame the bright midday sun.

"Can I make a suggestion?" he said as they picked up menus.

"Of course. But it doesn't mean I'm going to listen to you," Alison warned him.

"Don't read the social pages if they annoy you so much," he said.

She opened and shut her mouth a few times. "But it just irritates me that so many people lap that stuff up like it's gospel!"

"Yep. And you can't do a damned thing about it. So...don't worry about it," he said, spreading his hands wide to illustrate his point.

Alison stared at him a moment, an arrested expression on her face. "I guess that's why you're the millionaire in the family," she said grudgingly.

"Just common sense, Ally," he said drily.

"Still."

She smiled at him, and reached across to squeeze his arm. "You're looking better, you know. More relaxed, less stressed. Last time I saw you I thought you were developing a permanent frown."

Instantly his thoughts turned to the spectacular bout of stress relief that he'd enjoyed the night before. He cleared his throat and shifted in his chair.

"What are you going to have?"

Alison lifted dark eyes to him. Anyone seeing them together would have no doubt about their relationship, Marc thought. They shared the same olive skin and dark hair and eyes. She was tall for a woman, too. Almost as tall as Anna Jackson.

"Damn it," he cursed under his breath. Why did he keep thinking about her?

"Sorry?" Alison asked.

"Nothing. Just thinking of something," he said, waving a hand to signify the thought's irrelevance.

"Work?" she asked sympathetically.

To his everlasting amazement, he felt a blush heat his neck and cheeks. He kept his gaze firmly on the menu, avoiding his sister's eagle eyes.

But she'd already caught on. "Why, Marc, I do believe you're blushing!" she said archly.

Marc raised an eyebrow imperiously, trying to brazen it out. "Am I?"

"Oh, yes. What's going on?"

"Nothing."

"Come on now, you know that's not going to cut it with me," she said mockingly. She cocked her head to one side and studied him. "Looking relaxed…slightly rumpled…running late…"

She sat up straighter and clapped her hands together. "You've met someone!" she squealed.

Marc frowned. "Alison…."

"Tell me everything. Where did you meet her? What's her name?" Alison asked, almost rubbing her hands together with anticipation.

Marc signaled for the waiter to come over. "I'm having the croissants. What would you like?" he said, drawing a line under his sister's nosiness.

"The quiche and salad, please. And a slice of the gâteau."

"We are lashing out," Marc commented sardonically.

"Absolutely. And don't think you've changed the subject, mister."

"Alison, as much as I love you dearly, you are not getting a free pass into my private life. So just leave it, okay?"

She must have heard the warning note in his voice, because she bit her lip and began fiddling with a sugar straw.

"I'm not being gratuitously nosy, Marc. It's only because I care about you. I know you loved Tara, I know you're still upset about what happened. But life goes on. You're thirty-five, ridiculously good-looking, disgustingly wealthy—you should be having a good time, not having lunch with your sister on a Saturday afternoon."

"At this stage I feel honor-bound to point out that this lunch was your idea, to discuss Sally's progress with the job," he reminded her drily.

A wave of Alison's hand dispensed with this consideration. "You know what I mean, don't pretend you don't. Life goes on, Marc. There's still plenty of time to meet someone else, have a family."

"Perhaps I don't want a family," he said coolly.

"Which is why you bought a six-bedroom home."

Marc could feel all the familiar anger and hurt welling up inside him. Tara had thrown away so much when she'd betrayed

him with another man. All their plans for the future… He wasn't
going to risk that happening again.

"If it will make you happy, we can put a lid on this topic for
all time right here and now. Listen very carefully—I am not interested in marrying again."

Alison opened her mouth, and he headed her off at the pass.
"Or having a long-term relationship without marriage. Any future
woman in my life will be there for one thing and one thing only.
And right now, I'm not even particularly interested in that!"

Just to make a liar of him, an image of Anna flashed into his
mind—the one he'd been obsessing about all week after he'd
caught her changing before their opera house meeting. The slope
of her breast, the curve of her butt in lace, glimpsed for just a
second before she pulled her dress on….

"Are you telling me that you're just going to fritter away the
rest of your life having a series of affairs with women? Do you
have any idea how empty that sounds?" she asked.

Marc saw that there were actually tears in his sister's eyes.

"Ally. Don't cry for me. I'm a very happy, very contented man."

But she just shook her head. "I'm really going to need that
gâteau now. That is the saddest thing I have ever heard."

Marc tensed his jaw and looked off into the middle distance.
She didn't get it. Perhaps if her husband had pulled the rug out
from beneath her, destroying everything she'd built around them
to make their lives work—perhaps then she'd understand the pain
and anger he'd been through in the last six months. And why he
was never going to put himself in a position where it could
happen again.

ANNA PUSHED THE COUCH another few inches forward, then
stepped back to admire her handiwork. Perfect. She took another
couple of steps back, eyes running approvingly over the soft
chocolate leather of her new couch. It was accented perfectly by

the rich burnt orange of the newly painted feature wall behind it, and by the luxuriously thick ruby red rug in front of it.

She knelt and ran her fingers through the rug's soft, velvety tufts. Silk and wool, the man in the shop had said. In winter, she could steal cushions from the couch and curl up on the rug with a book and a glass of red wine. And it would be great for yoga—if and when she ever got around to watching the exercise DVD she'd bought recently. And, of course, it would really come into its own for making love. Instantly she pictured Marc, naked, hard and hot for her, stretched out across the rug like an offering to the gods.

She snatched her hands off the rug as though she'd just been electrocuted.

"Damn it!" Pushing her hands against her thighs, she exploded to her feet in a burst of frustrated energy.

She had done everything in her power to forget the man, and still he kept popping up in her subconscious. What was it going to take?

Gathering the plastic wrap that had protected the couch during delivery, Anna stuffed it into a garbage bag. It had been a week and a day since the encounter on her car. A good week, too, she told herself. She'd decided to learn from her lesson with Marc, to see it as the next, if maybe slightly extreme, step in her new life plan.

Hence the new couch. She'd always secretly longed for a colorful, comfortable nest to come home to. Her previous furniture had been a mixture of hand-me-downs, practical acquisitions and loans. Clean, neat, tidy. Boring. She'd always planned to invest in something more dramatic and interesting. But somehow, like so many other things, she'd never gotten around to it. So when the catalog came in the mail, she'd stared at the gorgeous couch in classic Art Deco clubman style and decided to just go for it. Life was short, right?

Two hours and a drive to the furniture outlet later, she'd

dropped a large chunk of change on the rug, the couch and a number of other accessories for around her home. Then she'd gone straight to the hardware store and picked a delicious deep orange paint to accent her new purchases. The whole lot had come together today, and it looked amazing—her own take on Morroccan nights.

She was changing, she really was.

Now, if she could just get Marc Lewis out of her head!

Even if she succeeded in going a whole day without indulging in a flashback fantasy about her time with him, she couldn't stop him from stealing into her dreams. As soon as she was asleep she was with him again, each touch a flame on her skin, each caress urging her toward an orgasm that she knew was going to be so intense, so mind-blowing that she'd never be the same again. In her dream she'd strive and hold her breath and strain…but the orgasm never came and she woke each morning feeling damned cranky and damned horny and knowing full well that there was precious little she could do about it.

Because calling him was out of the question. She wanted to. She dreamed about making that call. But she couldn't. She just… couldn't.

What had happened had happened. But it was a one-off. Definitely.

She'd been over his side of the city many times since that fateful Friday night a week ago. Twice she'd even driven right past his corporate headquarters. Both times her skin had prickled and she'd felt ridiculously self-conscious—just from driving past a stupid building! It was too much. Too ridiculous.

But no urge this strong could sustain itself. She'd reassured herself of that fact every morning as she stepped under the cold spray of her shower. It was just a matter of time. And of distracting herself from obsessing about him.

So as well as giving her apartment a new look, she'd reconnected with a number of her girlfriends from her lawyer days. They'd been flatteringly pleased to hear from her, and she'd been surprised at how much she'd enjoyed catching up with them. She'd cut a lot out of her life after her cancer diagnosis, and some of it had been good stuff. A case of throwing out the baby with the bathwater, perhaps.

Checking her watch, Anna pulled a face. She had to hustle if she was going to be ready in time. Dropping the garbage bag by the front door to take out when she left for the evening, she padded barefoot into her bedroom and pulled open her underwear drawer. Tossing a bra and panties onto the bed, she turned to head into the bathroom, only to find her attention caught by her new dress.

She was going to an exhibition opening with Leah and Jules, two friends from law school, and she'd added to her post-surgery wardrobe for the outing, purchasing a deep crimson sheath that hugged her curves and ended at midcalf. The front dipped dangerously low, showcasing the swell of her breasts but not prohibiting the wearing of a bra. Somehow, this small saving grace gave the old Anna some comfort. Baby steps, she reminded herself. Lots of baby steps.

She showered quickly, then did her makeup and hair in record time and was wriggling into her dress with a whole ten minutes to spare before her friends were due.

She whirled in front of the mirror, inspecting herself from every angle. She looked nice, definitely presentable. Maybe even a bit sexy, dare she say it? She stared at the large expanse of cleavage on display. Perhaps the dress was too sexy? It was the old Anna talking, she knew, but it made her move to her wardrobe and stare at the clothes hanging there. Was it too late to change?

The doorbell sounded. Her mouth twisted wryly—decision made, obviously. She opened the door, and her apartment was quickly filled with the sound of feminine laughter and chatter as they greeted each other.

"My God, Anna, that dress is incredible!" Leah said. "And your hair! You look so different!"

"Hell, yes. But it really suits you. You've got such great cheekbones," Jules chimed in.

Leah was still shaking her head, obviously incredulous. Anna spared a sympathetic thought for the woman she used to be—she of the uptight wardrobe and conservative blond bob.

"Thanks, guys. I thought maybe the dress might have been a bit too much…?"

"Are you kidding? You look like a movie star," Jules said.

"You should have done this years ago," Leah added enthusiastically. Then she blushed deeply, and clapped a hand over her mouth. "Anna—I'm so sorry!" she said contritely. "I didn't mean…"

Anna laughed, keen to dispel any awkwardness. That was the thing with cancer—other people were always more uncomfortable about it than she was.

"It's okay, relax," she said. "I know exactly what you mean."

Leah looked relieved, and Jules lifted envious eyes from the intent study she'd been making of Anna's dress.

"Such a gorgeous red, Anna. I'd rip it off your back if I thought I could squeeze more than one thigh into it." Jules pulled a face, indicating her fuller figure ruefully.

Her confidence well and truly bolstered, Anna collected her evening bag and house keys. "Well, if I'm not ready for a night out after that, it's never going to happen," she joked.

They laughed and talked in the taxi as they traveled across the city to the inner-west suburb of Glebe. Jules filled them in on her friend Maxine, the artist behind tonight's exhibition. She was a childhood friend, and Jules explained her style was abstract, but "not in a horrible elite wanky kind of way." Since Anna knew just enough about art to fill the back of a postage stamp, she wasn't particularly fussed. Tonight was about fun—doing something different, and catching up with her friends.

The exhibition was being held in a Victorian-era mansion set well back from the road in a busy café district. Their taxi dropped them at the curb, and they click-clacked their way up the garden-bordered path and into the foyer of the old house. All three of them gasped with admiration as they stepped through the stained-glass entrance door. Floorboards gleamed around them, a huge chandelier sparkled high above and a staircase swept grandly up to the second floor.

They grinned at each other, a bit embarrassed by their gauche responses. Leah pulled her jacket off with a flick of her wrist.

"Darrrrrrlings, I think we've arrived," she said in a really bad imitation of an upper-class English accent.

Anna muffled a laugh. Making contact with her old friends and coming here tonight was the best thing she could have done. Already things were assuming a more normal, rational perspective. Like Marc Lewis, for example. She could barely remember the smell of his aftershave anymore. A huge step in the right direction. A few more weeks of determined socializing, and he'd be nothing but a short, hot flash of memory.

Realizing that Leah and Jules had moved off ahead of her, she followed them into the main exhibition space. There was a good crowd, a very respectable showing for a young artist. But it only took a second for Anna's eyes to hone in on one tall, broad-shouldered figure standing at the far end of the gallery. Even as her stomach dipped with nerves, he turned his head toward her—almost as though he'd *known* she was there. Perhaps he had, in the same way that she'd sensed his presence the moment she walked in.

Across the room, dark, depthless eyes met hers as she froze in place, her breath stuck somewhere between her lungs and her throat.

Marc Lewis. Wouldn't you know it?

5

EMBARRASSMENT WASHED OVER HER. World-class embarrassment. Her body was so hot a troop of Boy Scouts could toast marshmallows on her. Astronauts could probably see her from the moon. The last time she'd seen this man, she'd torn his clothes off and done... *things* with him on the trunk of her car. She wasn't supposed to run into him like this. In fact, in a perfect world, Marc would have ceased to exist the moment she dropped him off at his house just over a week ago. That way she would never have to face up to the reality of what had happened between them that night.

But here he was, larger than life. In the flesh. Tall and handsome and vitally attractive.

Of their own accord, her eyes took a lingering tour of his body. He was wearing a dark charcoal casual shirt with a stylized floral pattern printed on it in dark brown and black. His long legs were clothed in dark jeans, and his hair was more tousled, less tidy than his workday look. He was stunning. Dangerous. Sex on legs.

She tore her eyes away from him. She had to go. That much was obvious. She couldn't possibly live this down. She had no idea what the etiquette was for the first time you met your one-night stand after the event. Polite chitchat? Ignore each other? Or were they supposed to greet each other like old friends?

Much easier to go. Absolutely.

She turned back toward the foyer, ready to just hightail it out of there.

"Anna, where are you going?" Leah asked from behind her.

Anna blinked, astonished that for a few seconds there she had actually forgotten her friends.

"Um…" she said, her mind a complete blank as far as handy excuses went.

Jules waylaid a passing waiter and held out a champagne flute to her.

"There you go," Jules said.

Anna stared wide-eyed at the drink, then her gaze flickered past her friends to where Marc stood talking to a younger man and woman at the other end of the exhibition space. He was still watching her. Her heart picked up its pace, banging against her ribs.

"Um…" she said again, feeling like a bunny frozen in the car headlights.

Jules and Leah didn't seem to notice; Jules just slid the cool glass into her hand, then turned to Leah. "Good turnout. Maxine must be rapt," she commented, sipping from her own champagne flute.

"This all looks great. I've been meaning to buy some art. I don't think my old Picasso prints cut it anymore," Leah said.

The two of them moved closer to the nearest painting in order to study it more closely, and somehow, Anna found herself following them.

So, she wasn't going. What was she doing, exactly? She wasn't sure. She still felt shell-shocked from that first moment of eye contact with Marc. How could a glance across a room affect a person so much? Confused, overwhelmed, she took a hearty slug from her champagne glass.

I can handle this, she told herself firmly as the alcohol burned its way down her throat and warmed her belly. *As long as I don't have to look him in the eye and talk to him, I'll be fine.*

MARC TRIED TO CONCENTRATE on the conversation he was supposed to be having, but it was impossible now that he knew she was here.

Anna Jackson.

A week of pounding the pool, punishing runs and working late had finally pushed her image from his mind. For the most part. There had been that one hot flashback to the parking lot as he was showering this evening. Perhaps it was the steam, or the hot water, or the slick slipperiness of the soap. Whatever, one minute he was enjoying the water massaging the tense muscles across his shoulders, the next he was thinking about Anna, how tight and hot she'd been, how she'd moaned in his ear as he plunged inside her, the way she'd held his head to her breasts as he sucked her nipple into his mouth.

Now she was standing across the room, and he couldn't take his eyes off her. She was wearing a dark red dress that hugged her curves, and high, strappy sandals that made the most of her long legs. Even at this distance he could see the smooth, creamy skin of her cleavage. He knew what her breasts looked like now, knew that her nipples were a pale coral pink to match her fair complexion, and that they puckered readily to his touch. He knew that if he ran his hands down her hips he would find the perfect curve of her butt, and he knew just how soft and yielding she would be if he pressed all his hardness up against her.

"...if that's okay with you, Mr. Lewis?"

Marc gave himself a mental slap as he registered that Jacob had been talking to him, suggesting they take some time now to get their business out of the way. He smiled, forced his gaze away from Anna.

"Of course," he said smoothly. A spurt of self-directed annoyance cleared a path through the fog of lust he'd sunk into. He was here to finalize the last stages of a deal that had taken more than a month to set up. He couldn't afford to lose focus like this.

"I'll leave you to it, then," Maxine, Jacob's girlfriend, said. "An old friend has just arrived, anyway."

Despite his determination to ignore Anna, Marc couldn't help noting that Maxine made a beeline for her and her friends. Did Anna know her? Was that why Anna was here?

Not that it mattered. It didn't mean anything at all. It was just that he hadn't expected to see her. That was the only reason he was feeling so unsettled. After all, what had happened between them was hardly run-of-the-mill. There was bound to be some awkwardness attached to seeing each other again.

But the tightness in his trousers belied all rational argument. He didn't feel *awkward* about seeing Anna again. He was aroused. Turned on beyond all belief. And hungry for more of what he'd tasted a week ago.

He swallowed the last mouthful of his champagne and handed his empty flute to a passing waiter. Pushing his fascination with Anna to one side, he focused very deliberately on the man standing in front of him. Business. Tonight was about business.

"Have you thought any more about my offer?" he asked bluntly.

Jacob laughed nervously. "As if I've done anything except think about it."

"And?"

"I have a few questions. If that's okay?"

Marc smiled, knowing then and there that he would get what he wanted this evening.

"Fire away," he encouraged.

Jacob launched into a series of questions, all of which ranged around the one concern—he wanted to sell his small hothouse software development business to Lewis Technologies, but he was worried about losing his innovative edge within the bigger corporate structure.

"I understand your concerns," Marc responded. "If you come onboard, you and your team will run as a separate arm of the research and development department. You'll report directly to me, and you'll have the ability to be as flexible, responsive and innovative as you are now—with the resources of a major player at your back. It's a win-win, Jacob. You'll get royalties on any software you author, and we have a generous superannuation and bonus scheme. I believe in rewarding effort."

Jacob's cheeks were flushed, his eyes shining as he began to imagine his new role. Marc's instincts told him he was almost home. Then he glanced up and his eye was caught by the red flare that was Anna's dress.

She was talking to a waiter, accepting another glass of champagne. Marc narrowed his eyes as he watched the other man glance down at Anna's body, his thoughts more than obvious. The waiter said something, and Anna threw back her head and laughed. The sound was pure and honest, and Marc found himself arrested by the sheer abandonment of it.

"...is the one who's been the most resistant, but I'd hate to lose him. I think he'd be a real asset to your business," Jacob said.

Marc snapped his attention back to the here and now, realizing that once again he'd been distracted from the matter at hand. Fortunately, he was familiar enough with Jacob's business setup to guess what—or, more correctly, who—he was talking about.

"I agree that Benji is an asset," he said crisply. He had to get Anna out of his mind. "What's his sticking point?"

Jacob looked uncomfortable. "This is going to sound pretty lame to someone like you...but Benji thinks that us shacking up with Lewis Technologies is selling out. He figures you'll be expecting us to wear suits and do the whole nine-to-five thing. He doesn't work like that."

"Tell Benji to relax. As long as the work gets done, I don't care when or how. Bring him in for a tour of the R & D suite next week. I think he'll see enough torn denim and bad personal hygiene to make him feel at home."

Jacob allowed the grin he'd been suppressing for the last few minutes to break free at last.

"In that case, Mr. Lewis, you've got a deal!" he said enthusiastically.

Jacob offered his hand, and this time his handshake was firm and certain.

"Welcome onboard. And it's Marc."

Jacob pumped his hand even more enthusiastically. "Marc, then. Cool."

As soon as his concentration slipped, Marc's eyes found their way back to Anna. She was standing with her hand on one hip, head cocked to one side as she contemplated one of Maxine's floor-to-ceiling paintings. Maxine was standing beside her, gesticulating broadly as she talked. The line of Anna's neck was elegant and alluring, the curve of her hip even more so. She looked stylish and sophisticated—but he knew just how hot she could be.

"I can introduce you, if you like," Jacob said beside him.

"Sorry?"

Jacob gestured toward Anna. "Maxine obviously knows her."

Marc smiled coolly, unhappy that his fascination was so obvious. "Thanks, but I'm fine," he said.

Jacob nodded, embarrassed now. "Sorry. It's just, the way you were looking at her…"

"I know her," Marc explained. "An old acquaintance."

"Oh. Right."

Across the room, Anna laughed again. He forced himself to stay focused on Jacob.

Business. Tonight is about business, he reminded himself.

If only his body would listen, he'd have half a chance of walking away from this evening with his pride and self-respect intact.

ANNA FELT AS THOUGH her cheeks were going to crack in half if she smiled one more time. She just wanted to get the hell out of there. No matter what she did, where she looked, or who she was talking to, every sense, every fiber of her being was focused on the man standing at the other end of the room. And it was driving her crazy.

Why hadn't she gone home the second she saw him standing there? It was the only sane, self-preserving thing to have done. Yet here she was, allowing Jules's artist friend, Maxine, to drag her farther up the gallery so she could show her another painting. She glanced toward Leah and Jules, wondering if she could convince them to bail early. They were chatting to one of the waiters, a tall blond guy with green eyes. She got the definite sense that suggesting they go elsewhere would not be welcomed.

"This was the first sale of the evening," Maxine chattered, her cheeks rosy from excitement and champagne. "My boyfriend's new boss bought it," she confided happily. "He said he's going to put it in the foyer of his building. Can you believe that?"

"That's great. I hope it's a nice big building, so lots of people will get to see it every day," Anna said. Out of the corner of her eye, she saw Marc flash a smile at the man Maxine had been talking to when she first arrived. She almost blinked and stared, the smile transformed his face so much. He went from brooding and sexy and dangerous to approachable and fun and dangerous.

"It's huge. Jacob's going to be so much better off working for a big company instead of having to worry about making ends meet all the time," Maxine said. "He's so clever—he deserves to be recognized."

The softness in the other woman's voice caught and held Anna's attention—no small feat given her growing obsession with the man standing across the room.

"Sounds like you guys get along pretty well," she observed.

"Jacob's the best," Maxine said, her eyes misting over. Then she glanced over Anna's shoulder. "You want to meet him?"

"Um…sure," Anna said.

The words were no sooner out of her mouth than Maxine had grabbed her by the hand and was towing her across the room.

Way across the room. Toward Marc Lewis's end, in fact. Or, more specifically, *straight to Marc Lewis!*

Before Anna could dig her heels in or object or even think of escaping, she was being pulled forward and introduced to Maxine's boyfriend. In his early twenties, Jacob was red-haired and freckled, with bright blue eyes that radiated intelligence and humor. Anna could barely comprehend a word that was coming out of his mouth, however, because Marc was standing a mere arm's length away and all of the blood in her body was rushing south. God help her. She kept her eyes fixed on Jacob with a conscious act of will, smiling and shaking his hand and hoping she looked remotely sane.

"And this is Marc Lewis," Maxine said brightly. "Marc, this is Anna Jackson."

Reluctantly she dragged her eyes up to meet his. His gaze was smoky, unreadable.

"Anna. How are you?" he asked.

"Good. Thanks. Marc," she managed to stutter.

Jacob handed her a fresh glass of champagne, and she accepted it automatically. It wasn't as though she needed alcohol. She already felt both sick and dizzy and her heart was beating a frantic tattoo against her rib cage.

"Oh—you two know each other already?" Maxine asked, curiosity sending her gaze zinging back and forth between them.

Why couldn't the ground open up and swallow her? Anna was painfully aware of everything about him, from the woody scent of his aftershave to the way the hair curled over his ears, and the fact that he had a faint after-five stubble darkening his jaw. He stood squarely, looking supremely relaxed, easily dominating their small circle with his presence, and she shot him a desperate look before answering Maxine's question.

"Marc used to be one of my clients," she said, taking a bracing mouthful of her champagne.

"Used to be? Have I been blackballed, Anna?" Marc asked.

She was swallowing—not a good time to gasp with surprise. She choked, pressing a hand to her chest and coughing violently.

Someone took the glass of champagne from her hand as she endeavored not to lose a lung.

"Are you okay?" Maxine asked.

"I'm...I'm fine," Anna managed to say, finally clearing her throat.

Her cheeks were radiant with embarrassment, and she glared balefully at Marc's back as he turned to grab a glass of mineral water from a passing waiter. It was all his fault for making that crack. And for being so sexy. And for being here in the first place.

"Here."

He slid the water into her hand, and she took a couple of tentative sips.

"That's much better, thank you," she mumbled, not meeting anyone's eye. Could she have made it any more obvious that something had gone on between the two of them? She didn't think so, short of hiring a billboard or having it written in the sky.

"Back to normal?" Marc asked. As if in slow motion, she watched as he lifted a hand and placed it on her upper arm—an inconsequential, polite gesture between acquaintances.

But the instant his hand was on her, about a million neurons fired off simultaneously throughout her body. Her stomach muscles clenched. Her knees went weak. Her heart started to race. And her nipples nudged against the silk of her bra, remembering his touch and wanting more. Between her legs, her sex throbbed with need.

She stared down at his hand where it rested on her arm. His olive skin looked impossibly tan against her paler complexion, his fingers long and strong.

Completely at sea, she lifted her gaze to his. His dark eyes burned into her, and she licked her lips nervously. His gaze dropped to follow the movement, then he locked eyes with her again. There was no mistaking the desire in him. His pupils were dilated, and the raw hunger in him sent a thrill through her. She squeezed her thighs together, all too aware that wet heat was already pooling there—all from just a simple touch and a not-so-simple look.

Suddenly everything in the world dropped away. It didn't matter that five seconds ago she had been practically writhing with self-consciousness, wishing she was anywhere but here. Or that she'd spent the past week trying to justify her reckless, wild response to him. Or even that she was still deeply ambivalent about the whole Marc Lewis phenomenon. There was nothing in the universe except the need to be with him again. Her body knew him. And her body wanted him. Bad.

As if he could read her thoughts, Marc's fingers tightened on her arm. A delicious surge of heat raced along her veins. She had to bite back a moan of desire.

She had to be alone with him. Now.

Her heartbeat sounded loud in her ears as she put her water glass down carefully on a nearby table.

"It was nice meeting you, Jacob. If you'll excuse me, I might just go powder my nose," she heard herself say.

Then she was putting one foot in front of the other, walking toward the archway that led into the administration part of the building. She didn't need to look to see if Marc would follow her. He would come. Every instinct in her told her he would come.

The air in the corridor was cool on her heated skin, and she stepped toward the first closed door on her left. The handle turned beneath her hand, and she stepped into a darkened office. Leaving the door open, she walked across the carpeted floor to survey the wide leather-topped desk. Perfect.

She sensed rather than heard him enter the room behind her. She was shaking with need by now, and the sound of the privacy lock being engaged made her catch her breath. Soon, soon she would have him inside her again....

A faint click, and a pool of light illuminated the leather top of the desk as he turned on the lamp.

"Take your dress off," he said.

Despite the lamplight, his face remained in darkness. She obeyed him, because she wanted to more than anything in the world. Already the muscles deep inside her were tightening in anticipation of his penetration. Remembering the full, hard length of him, she closed her eyes and shuddered.

Her zip undone, she pushed the dress off her shoulders, then shimmied it over her hips. She could feel the heat of his gaze as it traveled across her body, exposed now in a few bare scraps of silk and lace.

Without hesitation she slid the clasp of her bra loose and flung it to one side, quickly adding her panties to the growing pile of her clothes.

Then she was standing there, naked bar her stiletto sandals, hot and panting for him.

His gaze raked her, and the raw need and desire in his eyes was almost frightening—but she was too busy being excited by it to care.

He made a low animal sound in the back of his throat and reached for her. They came together as though they wanted to devour each other, tongues dueling, lips almost snarling as they strived to become one and satisfy the need that burned in both of them. His hands slid down her back, then swept smoothly over her hips and butt. She felt the tension ratchet tighter in his body as his hands explored the dips and curves of her backside, molding her to him. She ground herself against him, the action a pale imitation of what she truly desired.

Then suddenly he was grasping her, lifting her and turning to place her on the desk so that he was standing in front of her. He stared down into her eyes for a heartbeat before his hands brushed down over her breasts, her belly, and finally, to her thighs. She didn't wait for him to push them apart, spreading them eagerly for him. Her heart slamming against her ribs, she watched his face as he stared down at the nest of curls at the juncture of her thighs.

His mouth parted, and his tongue darted out to lick his lips. Her stomach muscles clenched. He ran his hands up the smooth skin of her inner thighs, pushing them wider but stopping just short of touching her heat. His thumbs caressed the tender skin of her upper thighs, back and forth, back and forth. She sucked in a breath, then let it out in a rush as he at last slid a finger into her slick folds.

"You're very wet, Anna," he murmured, dark eyes skewering her.

"You make me hot," she murmured back, reaching for the hard, straining bulge in his pants.

She gasped as he unerringly found her clitoris, his knowing fingers teasing over and over the tight bud. All the while he was watching her, his gaze intent on her face.

"I want you inside me," she said, her voice thready with need.

"No," he said, but the word was more a promise than a denial.

Very deliberate, he sank to his knees, and she sucked in a lungful of air as his dark head moved toward her wide-spread thighs.

"*Ohhhh* yes!" she moaned as his tongue made its first sweep across her wetness.

His hands gripped her thighs firmly, holding her in place as he began to lave her with skillful intensity. His tongue was by turns firm and rasping, then slick and darting, then warm and wonderfully wet as he suckled her.

She forgot her name, where they were, who they were. The whole world narrowed to the spiraling heat that was building inside her and the remorseless, delicious pressure of his tongue. She gripped the edge of the desk, knuckles clenched white as she writhed.

Her thighs found their way onto his shoulders, and just when she thought she was going to explode his hands slid under her butt and he lifted her up, his tongue firmer and harder than ever before.

She came hard, her thighs clenching, her back arching, a low moan groaning out of her throat as her orgasm shook her. It seemed to go on and on, his skillful tongue teasing more and more response from her.

Finally she fell limply onto the desk and there was only the sound of her harsh breathing. She was totally spent, boneless with satisfaction. Her thighs were wet with her desire and his saliva, and she felt swollen with passion. Somewhere, deep inside, she knew she should feel self-conscious about the fact that she was slumped, thighs wide, on a stranger's desk, having just had the best oral sex of her life. But she was beyond caring, and when he sat back on his heels and simply stared at the glistening heart of her she felt nothing but a fierce satisfaction that he liked what he saw.

His eyes were full of desire, so full that she didn't protest when he reached out to touch her again, even though she knew she was too sensitive to stand any more.

His finger slid inside her with practiced ease, and she was stunned to feel her muscles tense instinctively around him. As though she'd told him all he needed to know, he stood and leaned over her.

"You want me again already," he told her, and before she could confirm or deny he was kissing her.

She could smell her own sex on him, but the faint musk only added to the eroticism of the moment. He pressed her back onto the desk, his hands sliding down to cup her breasts. He plucked at their straining peaks with increasing firmness, the pleasure almost painful, then he ducked his head and sucked a nipple hard into his mouth.

He had too much clothing on. She needed his skin against hers. Her hands tore at his shirt buttons, fumbling them clumsily as she raced to reveal the hard breadth of his chest. No sooner had she won this battle than she moved on to his belt buckle. Desire lent her dexterity now, and she slid the buckle loose and released his fly in a matter of seconds. The taut, hard length of him sprang into her waiting hands. She smiled hungrily as she weighed his desire, sliding her hands up and down his shaft.

He stiffened further still, if that were possible, and she could see the muscles of his shoulders and belly tense as he fought for control. She licked the palm of her hand and slid her newly-licked hand up and down him, her grip firm and sure.

He made a guttural sound in the back of his throat. She liked the way his eyes glinted down at her, liked the hunger in his gaze as it roamed from straining breast to straining breast, then down her belly to where she was already aching to be joined with him.

She didn't protest as he slid her off the desk and gently but firmly turned her so that her back was to him. She heard the slither of fabric as he tugged off his jeans, then felt the warmth of his thighs against the back of her legs as he molded himself to her body. The hair on his legs and chest rasped sensually against her skin, and she bit her lip as his hands slid around her rib cage to possess her breasts. He plucked at her nipples as he ground himself against the curve of her butt, and she slid a hand behind herself to grab the length of him.

His breath was hard and fast in her ear, and she made an impatient sound as he pulled away for a brief second to protect them. Knowing exactly what he wanted, she leaned forward, reaching for the edge of the desk and arching her back as he plunged inside her from behind. It felt so good she couldn't stop herself from crying out. Then he began to move, his rhythm sure and smooth, his strokes powerful. His hands gripped her hips, and Anna closed her eyes and gave herself over to the experience. He was so thick and hard, and her muscles contracted around him, urging him on. Just when she thought it couldn't get any better, he snaked a hand over her hip and between her legs and zeroed in on her clitoris. She bucked as a bolt of pure desire rocketed through her, and then she was pulsating around him, her breath coming in shuddering gasps as she rode the peak of another orgasm.

As she tapered off Marc's rhythm increased, and then his grip firmed on her hips, and she felt him tense and shudder as he spent himself deep inside her. The moment seemed to last forever, until finally the tension dropped out of him and his grip slackened.

A moment passed, a few heartbeats as they remained connected, his breath in her ear, his body warm against her back. Then he sighed, and her head drooped forward. She felt a small moment of loss as he withdrew from her. Her flesh was cool where his had been, and all the bad memories from last time came rushing back—the awkwardness, the embarrassment, the uncertainty.

She straightened and with shaking hands reached for her bra. It took two attempts to fix the clasp in place, and she glanced across at him as she walked to where she'd flung her dress. It was the first time she'd had a chance to appreciate his powerful physique. He was in superb shape, a man in his prime. Despite what had just happened between them, her body tightened at the sight of him. She bit her lip and pulled her dress over her head.

She could hear him dressing, also, but she didn't look at him again. Why did this keep happening between them? She clenched her hands, trying to hold back the tide of regret. Half an hour ago she'd been standing in an art gallery trying to come up with a good exit line. Then Marc had touched her, and her thighs had gone up in flames and nothing in the world had been as important as getting her hands on him as soon as possible.

A panicky feeling gripped her. It was as though she wasn't in control of herself anymore. As soon as Marc Lewis was in the room, she turned into some kind of sex-mad robot, obsessed with getting off and nothing else.

It was one thing to tell Danny she wanted more passion in her life, but these…encounters with Marc Lewis were so far removed from anything she'd ever imagined. She felt out of control. Completely out of control.

He was pulling on his pants, and she heard the clink of his belt buckle. The air was thick with unspoken thoughts and feelings. Now that the tide of desire had receded, she just wanted to get out of there, but her hands were shaking so much that she couldn't do up her zip.

"Let me."

He brushed her hands away from the zipper tab, and she felt the heat of his hands through the fabric of her dress as he slid the zipper closed. His hand lingered on her back, and she stepped forward to break the contact.

"Anna," he said, but she shook her head.

"I'm going to tell my dispatch service that I'm no longer available for work with your company," she said. Her voice was as shaky as she felt inside.

"That won't be necessary," he said after a short silence.

"This can't happen again."

"It won't." There was a world of clipped determination in his voice.

"Good."

Without looking at him, she unlatched the privacy lock and pulled the door open. Two women were exiting a room a few doors up the corridor, and they looked at her curiously as they walked past. Anna avoided eye contact and retraced their steps. As she'd hoped, they'd emerged from the ladies' room. She pushed the door open and stared at the woman reflected in the wall-to-wall mirror above the vanity. Her hair was a rumpled mess, her cheekbones stained with hectic color. Her eyes glittered strangely, and a dull red flush of desire still colored her chest.

She filled the sink with water and sluiced great handfuls onto her face, then used some paper towel to dab moisture onto her chest. Slowly her color went down. She finger-raked her hair into some semblance of order and thought of Leah and Jules. They were probably wondering where the hell she'd got to. She'd be lucky if they hadn't abandoned her—it would be nothing less than what she deserved.

She met her own eyes in the mirror, and was forced to acknowledge that she didn't know the woman staring back at her. She'd never thought of herself as sexy or even particularly sensual. She was just average. A normal, everyday woman.

But what had just happened with Marc was not a normal, everyday experience—unless she'd been living a far more cloistered, secluded life than she'd ever imagined. Never in her wildest dreams had she thought she was capable of the kinds of things that had happened over the past hour. A wash of heat rushed through her as she remembered how abandoned she'd been as Marc went down on her. She had not spared a single thought for repercussions or reputation or anything. She had just given herself over to the moment and absolutely reveled in it. Lord only knew how much noise she'd made as she came— she had the uncomfortable feeling that she'd been extremely vocal.

She stared despairingly at herself in the mirror. She just wasn't cut out for this kind of thing. It was all very well for Danny to talk of flings and fun, but she was made of sterner, more prosaic stuff and she didn't bounce back from these encounters the way he did.

The door swung open, and Jules and Leah bustled in.

"There you are! We were wondering where you'd got to," Leah said.

They were both a little flushed and bright-eyed, and Anna realized with relief that they were tipsy. It would make it much easier to do what she was about to do.

"I'm sorry—but I think I might have picked up a bit of tummy bug," she fibbed.

"Oh, Anna, no," Jules said sympathetically. "Do you want to go home?"

"I think so, but I'll grab a cab on my own. No need for you guys to have an early night because of me."

"No way—we'll take you home," Leah insisted.

"Seriously, I'm just going to go straight to bed," she assured them hastily. "You guys seem like you're having a pretty good time."

They exchanged guilty looks. "There is this very cute waiter," Jules admitted.

"And he has a brother," Leah added.

"Then you should definitely stay and chat him up. I'll give you a call next week, okay?"

After making her promise to drink lots of water and have some dry toast when she got home, they finally let her leave. In three minutes flat she had congratulated Maxine on her exhibition, made her excuses, collected her bag and was standing on Glebe Point Road, waiting to hail a taxi.

It was a busy time of night, and there were plenty of cabs cruising for fares. She flagged one down and slid into the back seat with relief. Telling the driver her address in Rose Bay, she sat back against the upholstery and relaxed for the first time in hours. She just wanted to be home so she could forget tonight's mistake.

As the cab pulled away from the curb, a low-slung sports car shot past. She recognized the dark, familiar profile of Marc Lewis and hastily turned away, hoping he hadn't seen her. She couldn't stop the wave of remembered desire that the mere sight of him provoked, however. It seemed that no matter what happened, her body would always want Marc Lewis.

Tough luck, she told herself. *I want my life back. I want* me *back.*

No more out of control. It was too much, and she wasn't cut out for it.

MARC PARKED HIS CAR and slammed the door behind himself as he exited. The house was in darkness and he left it that way as he stalked his way through the garden and onto the back terrace. He was filled with anger—at Anna for having so much control over him, and at himself for having so little. He still couldn't believe that they'd had sex just meters from a packed art gallery. He knew some men would revel in the sexual conquest, but he wasn't one of them. His father had been an inveterate womanizer, a man who never denied his passions. Marc had learned early on what kind of damage such self-indulgence could wreak. He'd worked hard to prove to himself and the world that he was not his father's son.

Now here he was, being led around by his cock, just like his father. Why hadn't he just walked away from her? But he knew why—the moment he'd touched her, he'd been gone.

He reminded himself that it was over now. Even if he'd wanted to pursue things with her—which he didn't—she'd made it clear that she wasn't interested.

Swearing under his breath, Marc began stripping his clothes off angrily. He dove into the pool, the cold water like a slap in the face. He wanted to wipe the night out, just erase it from his mind and body.

Kicking off from the wall, he started swimming.

6

"JACINTA, WHERE THE HELL is that file I asked for?" Marc demanded.

He braced his arms against either side of the door frame, leaning out into his assistant's domain aggressively.

She flinched at his surly tone. "I'm still waiting for it to come back up from R & D."

"And do we think that's going to happen sometime this century?"

She blinked at his sarcasm. "I'll get straight onto them."

She swiveled abruptly in her chair and reached for the phone, turning her back on him deliberately, he guessed. He stared at her hunched shoulders for a moment, guilt stabbing at him. Since when had he become the kind of grade A arsehole who took his moods out on his secretary?

Sighing heavily, he pushed himself away from the door frame and back into his office. Huge floor-to-ceiling windows covered one wall, but he stared blindly out at the view.

He owed Jacinta an apology. In fact, if he put his mind to it he was sure that he could probably come up with a lengthy list of people he owed an apology to. Gary, his personal trainer, his lawyer, his sister…all of them had copped the brunt of his temper in one way or another over the past few days. Hell, he'd even had a go at his niece, Sally. And now Jacinta.

He rubbed the bridge of his nose and turned away from the window. It wasn't as though he didn't know what his problem was: frustration. In the enticing, hourglass form of Anna Jackson.

He was thirty-five years old, newly single, wealthy and in charge of a large private company. He employed more than five hundred people, he owned one of the best views in Sydney and this year's after-tax profit looked on target to set a new all-time record.

And, despite himself, he was fast becoming sexually obsessed with a certain platinum-haired chauffeur.

He swore, furious that his thoughts had drifted toward her yet again. This was the last thing he wanted or needed in his life, but he'd been like this since Saturday night. Sure, he could concentrate on work for minutes, even hours at a time. But as soon as he relaxed his vigilance, in she crept, with her silken thighs and her panted demands and hungry hands.

He didn't want to want her, and she obviously shared his wariness regarding their explosive sexual chemistry. She also resented her lack of control over it, he guessed, just as he did. Which left them…nowhere. He dug his hands into his pockets and stared hard at the plush carpet beneath his feet.

His nights were peppered with fantasies of having Anna again. He knew what she tasted like now, the texture of her skin, the sound of her desire. The scent of her, the essence of her. His dreams were incredibly explicit, and every morning he woke with a raging hard-on. He'd even reached for the phone a couple of times to test whether she really had barred herself from taking jobs with his company. He told himself that if he called and she'd barred him, that was it, he wouldn't pursue it any further. But if she hadn't followed through with it…well, then she was fair game and he could seek her out and quench his need for her.

That was when he'd yelled at Gary, he remembered. He shook his head at his own behavior. He was not his father. He would prove it to himself if it killed him.

Running a hand through his hair, he crossed to his desk and

sat. A click of his computer mouse, and the online version of the
Yellow Pages came on screen. He found a local florist's number,
and made a quick call. A generous arrangement of oriental lilies
would hopefully put him back in the good books with Jacinta.
As for the rest of the people in his world—perhaps he should just
do them a favor and take himself off to a desert island until
this…*thing* he had for Anna Jackson had burned itself out.

ON FRIDAY ANNA WALKED through the double glass doors of the
advertising agency where her brother worked and blinked dully
in the halogen lighting. Color assailed her from all sides, and the
frown that had become a permanent fixture on her face over the
past week deepened. The foyer was filled with bright and chirpy
people to match the bright and chirpy decor, and Anna gritted
her teeth and dodged her way through the people to the elevator.

This was the first time she'd ever visited her brother at work,
but he'd invited her out to lunch and one of the perks of owning
her own business was that she could decide when and where she
lunched. Negotiating her way into an almost-full elevator, she
watched impatiently as the numbers on the floor indicator slowly
crawled by, one foot tap-tapping away as the doors opened and
closed, opened and closed on what seemed like every floor.

"Come-on-come-on-come-on," she muttered under her
breath, nearly rolling her eyes with frustration. What was with
the world all of a sudden? Lately everything seemed either too
slow, or too fast, or too loud, or too expensive, or just plain old
annoying. She felt as if she was on the perpetual verge of a
primal scream, and that any tiny miscalculation on someone
else's behalf might just push her over.

Kind of like PMS to the power of a million. Fortunately for
her, Australia had strict rules on gun control, so the only weapon
she had to hand was her tongue—and oh, how she'd used it this
past week. The dry cleaner had got an earful for shortchanging

her. A young kid in a purple hatchback had scored some abuse for swerving dangerously across her lane on the freeway. And she'd treated a parking inspector to a public rant on the failures of government when she'd found him writing up her car for being one minute over time on the parking meter.

Maybe it *was* PMS. She did a quick mental calculation, but the math didn't add up. Maybe it was a full moon. Or maybe her frustration tolerance was just at an all-time low.

Another possible cause for her unusual bout of crankiness occurred to her, but she resolutely refused to consider it. Saturday night was an aberration. Marc and her response to him was an aberration. She simply wouldn't let herself go there.

The doors pinged open and she stepped out onto the creative level where her brother worked. He was loitering near the elevator bank waiting for her, and they embraced briefly.

"Sorry I'm late. Stupid lift had to stop on every floor," she explained.

"It's cool. I'll just grab my phone and wallet from my desk," Danny said, gesturing for her to follow him up the hallway.

He showed her into a spacious corner office full of groovy furniture and more jewel-toned colors.

"How can you stand all these bright colors all the time?" she asked, poking a finger at his purple mouse pad.

"It's nice. Most people like it," he said, giving her a peculiar look.

"Is that what some focus group told you? Or is it just what the interior designer said to justify his bad taste?"

Danny made a show of looking taken aback. "Yow! Saucer of milk, table two. Someone's in a bad mood today."

Anna opened her mouth to protest, but she knew he was right. Hadn't she just been thinking about how annoying she was finding everything all of a sudden?

"I think I got out of the wrong side of the bed this week," she said apologetically.

"Hmm, I wonder," Danny said, then his eyes slid over her shoulder and narrowed slightly. The look he refocused on her was speculative as he scanned her from head to toe. Then he nodded, and took her arm confidentially.

"Anna, I need a favor. No time to explain, but I need you to just play along with me for the next few minutes, okay?"

She'd barely nodded before Danny reached for the top button on her shirt and slipped it loose. When he reached for the next one, she slapped his hand away.

"Danny! What are you doing?" she hissed at him, fingers automatically reaching up to redo her buttons.

"Just work with me here. I need some cleavage. Come on, Anna—I'd do it for you," Danny wheedled.

Anna glared at him, and he put on his best little-boy-lost look. She'd never been able to resist it.

"This had better be really good," she said grumpily as she slid another button free and pulled her lapels wide so that a substantial amount of bosom was exposed in the V of her shirt.

She turned to Danny for approval, but he was focused on the man emerging from the office across the hall.

"Hey, Ben, wait a minute," Danny called out, his tone super-casual.

A young guy in his early twenties popped in the doorway, a smile on his tanned face.

"Hey, what's up?"

Danny shrugged. "Just wanted to ask where that new sushi place is you were talking about the other day," he said.

"Just opposite Circular Quay. Near the McDonald's," Ben said easily.

"Right. Thanks for that," Danny said.

Then, before Ben could move off, Danny knocked a pile of papers off his desk and onto the floor. Anna stared at him, sure the move had been deliberate.

"What an idiot!" Danny said self-deprecatingly.

Laughing at Danny's clumsiness, Ben stooped to pitch in and help collect the papers. "Hope this isn't the Arnott's account," he said.

Danny cut his eyes across to Anna and jerked his head, signaling for her to join Ben in collecting the papers. Anna frowned at him, and Danny grimaced, then pointed at her cleavage, then at Ben as though the connection should be obvious. Sighing heavily but knowing she owed Danny for all his vixen counseling, Anna stooped down beside Ben.

"My brother's always been a doofus," she said as she started stacking papers.

Ben glanced up, a smile in his bright blue eyes. He was very good-looking in an aftershave-ad kind of way, with a nice straight nose and carelessly tousled blond hair.

Behind her, Danny nudged her meaningfully, and Anna took advantage of the moment to lean forward, treating Ben to a panoramic view of her supercleavage. "Not the same Danny who made the photocopier explode? I find that hard to believe," Ben joked.

"Yeah, yeah, you're both hilarious," Danny said, finally stepping in and taking over. "Thanks, Ben, but I can clean up after my own disasters."

"Just as well," the other man said as he stood. Then he waved a friendly acknowledgment to Anna and exited.

Anna waited until Ben had been gone a good few beats before she spoke.

"You want to tell me what that was all about?"

Danny finished collecting the last of the papers and returned the now-messy stack to his desk.

"Once we're outside the building, absolutely," he said, eyes sparkling mischievously.

Biting her tongue, Anna rebuttoned her shirt and let him lead her back to the elevators and down to the street. As soon as they hit the pavement she punched him on the arm.

"Well?"

"Ow. What is it with you today? Is it that time of the month or something?"

"No! Why is it that men automatically assume that just because a woman is feeling a little emotional it's got something to do with her hormones?" she said defensively.

"I don't know—maybe because it usually does?" Danny returned flippantly.

Anna punched him again.

"You can stop that any time you like," Danny said, glaring at her now.

"Are you going to tell me what that little performance was all about or not?"

He shrugged. "It's no big deal. Ben's our new gun in creative, fresh out of university, full of vim and vigor, blah, blah. The next wunderkind to storm the ranks."

"And the reason I was throwing my breasts in his face was…?"

"You saw him. He's very cute. But I can't get a read on him, and usually my gaydar is spot on. Sometimes I think yes, then he does something or says something that just throws me right off…." Danny rubbed his chin thoughtfully, lost in the conundrum.

Anna stopped in her tracks. "Please tell me you weren't just using my breasts to find out if your new work colleague is gay," she asked warningly.

"They're very nice breasts, Anna Banana, if it's not too creepy for me to say so. I figured if he didn't go for them, he's either gay or he's just got a little plastic mound like a Ken doll."

She couldn't believe it. Her brother really was completely beyond the pale.

"What? It's not like they're going to wear out or anything. It's not like I just used up one of your breasts' nine lives," Danny said, arms spread wide in appeal.

"It's just *wrong*, Danny."

"Peanut-butter-and-honey wrong? Or dogs eating their own sick wrong?"

She couldn't help herself: she laughed. He always got her like this, and always had. "You are so lucky you're a funny guy," she told him as they crossed the street and entered a busy downtown food court.

"What do you feel like? Sushi, burger, souvlaki? My treat," Danny offered.

"Sushi's fine, since that's the line we fed Ben," she said.

"Hmm. The mysterious Ben Grayson," he mused as he began selecting sushi from the open display.

"Well, what was the verdict?" she said as she added some double-avocado and teriyaki chicken rolls to her brother's selection.

"Well, he looked. He definitely looked," Danny said.

"They were right in his face, Danny. I nearly took his eye out."

"That's true. I don't know. Maybe my methodology was flawed."

"You could always just ask him out. Revolutionary concept, I know."

"And out myself at work? I don't think so," Danny scoffed.

Anna shot him a curious look. He always seemed so on top of things that it was easy to forget that there was a big part of his life that he kept under wraps from most of the world. He was like a human version of an iceberg, with most of his truth lurking beneath the surface.

"Would it be a problem if your work knew?" she asked. "I thought advertising was a pretty broad-minded industry."

"Oh, they are, they are. Just ask all the straight men at the top of the pile," Danny said sardonically.

"But you don't care about that stuff. You've told me over and over again that you love your job and you don't have any ambitions to be in management," Anna said shrewdly, guessing Danny wasn't being completely honest.

He shrugged, spearing a piece of sushi with his chopsticks. "Look, my sexuality isn't that important, you know. People don't have to know about it. It's not like you wear a T-shirt saying 'I'm straight' or anything."

Danny stopped suddenly, then shook his whole body, like a dog shaking off water after a swim. "Right, no more on that old chestnut. Let's tackle something a little less boring—like your love life."

Anna frowned. "Next topic."

She reached for a piece of sashimi, but it slid off her chopsticks slickly. Her frown deepened as she tried to pick it up again, and yet again, and still it eluded her.

"Bloody hell!" she swore, finally giving up and stabbing the darned thing repeatedly with a single chopstick until at last it stuck.

Dipping the fish into her soy bowl, she raised it to her mouth to find Danny staring at her in amazement.

"What?"

"You are wound tighter than a rattrap, my dear. What's going on?" he asked.

"Nothing." She shrugged, keeping her attention on the sushi platter. She'd told Danny the bare basics of her last "encounter" with Marc, but she'd also told him it was over and done with for good this time. The last thing she wanted was to rehash the whole stupid mess.

"Nothing. Right."

She sighed, knowing what was coming. "This has nothing to do with Marc Lewis, okay? So we tore each other's clothes off in public again. Big deal. It's history, Danny, like I told you. The stupid dreams will disappear soon, I'm sure."

"Ah, now we're getting somewhere. Tell me about these dreams you've been having."

Anna colored, realizing she'd given a little too much away. "You're not my psychologist, so just give it a rest," she snapped.

"Hmm. Irritable. Sleep-deprived, if I don't miss my guess. Snappy. Defensive. I'm afraid I'm going to have to diagnose this as a severe case of sexual frustration," Danny said.

"I am not sexually frustrated!" Anna screeched, remembering they were in a very crowded food court a few seconds too late.

"Of course not. Forgive me," Danny murmured, eyes wide at her outburst.

Anna pushed back her chair. "Look, I'm just going to go. You're right, I am tired. I'm not very good company, sorry," she said.

She started to walk away, but Danny's hand shot out to grab her wrist before she could move off.

"Why don't you just call him if you can't stop thinking about him? What have you got to lose?"

"Me," she said starkly.

Danny pulled on her wrist, obviously wanting her to sit back down. She obliged reluctantly, not wanting to even think about any of this stuff, let alone talk about it.

"Can't I just stay in grumpy denial?" she asked wistfully.

"'Fraid not. Why would you lose yourself if you had a fling with him?" Danny asked.

"I'm not like you, Danny. I realized after the first time with Marc that there's a reason why I haven't had a lot of men in my life, why I've never had one-night stands or sex outside of a bedroom," she said.

"Until recently," Danny inserted pedantically.

"Until recently," she corrected herself. "I'm just not cut out for it. I can't pull it off. The main course is delicious, sure, but dessert is a big fat serving of regret."

"Anna, it's not like you're running around town with a different guy every night. You just happen to have discovered great sexual chemistry with a guy, and the inevitable has happened."

"In a garage and on some poor person's desk," Anna muttered.

"So make sure you don't get caught short again. Call the guy, ave a fling with him. You said it yourself—you're not cut out or one-night stands. I really think a fling is more your style."

"When it comes to sex, I have no style," she said.

"Stop being such a scaredy-cat, Anna. What's so bad about iving in to your desires?"

"I'm not scared of my own desires!" she said, keeping her oice low. "I'm just not interested."

"Okay, I give up. Go buy yourself a kick-arse vibrator and orget Mr. Studly and get over it," Danny said, throwing his ands in the air.

Anna felt her mouth drop open and her shoulders creep up round her ears. She shot embarrassed glances to the right and left.

"Danny!" she snapped warningly. "Do you mind? What will eople think?"

"Whatever they like. Does it matter?"

Suddenly she was sick of her brother's pushing, well-inten- oned or not.

"You're the one who lives the big double life, Danny," she aid, standing so fast that her chair slid back with a toe-curling creech. "Most of the important people in your world have no lea who you really are. And you're giving *me* a hard time ecause I feel uncomfortable about abandoning the morals of a fetime?"

All the color drained out of Danny's face. He blinked a couple f times, then took a deep breath.

"You're right—you're not very good company right now," he aid, pushing his own chair back.

Anna was instantly swamped with a rush of remorse and guilt.

"Danny, I didn't mean it," she stuttered, reaching out a hand.

He shrugged it off. "It's cool. I'm not made of glass, Anna." le checked his watch. "I'd better be getting back to it, anyway."

Giving her a perfunctory kiss goodbye, he left her standing there, wallowing in her shame.

She was turning into an out-and-out bitch! How could she have said those things to Danny? Even if they were marginally true, it was none of her business, and certainly not relevant to anything they'd been discussing.

Feeling thoroughly disgusted with herself, she trudged back to her car. It didn't take long for Marc to insert himself into his thoughts. As always over the past week when her guard was down there he was, with his breath hard in her ear and his firm, knowing hands on her body. She saw him everywhere—in the broad shoulders of a man getting out of a cab, in the confident stride of another man racing across the road. She shook her head angrily.

It's all your bloody fault, Marc Lewis, she thought. *I wish I'd never met you.* She'd never have said those things to Danny if she hadn't been tired and cranky and horny as hell. Damn it.

She beeped her car open, but didn't get in. How on earth was she going to get rid of all the unwanted emotions and desires whirling around inside her body? Frustrated with herself and her unruly body, she actually kicked her car tire, scuffing her patent leather pump in the process.

"Great," she said dully. Then she felt a prickle of awareness. She glanced down, and all the small hairs on her arm were standing on end.

Her head shot up, and she saw him, standing in the middle of the sidewalk on the other side of her car, an arrested expression on his face as he stared at her. He'd just exited the building behind him, she guessed, and was carrying a briefcase in one hand and his suit jacket folded over his other arm. The crisp white of his shirt highlighted his olive skin and the darkness of his hair and eyes. His shoulders looked impossibly wide. A surge of pure lust raced through her, and she had to place a hand on the roof of her car because her knees suddenly felt like rubber.

A second passed, then another as they stared at each other. He didn't move, and she didn't, either. Neither of them wanted this—they'd already established that. Yet she couldn't take her eyes off him.

He was so damned sexy! The way he held himself. The tilt to his chin. The glint in his eye. The dark stubble of his beard, already showing despite the fact that it was only one o'clock in the afternoon. She knew that if she touched him, his skin would be firm and hot to the touch, and she knew the exact low, satisfied noise he'd make if she pressed herself against him….

Still he didn't move, but she could see a muscle flicker along his jaw, and knew that he was having as hard a time staying put as she was.

Then a car horn sounded behind her, rude and intrusive.

"You leaving, lady, or what?" a cabbie called out, his tone impatient.

Suddenly she found her willpower. Fingers curling around the door handle, she pulled the door wide and got into her car. She didn't dare look back at him, but she knew that he'd gone, anyway. The moment had passed. Thank God.

She started the car and pulled out into the stream of traffic. Her heartbeat sounded loud in her ears. She was gripping the steering wheel as though someone might try to take it away from her.

"Oh, boy," she said into the silence of her car.

Close call. Very close call.

MARC SLID INTO the seat of his Jag and sat staring straight ahead for a few beats. She looked incredible. Even in her conservative business uniform, she looked nothing short of sensational. Those curves. The pout of her mouth. The litheness of her tall body.

It's been almost a week, he told himself. *Don't blow it now.*

But his hand was punching numbers into his phone.

"I'd like a number for a business, please. Lady Driver. It's based in Sydney, I'm not sure what suburb," he said.

Before he could self-edit, he selected the option to be instantly connected to Anna's phone, and listened to it ring on the other end.

She answered almost straight away. "Thank you for calling Lady Driver. How can I help you?"

Just the sound of her voice was enough to make him hard. Again.

"It's me," he said.

There was a long pause on the end of the phone. "I don't think this is a good idea," she said at last.

No kidding. "I can't get you out of my head."

He couldn't believe he'd just said that. Was he this much of a slave to his libido?

"It'll pass. It's got to," she said, and he felt a thrill of triumph at the desperation in her tone.

"Meet me," he said.

"When?"

"Anytime. You name it."

He held his breath, waiting. She had to say yes. God, if she said yes, right now, let's go, he'd cancel his afternoon's appointments and be with her in under five minutes. They could check into a nearby hotel—whatever—just as long as he could be with her again.

"I—I can't," she finally said after a long, long silence.

He closed his eyes and rested his forehead against his steering wheel, suppressing the urge to groan with frustration.

Then he opened his eyes. She was right to say no, he knew that.

"Okay," he said and ended the call. There was nothing else to say, and they both knew it.

He put his head against the headrest and stared at the canvas roof of the car. She'd better be right. This…obsession had better pass soon. Or he was in serious danger of becoming a crazy man.

ANNA WAS CHOKING the steering wheel again. Seeing a parking space up ahead, she flicked her indicator on and pulled into it. Then she let out the breath she'd been holding ever since he'd ended their call.

I can't. The hardest words she'd ever said when all of her was already on fire for him. But she wanted him so much—it was terrifying, absolutely terrifying. She couldn't handle it.

Very deliberately, Anna ran both hands through her hair, then reached for the clipboard holding her day's jobs. She had a pickup in fifteen minutes near the top of George Street. Keeping her mind carefully blank, she put the car into drive and signaled to pull out.

She'd said it to him herself. This had to pass. It had to.

By five o'clock the next evening, she felt she had some kind of insight into how an addict must feel when craving their drug of choice. Seeing Marc yesterday, hearing his voice—it had switched on that part of herself that hungered for him, and it only seemed to be getting worse.

Her clothes felt too tight, and every inch of her skin seemed acutely sensitive. She'd tried everything, from stuffing her face with chocolate to taking the matter in hand, so to speak. The former made her feel sick, the latter even hornier. She truly was going around the bend.

Now she'd been reduced to the only thing she could possibly think of to ward off her need. Pulling up the collar on her coat, she shot a self-conscious glance over her shoulder, then chastised herself. She was allowed to go into an adult shop. She was an adult. With needs. There was nothing to be ashamed of. Chin high, she stepped into the darkened doorway of the shop.

Immediately she could smell an overly sweet berry odor, and she registered that the carpet beneath her feet felt faintly sticky.

That alone was almost enough to turn her on her heel, but she was a desperate woman. She rounded the corner of the dog-leg-shaped entrance to the shop and emerged into a dimly lit space lined with bookshelves and filled with large display trays. A young guy was lounging behind the counter to one side, and a number of people were browsing at the magazine racks. No one so much as flickered an eyelid at her, and she took a steadying breath.

Elaborately casual, she picked up the nearest DVD. *Riding Miss Daisy.* She put it back down again. Perhaps she should just cut to the chase. Her gaze zeroed in on the display case to her right. She moved closer and inspected the merchandise on offer: a large lime green rubbery-looking vibrator; a smaller, bullet-shaped chrome-finished one; and a virulent purple device with a strange sea-anemone-like protuberance on its shaft. She leaned a little closer, frowning. What on earth could the sea anemone be for? Then she saw the neon pink wording on the packaging displayed behind it—complete with state-of-the-art clitoral stimulator. She stared at the sea anemone. Well, probably it could work.

Problem was, she'd come here seeking relief, be it of the battery-operated kind, but suddenly she knew that there was nothing in the case in front of her that was going to stop her from wanting Marc Lewis. She could close her eyes and fantasize and put the sea anemone or any of his rubbery friends to work, but she knew, absolutely, that she craved a *man,* not an orgasm. She wanted the heavy weight of a warm body pressing against hers. She wanted touch and taste and smell, not just stimulation for one part of her anatomy.

She stared blindly at the purple vibrator, feeling slightly dizzy for a moment as she allowed herself to consider the other possible solution to her situation.

She could call Marc. Or better still, go see him. She could have a fling with him, get this…*urge* out of her system. Her thighs trembled at the very thought of allowing herself to explore the dark attraction that existed between the two of them.

All of her objections rushed to the fore. This wasn't what she really wanted. She wasn't this kind of person. It was all very well to say she wanted to get more out of her life now that she'd had a reprieve, but a person couldn't change who a person was. That wasn't the way the world worked.

But what if a person had parts of herself that she'd never explored? Parts that had always been out of bounds, tightly packed away, hidden? Danny had said it—she was scared of her own desires.

At last she admitted to herself that Marc hadn't made her feel the way she felt; he hadn't forced her to want him, to dream about having sex with him, to crave him so badly that she was even now standing in a sex shop staring at pale imitations of what she really desired. That was all in her, part of her. And she had the bewildering feeling that she was about to untie the bonds and let that part of herself loose.

She turned away from the display case. She didn't care about the rest of the people in the shop anymore. Hell, twenty of her most lucrative clients could be standing there drooling over the magazines and videos, and she wouldn't give a hoot. The only thing she could think of was getting her hands on Marc Lewis.

Her body felt strangely hot and heavy as she stepped back out into the street. She got into her car, operating on a sort of semi-aware remote control. It was a Saturday night, and he was a busy man, but he had to be home. He just had to be, because now that she'd made her decision, she didn't think she could wait.

The smooth, powerful hum of the motor played below her thoughts as she drove. She would tell him exactly what she wanted, in no uncertain terms: a fling. Nothing more. She wasn't up for anything more permanent, and she was pretty sure he wasn't, either. This was about sex. Carnal desire. Nothing else.

The fading light of day became darker still as she turned into the tree-lined streets of Point Piper. She bit her lip as she pulled up outside the nondescript wall bounding his yard. Did she have the courage to do this?

She was poised on the edge of indecision when her cell phone rang. She stared at the caller display. It was Danny. This was the first time he'd called since she'd savaged him on the previous day. She pressed the button to take his call with relief.

"Danny!"

He laughed. "You don't have to sound so relieved. I wasn't about to cross you off my Christmas list or anything."

"Still. I was a bitch. I'm sorry."

"So your five phone messages said. It's okay, Anna."

"Really?"

"Really. I was actually calling to see if you wanted to go see a movie or something. My date canceled."

Anna cut her gaze to the wall hiding Marc's house.

"Um…I can't. I mean, I hope I can't. I could call you back…?" she stumbled.

"What's going on? You sound weird," Danny said.

She took a deep breath. "I'm out the front of Marc's house. I was going to go talk to him. At least I think I am. If I can find the backbone."

Danny let out a whoop of congratulations. "Anna Banana! Go for it, girl! Fling your thing—you'll never look back, I swear it."

She couldn't help smiling at Danny's untrammeled hedonism. "You're a complete slut, you know that?" she said.

"Must run in the family. My God, I'm so glad I called. You need to know the three golden rules of flings before you go in there. Otherwise it's like sending Little Bo Peep into an abattoir."

"Nice analogy."

"Listen up. Rule number one—never stay overnight. Overnight leads to toothbrushes and breakfasts and familiarity. Flings are about excitement. Mystery. Intensity. Got it?"

"No overnight. Check."

"Rule number two—no plans for the future. Anything longer than a few days away is a no-go zone."

"What, so I can't even agree to meet him in a week's time?" she asked, surprised by the rigidity of Danny's instructions.

"No. Next week, you could be with some other hot guy. Or at least he should always think that. Uncertainty is the spice of life. Keep it unpredictable."

"Unpredictable. Check."

"Now, rule number three—never, under any circumstances, do you talk about your feelings or the relationship. You both know what the relationship is about—sex. No discussion required. You with me?"

"I'm with you. That's it?" She would have been happy to listen to a hundred rules if it meant putting off the moment of no return.

"That's it. Stick to those little puppies, and you can't go wrong."

"Okay. All right." She took a deep breath. Was she going to do this?

"I'm going in, Danny."

She was.

"Good luck, girl," he said.

She took another deep breath and stepped out of the car. Her hands were shaking so much it took two clicks to get the car to lock itself, then she was standing in front of the intercom beside the pedestrian gateway to Marc's property.

She took a quivering breath, and pressed the glowing golden light on the intercom. A long beat of silence, then, "Yes?"

His voice was deep and resonant. A curl of desire unfurled inside her.

"It's me, Anna," she said.

There was a stunned silence, then he said, "Wait there."

She gripped her hands together to stop them from shaking.

Was she really going to do this? Could she really hand herself over to her desires like this?

She heard footsteps on the other side of the gateway, and then the door swung open, and there he stood.

7

HE COULDN'T BELIEVE she was standing there. He'd been pacing the house all day, coming up with then discarding schemes for getting her out of his system. He'd even dug out his little black book, but all the entries were well out of date; he doubted if any of his old flames were still available after ten years.

Twenty lung-busting laps of butterfly stroke in the pool, and several hours of mindless program debugging had also proved completely useless. He'd been at the point of ringing Gary and finally agreeing to one of the many blind dates his wife had been advocating for the past few months when the doorbell rang.

Now she was standing on his doorstep, her long legs in faded denims, her face pale as she stared back at him.

"Can I come in for a moment?" she asked, her voice low.

She looked tense, uncertain. He opened the door wider and stood back to allow her to pass. Her perfume came with her— musky, spicy. Alluring.

Wordless, he gestured for her to follow him up the covered walkway to the front door of the house. Every muscle in his body was on high alert. Why was she here? He wanted to leap to conclusions—well, The Conclusion—but he couldn't presume anything. He knew enough about women to know that.

She wiped her feet politely on the front mat, then trailed him into his home.

"Wow," she said, eyes wide.

He followed her glance, seeing the broad, airy entrance hall with new eyes. To one side, a wide staircase swept up to the second story. In front, double doors led into the first living area. Huge windows let in light on either side of the front door behind them, flooding the sandstone floor with the sun's last golden rays. The walls were painted a soft wheat, and polished timber glowed from the window frames and the stair balustrade. It was an impressive space, an impressive house. And he didn't give a fig for any of it right now.

He led her into the living room, then turned to face her.

"Can I get you a drink?" he asked politely, unable to stop himself from eating her up with his eyes.

Under her casual denim jacket she wore a bright grassy green T-shirt which stretched across her full breasts in a way that made it almost impossible for him to look away.

She cleared her throat, and he watched as her hands clutched at each other nervously a few times before she finally shoved them into her pockets. Which only dragged his attention to her thighs, sleekly outlined by the washed and worn denim…

"I wanted to ask you something," she said.

He shoved his own hands into his jean pockets so they wouldn't be tempted to reach for her.

"Yes?"

She cleared her throat again, and her cheeks colored up attractively as she lifted her gaze to make eye contact with him.

"I wanted to know if your offer was still open. To…meet you?" she asked in a rush.

He almost laughed. "Are you kidding?" he said on a tidal wave of relief and lust.

If only she knew how much she'd haunted his dreams, how much he'd been fantasizing about this exact thing happening.

She frowned uncertainly. "Is that…is that a yes?" she asked.

Marc let out an explosive breath and crossed the space between them in three long strides. Her eyes widened slightly, then she was in his arms and he was kissing her the way he'd wanted to all week. Her hands clutched at him, and she made a low, needy sound before letting her head drop back and giving herself up to the kiss. Her tongue was deft and just as eager as his as they explored one another's mouths in a greedy, grabby kiss that was all lust and no finesse.

He was instantly hard, absolutely ready for her, and he broke the kiss to start undressing her. He needed her now, right now.

"That's a yes, by the way," he told her, his voice low as he reached for her jacket.

"I got that," she said, helping him peel her jacket off and fling it to one side.

He reached for the hem of her T-shirt and tugged it unceremoniously up over her torso. She lifted her arms and tilted her neck to make it easier for him to pull it over her head. Her breasts were already tight and aroused, the nipples poking through the silk of her bra.

"We need to get a few things straight before this goes any further," she said, reaching for the hem of his own T-shirt. He tore it over his head impatiently.

"Sure, whatever," he said, sliding her bra straps off her shoulders and exposing one creamy breast to his touch.

"I'm not looking for commitment or anything permanent. This is about sex, that's all," she said, the last word dissolving into a gasp as he ducked his head and sucked her nipple firmly into his mouth. Her hands clutched at his head as he ran his tongue over and over the straining peak. His hard-on throbbed against the zipper of his jeans, eager to join the party.

"Sex. Absolutely. No commitment," he murmured as he transferred his attention to her other breast.

She made a guttural noise and grabbed his belt buckle. "No

future. No feelings, one of us says it's over, it's over," she panted as she pulled his jean stud free and grasped his zipper.

"Couldn't agree more," he said, reaching for the stud on her jeans.

They were both panting by now, tugging at each other's jeans. They bumped heads, and she laughed suddenly.

"This might go easier if we take our own jeans off," she suggested.

"Excellent idea," he said, sticking his thumbs into his waistband and shucking his jeans as though his life depended on it. She followed suit, and then they were standing naked in front of each other.

He groaned as his eyes ran over her full curves. "You have no idea how much I want you," he said.

Her eyes dropped to the throbbing evidence of his desire. "I'm getting the picture," she said.

Then they came together as though they'd just been told that they had two minutes before the earth exploded.

ANNA STRETCHED LANGUIDLY, pointing her toes and pulling her arms tight over her head. She felt fantastic. A little tender in places, but three bouts of intense lovemaking in as many hours would account for that. The instinctive, relentless drive inside of her was gone—for the moment. She had no doubt now that it would return. All Marc had to do was look at her, his eyes smoky and intense, and she was hot and ready for him again. But she had the solution to that problem now—she had Marc. She had embraced the fling, and as far as she could tell just three hours in, the fling had embraced her back.

Beside her, Marc stirred in his sleep, his thigh shifting to rub against hers. Right on cue, her body sat up to full attention. She didn't need to look down to know her nipples were already puckering, ready for his touch. And she could feel the wet heat pooling between her thighs. As though he could read her mind, Marc rolled toward and pulled her close.

She could barely see his face in the darkness as he began kissing her again. Long, slow, lazy kisses, because he knew they had time now. The first time they'd made love tonight, they'd both been so desperate for completion there'd been no frills, just hard, driving sex, the two of them straining to get as close together as possible. Then they'd made their way upstairs to his enormous, decadent double shower, and he'd made love to her more slowly against the cool tile of the shower wall. When they emerged from the steam he made them soup and toast in the kitchen—then lifted her onto the kitchen counter, spread her legs wide and showed her exactly how good he was with his hands and mouth.

Now his hands drifted lazily over her body, touching here, plucking there, smoothing over her hips. He was a consummate lover, but she'd known that already. Focused and assured, his touch by turns gentle and demanding. He seemed to know exactly what she needed, and when.

But Anna was used to being an equal in all things in her life. Despite the delicious desire building inside her, she nudged his hand away from between her legs and his mouth away from her breasts.

"Lie back," she told him instead.

Then she took him in her mouth, using her tongue and hands to drive him crazy. She swirled her tongue over the straining head of his penis, enjoying the way his body tensed in reaction. She wrapped her hand around his hard shaft, working him slowly, languidly as her tongue teased and taunted the tip of his penis. When she judged he'd had almost enough, she slithered lithely on top, slipping a condom on quickly before sliding down onto his hardness in one smooth action. His eyes glinted dangerously as she rode him, her breasts swaying with the movement.

Afterward, he smoothed the short spikes of her hair away from her damp forehead. Their legs were still tangled, and she felt his ribs expand and contract with his breathing.

Her stomach rumbled, and he laughed.

"Hungry?" he guessed.

"Starving," she said.

"Don't move," he said, sliding to the edge of the bed. She watched avidly as he stood, loving the play of light and shadow over his body. He was so damned hot. And he was hers to play with for as long as she needed him.

"Don't be long," she called after him as he dragged on a pair of boxers and padded out of the room.

His low laughter echoed back up the hallway, and she collapsed back onto the pillows with a smile on her face.

It was so good not to have to second-guess herself anymore.

She dozed lightly for a few minutes, then woke to the rattle of crockery. She stared in amazement as Marc entered the room with a loaded tray, his biceps bulging as he carried it to the bedside table.

"Okay. Scrambled eggs with smoked salmon, toasted bagels, cream cheese and capers on the side if you're that kind of girl. And pancakes for dessert, of course," he said as he handed her a linen napkin.

"Wow. You made all this?" she asked, seriously impressed.

"Don't sound so surprised."

"I can't cook at all," she admitted. "Can't even boil an egg properly."

"My mom worked a lot when I was a kid. It was learn to cook, or learn to like baked beans."

He said it casually, but she wondered if the fact that he hadn't mentioned his father meant anything. It was on the tip of her tongue to ask, to probe—but then she remembered rule number three: no personal talk. She figured questions about sad family stories definitely counted as personal. Swallowing the need to know more about this intense, exciting man, she scooped up a mouthful of scrambled eggs and made appreciative noises at their creamy, savory texture.

"You are *good!*" she said vehemently.

He breathed on his fingernails and pretended to buff them on his naked chest. "I try."

She rewarded his little joke with a smile, liking how comfortable she felt with him. It could have been incredibly awkward, after they'd gotten what they needed from each other. But he had a good sense of humor, she was learning. And he was considerate outside of the bedroom as well as inside it. And he could cook.

He spread cream cheese over half a bagel for her, and passed it over. Their fingers brushed, and she saw the way his eyes darkened instantly. It was like that for her, too.

"Hurry up and eat your bagel," he growled, polishing the last of his off with one big bite. The gleam in his eye told her he would like to do the same with her.

"What about the pancakes?" she said, teasing.

"Haven't you ever had cold pancakes? Manna from heaven," he said, whipping her napkin from where she'd lain it across her breasts.

"I'll take your word for it," she gasped as he took possession of her breasts.

Much later, she woke from a light sleep and caught sight of the clock on his bedside table. It was nearly five o'clock. She stiffened, remembering Danny's rule number one: never stay the night.

Good grief—she'd almost broken two rules and her fling wasn't even twenty-four hours old!

She didn't quite know how to go about politely extricating herself from Marc's bed without tortured explanations or excuses, so she opted for the cowardly route: sneaking out. His leg was thrown over one of hers, his hard, hairy male arm across her belly. Slowly she eased out from under him, then slid from the bed. The first gray light of dawn was showing on the horizon, and she glanced down at his sleeping form as she pulled on her clothes.

He looked younger asleep, more vulnerable. A dark lock of hair had flopped across his forehead, and she felt an absurd desire to smooth it back. She frowned. She shouldn't be standing here staring down at him like some moony teenager. She rolled her eyes at her own behavior. She could practically hear Danny's voice in her ear, "Typical girl, having to make everything all pretty pink and perfect."

Marc Lewis was her lover, not her partner. Not her friend, even. He was her fling, a walking penis who existed to satisfy her base carnal desires and nothing else. And that was exactly what she was to him, too. She needed to keep reminding herself of that, or this fling of hers was going to go seriously off the rails.

It would be easy, she suspected, to become addicted to Marc's touch. To give in to her curiosity about him and his world. To fall for him in a big way. An iron band tightened across her belly at the very thought. He was very charming, very good in bed, very seductive. But she couldn't contemplate having a relationship with anyone. It just wouldn't work right now.

There was a deeper, darker reason lurking, but Anna didn't want to go there. And she didn't have to, either. She and Marc were having a fling—they even had rules to ensure it stayed that way. She was just going to sit back and go along for the ride, and at the end she'd say thanks with a smile and be on her way.

On her way to the stairs, her eye was caught by a stack of boxes visible in one of the rooms running off the hallway. Feeling incredibly nosy, she paused to peek inside. It was a bedroom, she guessed, and it was empty of everything except the boxes. Two more open doorways revealed empty rooms, also, before she got to the stairs. She frowned as she padded down to the ground floor. Everything else was so nice—the kitchen was a paradise of stainless steel and granite, the living room where they'd first talked was fitted out in neutral-toned couches and beautiful timber pieces. But half the house was empty.

It made her wonder, again. And again she told herself that it was none of her business. His life was closed to her—and it was only his bed she was interested in, anyway.

She let herself quietly out of his house and inhaled a deep lungful of early-morning air. She felt good, she decided. Things *were* good. She was her own boss, pulling in a respectable income in a low-stress job doing something she enjoyed. She had plenty of savings, a clean bill of health—and now she had a hot lover who knew exactly how to please her. She just had to remember Danny's rules, and all would be well.

MARC WOKE when he shifted in his sleep and registered the chill, empty sheets on the other side of the bed. He sat up and blinked in the early morning light. She was gone. There was a hollow in the pillow from where her head had rested, and he could still smell her perfume on the sheets, but she was definitely gone.

He checked the clock. Just past six. Flopping back down onto the bed, he flung an arm across his eyes and wondered why she hadn't woken him to say goodbye. Then he frowned at his own stupidity. She'd outlined the rules very simply and clearly before they'd leaped on each other last night. No commitment, no feelings, no future. And when one of them said it was over, it was over.

The perfect deal for a man who had just declared his complete lack of interest in ever settling down again. He couldn't have arranged it better himself. Smiling, he rolled out of bed and padded into the en suite bathroom. He hadn't exactly caught a full eight hours last night, but he was feeling better than he had in weeks. Turning the shower on, he realized he was even humming to himself as he stepped under the warm water. He had a vague commitment to have brunch with Gary and his wife, and later in the day he'd planned on giving himself a break from weekend work by just bumming around. Hell, he might even read a book. Yesterday, the idea of being able to concentrate enough to read a book had felt like a far-flung fantasy. He'd been wound so tight with frustration and desire he'd been practically jumping out of his own skin. Now he felt great. Relaxed. At ease within himself. Having a short, hot affair with Anna was just what the doctor ordered.

SHE MANAGED TO GET an extra couple of hours of sleep when she got home. Marc's mansion was a convenient five-minute drive from her house—or a fifteen-minute walk, depending on how urgent a girl's need was. She giggled to herself as the thought crossed her mind over a late breakfast. She felt like the most liberated, decadent hedonist in the world. She, Anna Jackson, was having a no-holds-barred fling with a sexy, vibrant man. She'd acknowledged her adult desire, and pursued it. She felt sophisticated, and completely in charge of herself.

It wasn't until she was taking care of the week's ironing that she realized she didn't know his phone number. And he didn't have hers. In fact, they hadn't really discussed when they would next see each other at all. So…was she supposed to call him? Or wait for him to call her?

She chewed her lip, doubt assailing her. Then she remembered that he'd called her on her work line. So, he knew how to contact her. If he wanted to.

Suddenly she felt like a teenager again. What if she wanted him more than he wanted her? She'd been so sure of herself this morning when she snuck out of his bedroom, empowered by the fact that she was the one leaving him, and not the other way round. That put her in the driver's seat, right? But now she began to see that the fling thing had its downside, too. Sure, there was no risk of getting hurt because she definitely knew this was just about sex.

But there were other things to consider. Like pride, for

example. She'd laid herself on the line, going to his house and boldly propositioning him. His response had been gratifyingly instant and passionate—but there was nothing to say that that would continue. That he wouldn't get sick of her before she got sick of him. It was something that hadn't really occurred to her when she laid down the ground rules while they ripped each other's clothes off last night. Sure, it was over when one of them said it was over—but what if that person was him?

Anna stared at the shirt beneath her hands. She'd just ironed the same patch three times over. And she was obsessing about Marc when she shouldn't be. She was so used to analyzing and planning and negotiating everything. But part of finding a new way to live her life was giving up on some of that. She should just enjoy the afterglow of having had sex with a consummate lover, and forget the rest of it. Crossing to the stereo, she put on her favorite chill-out CD and returned to the ironing. Afterglow. She would enjoy the afterglow if it was the last thing she did.

By dusk the afterglow had been worn down to a nubbin and she was feeling distinctly edgy. She was almost embarrassed to admit to herself that she craved Marc's touch again. But there it was. She'd turned into a sex monster.

She flicked through holiday brochures, but she kept imagining making love to Marc on every deserted sandy beach. She tried some yoga, but every position reminded her of something they'd done in bed the night before. She thought about dinner, but food only made her think of Marc's scrambled eggs—and what had happened after the eggs. She was pacing the floorboards, wondering if going for the first run of her adult life would do any good, when there was a knock at the door.

She opened it to find Marc on her doorstep, a white paper-wrapped bundle in hand. He smiled sheepishly and lifted the parcel.

"Thought you might be hungry," he said. The delicious smell of fish and chips wafted toward her.

He shrugged a shoulder self-deprecatingly, and she noted that the hand he shoved into his front jeans pocket wasn't quite steady.

She smiled. This feeling inside her, this need—she wasn't alone. He felt it, too.

She stood back to allow him access. "Come on in. I was just thinking about dinner myself," she said.

She inhaled deeply as he brushed past her, loving the crisp yet mellow scent of his aftershave. He always smelled good. Good enough to eat, in fact.

He stood in the middle of her living room, looking around with an approving eye.

"This is great," he said.

She thanked her lucky stars that she'd splurged on the new couch and rug, then kicked herself. She didn't care what he thought about her apartment or anything else. The only thing she cared about where Marc was concerned was how hard he could get, how often.

She took the paper parcel from his hands. "I'll go grab some plates," she said.

She stepped into the kitchen and put the parcel on the counter. Who was she kidding? The fish and chips smelled fantastic—but all she wanted to do was rip Marc's clothes off. She let out a ragged breath, then returned to the living room where Marc was standing, both hands jammed into his jean pockets now.

"Anyone ever told you how great fish and chips are when they're cold?" she said lightly, eyes devouring his tall body hungrily.

"Couldn't agree more," he said, grinning widely.

She grabbed the hem of her T-shirt and pulled it over her head. She was wearing a stretchy tank top underneath in place of a bra, and she pulled that off, too. He was busy dragging off his own T-shirt.

Smiling, she leaned forward and tagged him on the arm.

"You're it," she said, then she turned on her heel and sauntered toward the bedroom.

MARC STARED AFTER HER, his arms still half in, half out of his T-shirt. She had the sexiest walk in all the world, especially in the clingy yoga pants she was wearing—part enticement, part provocation. It had been hard making the decision to come over here tonight, especially after last night. He didn't want her getting the idea he was a sex fiend or anything. But the plain truth of it was that he just couldn't get her out of his mind. And he didn't have to—he could have her now. There was no need to pretend or dress it up. But he'd still stopped for food on his way over. After all, she'd said she couldn't cook, and they were bound to get hungry at some point.

Shedding his jeans, he followed her into the bedroom, his erection nudging his stomach as he walked. She was on the bed, naked, her eyes hooded. As he watched, she ran her hands over her breasts, then trailed one down her belly until her fingers were delving into the folds between her legs.

"I've been thinking about you all afternoon," she said.

"I've been thinking about you, too," he said, feeling his erection harden further as she began to play with herself, her eyes never leaving him.

He moved onto the bed, felt the mattress dip beneath his weight.

"Why keep a dog and bark yourself?" he said into her ear as he swept her hand away from between her legs and pinned it to the bed beside her.

She laughed, but her eyes glinted challengingly at him as he moved on top of her, his penis finding its way unerringly to the hot, wet entrance he craved. Noting the condom box on the bedside table, he tore off a foil pack and quickly sheathed himself. She lifted her hips, spreading her legs wider.

"Now," she told him, and he stared down at her as he gave her exactly what she was asking for.

She clenched hot and tight around him, her hips sinuously tilting to prolong the slide when he withdrew. He plunged again, and she threw back her head, her throat long and vulnerable as she moaned her pleasure. Her hands clutched at the linen beneath them as he picked up his rhythm, and he dropped forward to tongue her nipples. She arched her back, crying out, her hips bucking again and again.

She was so hot. They were so hot. Already he could feel the urge to rush it coming on him. He pulled a nipple into his mouth, sucking hard. Her hands reached for his butt, and she gripped him tight, pulling him toward her, urging him to go faster, harder, longer, deeper.

Again, he gave the lady what she wanted, because it was exactly what he wanted, too. She was panting beneath him, her face taut with desire. Her intensity was almost enough to tip him over, and he deliberately slowed things down, trying to get a grip. He wasn't ready, not just yet....

Her hands clenched harder on his butt, urging him to step up the pace again, but instead he withdrew until just the head of his penis was inside her. She opened her mouth to protest, but he reached between them and slid his fingers deftly into the moist curls of her mons. Her clitoris was swollen and ready for him, and he slicked his finger over it, enjoying the way she flinched. He circled his hips, nudging the head of his penis against her inner lips, keeping up the pressure on her clitoris. She closed her eyes, breasts rising and falling dramatically as she tried to keep pace with the storm raging inside her. She clenched involuntarily around him, and he plunged all the way inside her again, hard and deep, keeping up a punishing rhythm as she came around him, her inner muscles pulsating, tight, so tight. He closed his eyes, dropping forward to cover her body as his own orgasm shook him. Her hands were still clutching at his butt, and he could feel her hot breath on his neck. After a few minutes, he realized that he must be heavy, and tensed to move.

"No. Stay," she said. He felt the distinct pressure as she flexed her inner muscles around him. He wasn't a bit surprised to find himself growing hard again. She always got him hot. He was getting used to it now.

Slowly, leisurely, he withdrew a few inches. Then slowly, leisurely, he drove back down. She matched her hip movements to his, her movements just as languid, her eyes hooded as she looked up at him.

He closed his eyes, reveling in the slick, slippery heat of her. He didn't know what it was that made them so good together, but whatever it was, it just kept getting hotter. Proof positive that you could never get too much of a good thing.

Afterward, they sat cross-legged on her living room rug and ate cold fish and chips with their fingers. Her hair was mussed, pressed flat on one side, and she wasn't wearing a scrap of makeup. She still looked dangerously attractive, her big toffee eyes alternately teasing or challenging as they talked. She'd pulled on a short silk robe, and every time she laughed he was treated to a tantalizing glimpse of a pale pink nipple as the gown slid open. Insatiable, his penis stirred in his boxers.

Reaching for another handful of chips, his eye was caught by the series of thick books filling one of the bookcases on either side of her open fireplace.

"Who did you used to lawyer for?" he asked impulsively, intrigued by the riddle that she represented. So clever and bright, yet she'd turned her back on a lucrative white-collar career.

"Gallagher, Worth and Jones," she said impassively, as though she wasn't naming one of the most prestigious firms in town.

He whistled, impressed. "Big time. Why'd you give it up?"

He could see her withdraw before she shrugged. "Didn't need the stress. Realized I was working when I could have been living."

She didn't want to talk about it. That much was obvious. He shut the door on his curiosity, recognizing that it had no place in their relationship. He deliberately turned his attention back to the bookshelf, following her cue to change the subject. What he saw there made him turn to her with a teasing smile.

"*Harry Potter?* Now there's a guilty secret," he said.

She blushed, smoothing her hand over her hair self-consciously. "Had to see what all the fuss was about," she said, shrugging.

"Overrated, if you ask me," he deadpanned.

She stared at him. "You have not read *Harry Potter!*"

"Only the first two. Got a bit sick of it by then," he said.

She eyed him narrowly. "I don't know if you're having me on or not," she said after a moment.

"One thing you should know about me, I never lie," he said.

She eyed him, then nodded, and he could tell she believed him. "Good. Neither do I," she said.

He liked that about her, the way she looked him in the eye, made sure he got the message she was sending.

Desire twisted inside him again. Registering that they'd both finished eating a long time ago, he rolled up the paper and crushed it into a ball. He levered himself to his feet, then stepped through to the kitchen, dumping the rubbish in the bin. Then he moved next door to the bathroom, where he found a face cloth. A minute later, he returned to the living room and offered her the hot cloth to wash her greasy fingers.

"Wow. Silver service," she said as she wiped her hands.

"You ain't seen nothing yet, lady," he said, leering comically.

She laughed, but he could see she was excited, too. A pulse flickered at her throat, and her nipples were hardening even as he watched.

Smiling to himself, he returned the cloth to the bathroom and hauled arse back to the living room in record time. She'd pulled some cushions from the couch down onto the big, fluffy rug, and was lounging back on them, gown open now, waiting.

"I was thinking of you when I bought this," she said, running her fingers through the rug's rich texture.

"Yeah?" he asked as he joined her.

"Yeah. I had this vision of you, stretched out, naked. Hard."

She slid her hands over his body as she spoke, one hand delving beneath the waistband of his boxers and reaching unerringly for his erection.

"Well, far be it from me to disappoint," he said.

She laughed, and he captured her smile with a kiss. Her mirth soon died as passion flared, and he pushed her back onto the cushions, his hands slow and gentle as he traced her creamy skin from the sensitive place behind her ear, down her neck, across her collarbone and onto the sexy slope of her breasts. Determined to take his time, he circled each nipple with his forefinger, then moved closer to gently suck and tease them with his mouth.

"You should do this for a living," she said drowsily.

His laugh was muffled by her breasts, and he continued on his voyage of discovery, cupping her in his hands, rubbing his thumbs over the coral pink tips as they strained upward for his attention. He kissed the curve of her breast where it met her arm, loving the taste of her. Everything about her drove him wild. Switching his attention to her other breast, he went to work. If a job was worth doing, it was worth doing well, after all.

SHE COULD NEVER GET enough of this, she thought hazily as he moved slowly over her breasts. Her hips lifted instinctively, seeking an invasion that was not yet there. But it would come, she knew it would come. And that knowledge was already swelling the sensitive folds between her legs, filling her with liquid heat.

"Oh, Marc," she whispered as he suckled on a nipple, biting it gently while his left hand plucked at her other breast.

She could feel her heartbeat echoing thickly between her thighs, and she shifted her hips again, increasingly gripped with need.

She knew the exact moment he saw the small, neat incision in the crease beneath her breast. Her surgeon had been brilliant, and there was no stiffness or roughness around the scar itself—just a thin, neat pale pink line, maybe an inch and a half long. Under normal circumstances, it was invisible. Indeed, even during several bouts of energetic, voracious sex it had remained undetected. But it couldn't survive the kind of attention Marc was lavishing on her breasts right now.

He ran a gentle finger over the scar, and she tried not to stiffen in reaction. This was the last thing she wanted to talk about. The very last. He raised his head, questions in his eyes, and she shrugged a shoulder lightly.

"Accident," she said briefly. She wasn't a practiced liar, and she didn't trust herself to elaborate. And she didn't want to, either.

To her everlasting relief, he accepted her explanation, ducking his head to kiss the scar briefly before shifting his attention back to her nipple. Relieved, she dropped back onto the cushions. She'd just told him that she didn't lie, yet she'd proven herself a liar at the first opportunity.

But he didn't need to know about her cancer. She didn't want him to know, better still. It had no place in the kind of relationship they had. Gradually the tension banding her shoulders relaxed and a new kind of tension took its place as Marc began licking and sucking his way down her belly.

It didn't matter. Nothing mattered, except for the fact that in a few seconds time she was about to receive head from a past master. That was what she should be concentrating on, and nothing else.

Life is about now, she reminded herself. Sighing, she gave herself over entirely to the moment.

8

THREE DAYS LATER, Anna stuffed her feet into high heels as a knock sounded at her door. She click-clacked her way across the polished floorboards to open the door to her brother. He let out a low whistle when he saw that she was wearing her black halter-neck dress again.

"The lady is dressed to thrill. Wait till my boss sees you," he said, grabbing her hand and spinning her so he could admire her from all angles.

Anna smiled and grabbed her shawl and evening bag. "I'm ready. Let's motor," she said.

"I'm not driving," Danny explained. "I've got a cab waiting downstairs."

"You should have said!" Anna exclaimed, pushing him out the door and locking it behind them. "Is the meter still ticking?"

Danny just shrugged. Anna gave him a poke in the ribs with her elbow as she made her way downstairs.

"You make too much money, that's your problem," she said.

"Not from where I'm sitting," Danny replied, adjusting his black tie.

He was taking her to an advertising industry award night, an annual gala that he'd invited her to a month or so back. One of Danny's print ads was up for an award for best creative, and she planned on embarrassing him if he won.

They settled into the back of the taxi and pulled on seat belts as the driver accelerated away from the curb.

"So, how're things?" Danny asked, winking suggestively. "You'll note I've been very discreet and not called once to see how your hot date with your big stud went."

Anna noted the way the driver's eyes flicked to the rearview mirror on hearing Danny's words.

"Danny, you have never been discreet in your life," she said, rolling her eyes.

"True. Which brings us back to my original question…."

"Things went well," she said. She couldn't stop the secret smile that stole to her lips.

"You dirty dog," Danny said, his tone light. "I thought you had the bright-eyed look of the recently shagged-senseless."

Anna choked back a laugh. "You have a real way with words."

"Tell that to the awards committee."

Danny was frowning, tweaking the French cuffs on his shirt. Anna studied him. Was he *nervous?* Surely not her Danny, king of cool?

"Got some butterflies in your tummy, little brother?" she teased.

He shot her a dirty look. "This is a big deal, you know. An industry award means more money, more prestige, a bigger office."

"Plus you get told publicly that you're the best," Anna added mischievously.

Danny grinned. "That, too."

She gave his hand a squeeze. "You're the best in my book," she said.

Danny snorted. "That's what you're supposed to say at the end of the night, after I've lost out to some wet-behind-the-ears graduate."

"But this way you know I mean it," she said.

Danny tweaked his cuffs again, obviously still edgy. "So where's the big man tonight? Hope I didn't cramp your style, but I had dibs on you first since we organized this ages ago."

"I'm not sure. I think he mentioned a work dinner." She

shrugged. It was none of her business what Marc did when they weren't together. And she'd seen him last night, anyway. And the night before. Every night, in fact, since she'd first laid down the rules for their fling.

She crossed her legs, thinking about the hours of intense sex they'd shared the previous evening. It just seemed to get better and better between them. So good that it was hard to stop herself from thinking about him during the day. That was probably part of the problem. She spent so much time thinking about him, about his body, and the expression he got in his eyes when he looked at her, that by the end of the day she was almost crazy with anticipation.

Fortunately, every night so far he'd felt the same way. They'd fallen into a pattern of sorts—they'd try to make it through the day, then one or the other of them would give in first. On Monday, it had been her. She'd arrived on his doorstep after dinner, heart drumming in her ears. Tuesday night it had been him, leaning against his car outside her apartment block when she arrived home from her last job of the day. And last night it had been mutual—they'd passed each other on the road that connected Rose Bay to Point Piper. Her cell phone had rung almost immediately, and she'd grinned and pulled a U-turn to race him back to her apartment.

It was pretty amazing, really. She'd gone from being a poster girl for celibacy and self-restraint to borderline sex addict in the space of a few weeks. Not that she *was* addicted, of course. She was just getting an urge out of her system. Fortunately she'd found a clever, talented lover to help her with the process.

As usual, just thinking about Marc made parts of her stand to attention. She recrossed her legs and tried to think about something else.

Problem was, if she was being completely honest with herself, she was actually feeling a little nervous at the thought of not getting her nightly fix of Marc's hot body this evening. It was pretty embarrassing admitting that to herself, but there it was. She had that distinct jittery, itchy and scratchy feeling she'd gotten when she wanted him and couldn't have him.

She shrugged. She'd survive. It was just one night, and she'd gone a whole thirty-two years without the man, after all. It just meant she was in for a long, cold shower when she got home after the awards ceremony.

"Okay, here we are," Danny said. His voice sounded tense, and she soothed a hand down his back as they got out of the cab in front of the hotel.

"Relax, you'll do fine," she assured him.

The first person they saw when they stepped into the hotel foyer was Ben Grayson, her brother's mysteriously oriented colleague. He smiled broadly when he spotted them.

"Danny! Cutting it a little fine, aren't you? They're just about to serve the entree," he said.

"What are you doing out here, then?" Danny asked wryly.

"Waiting for my date. Looks like she's a no-show, though." Ben shrugged.

Anna almost laughed at the sharp glint that came into her brother's eye. "Your girlfriend working late, is she?" he fished.

"Not my girlfriend, just a buddy of mine. She's a doctor—must have gotten stuck in emergency or something."

Ben didn't seem too fazed as he fell in alongside them and accompanied them into the hotel's ballroom where the dinner was being held. Waiting for a proper introduction, Anna realized Danny was too busy examining this new snippet of information from every angle to remember social niceties.

"I'm Danny's sister, Anna," she said, leaning across Danny to extend her hand in greeting. "We sort of met briefly the other day."

"Hi, Anna. Ben. I figured you must be related. You've got the same eyes and nose as Danny," Ben said.

Anna felt her eyebrows lift. He'd noticed her brother's nose and eyes? She shot a look sideways, wondering if Danny had picked up on the comment. The smug smile playing about his mouth told her he had.

"The agency's table is over here," Ben directed, and Anna trailed after him and Danny as they wove their way past dozens of large round tables, all set for twelve diners. Counting mentally, Anna estimated there must be about thirty all told in the room, which meant the hotel was catering for a staggering 360 people. She quietly resigned herself to cold vegetables and lukewarm chicken or beef.

She almost walked into Danny, realizing at the last minute that they'd arrived at their table. He shot her a triumphant look, his eyes inviting her to study the seating arrangements. Conveniently, she and Danny were sitting next to Ben. She guessed by Danny's increasingly cocky look that he didn't think this was a coincidence.

"Down, boy," she said in his ear as she bent to take her seat.

"Oh, come on. I couldn't have arranged it better myself. Date's a no-show my arse—he might as well have sent me flowers," Danny muttered back.

Shaking her head, she unfolded her napkin and turned to introduce herself to the man on her right.

As she'd predicted, the meal was barely warm by the time it got to her, but the real-life soap opera playing out on her left was more than enough to make up for it. Danny and Ben were plowing their way through the wine, their laughter and voices getting louder by the second. Since everyone else also seemed intent on tying one on, they didn't stand out too much, which was just as well if her brother intended on keeping his sexual orientation a secret at work. As his inhibitions fell by the wayside, Danny's speech became more relaxed, his gestures more languid. In short, the campy gay in him began to emerge—just flashes, enough for a like-minded individual to make the connection,

Anna judged. And unless she missed her guess, Ben was a like-minded individual. He exchanged innuendo with her brother, he slapped Danny on the wrist when he was too risqué, and he had a bright glint in his eye every time he looked Danny's way. By the time dessert was being served, there was definite sizzle in the glances being exchanged between her brother and his workmate. She had the distinct impression that her brother wasn't going home alone tonight.

The MC called the audience to attention at that point, and she struggled to keep her eyes open for a series of speeches and awards. But when Danny's category came up, she sat up straight and gave him a pinch on the arm to ensure he was paying attention and not just staring into Ben's bright blue eyes.

"Fingers crossed," she whispered to him as the announcer pulled the winning name from an envelope.

"And the winner is…Daniel Jackson for the Ultimate Airline print campaign!"

Anna felt a surge of pride and delight as she sprang to her feet and urged a shocked Danny to stand. Hugging him hastily, she turned him around and pushed him toward the stage. Danny wove slightly on his feet for a second, and she suddenly worried that he'd had too much to drink. But he quickly corrected his course, and calmly mounted the stage.

"This is great," he said into the mike. "But I wouldn't be here if it hadn't been for all the people who believed in me along the way, as well as the client services team, and the production gang. You know who you are—this is for all of us," Danny said.

Then, cheeky devil that he was, Anna saw him make eye contact with Ben and give him a saucy wink. She laughed. He really was incorrigible. It seemed impossible that they shared any genetic material at all—she was so conservative and self-conscious, and he was so outrageous. But then she remembered that e'd been guilty of her own share of outrageous behavior lately. aybe she and Danny weren't so different, after all.

There was lots of back clapping and champagne toasts when anny got back to their table, but Anna could tell that Danny's ind was definitely elsewhere—in Ben's pants, if she didn't iss her guess. She made a trip to the bathroom, and when she turned she spotted her brother and Ben standing near the edge the ballroom, heads close together as they talked intently. anny touched a hand low on Ben's back, not quite an ass grab, ıt close enough. Definitely time for her to go home, she decided.

She grabbed her purse and shawl from the table and cruised Danny and Ben on her way to the door.

"I'm outta here, Danny. Great to meet you, Ben. And congrat- ations again," she said to her brother one last time, giving him ›ig squeezy hug.

"Wait! How are you getting home?" Danny asked.

She just laughed and waved a hand. "I'm a big girl, Danny. »u have a good night," she said meaningfully.

Turning on her heel, she made her way out into the marble- ›ored foyer. The cool, quiet calm was very welcome after the bbub of the crowded ballroom. She slowed her step, nodding knowledgment to the well-groomed women behind the recep- ›n desk. A huge double staircase curved toward the second floor her right, branching off in opposite directions at a central ıding. All around her were huge glazed pots filled with exotic ›oms, and the ceiling glittered with chandeliers.

Now that she was alone with no distractions, the itchy- ratchy feeling was back with a vengeance. How could she be desperate for Marc's touch when it had been barely twenty- ur hours since she'd last had him?

Deciding to put off the inevitable frustration of going home an empty apartment, she veered away from the front entrance d into the hotel bar. Dark and discreet, it was dotted with small

tables and couches grouped in intimate settings. Everything wa
very elegant and of the highest standard, and she guessed tha
the rooms upstairs must be pretty spectacular. Running her ey
down the cocktail menu, she chose something creamy and ricl
banking on the liqueur settling her down and readying her for
good night's sleep. The waitress smiled as she took her order, ar
Anna settled back in her seat. The bar looked out on the busy cit
and she watched the car headlights come and go while sl
waited, one foot swinging as she unconsciously tried to work o
some of the unwanted desire in her system.

"Excuse me. Is this seat taken?"

Anna glanced up to see a good-looking middle-aged ma
standing next to her chair. He'd taken her by surprise, and sl
stammered.

"Um—n-no."

He smiled, flicking the button of his suit jacket open as he s
down opposite her. Anna suddenly realized what she'd just agre
to. This wasn't a bus or a train, for Pete's sake—he hadn't be
looking for somewhere to park his butt. He was looking for a resti
place for a very different part of his anatomy, if she had any gue

"I'm Kirk," he said, extending his hand across the space tl
separated them.

"Anna," she said, brain ticking over furiously. She'd really ju
wanted a quiet drink, but she had no idea how to extricate hers
from this situation.

"I have a confession—I saw you in at the awards dinne
Kirk said, smiling self-deprecatingly. "You're a very strikir
looking woman."

Anna blinked. Oh, boy. She so didn't know how to handle t
sort of thing.

"Um…thanks. Kirk," she wound up saying.

He laughed. It was a nice laugh, and she found hers
relaxing a notch.

"It's okay, Anna, I'm not going to try any moves on you. I just wanted to meet you, that's all," he said.

"Okay," she said, turning with relief to the waitress as she arrived with her cocktail.

"Do you work in advertising?" he asked as she eased her martini glass onto a coaster.

"No. I was here with my brother who does," she said.

"So there's not some guy who's going to get all bent out of shape if I ask you out for dinner sometime, then?" Kirk asked.

"Not exactly," Anna said cautiously. She studied him covertly under her lashes. He was probably midforties, with a square, chiseled jaw and bright green eyes. He had a faint tan, and a full head of midbrown hair that he wore brushed back from his forehead. He looked good in black tie, and she guessed he worked out or something because his belly appeared flat and his chest broad. All in all, an attractive man. A very attractive man, objectively speaking.

"Why don't I tell you a little bit about myself?" he said, surprising her. He picked up on it, and he shrugged again. "Is there an easy way to meet someone? Some way that doesn't involve awkward moments like this? 'Cause I'd love to know what it is. I was married for fifteen years when my wife died last January, and I've only just started getting my feet wet in the dating pool again. So I'm probably a bit rusty with all this sort of thing…."

Suddenly Anna liked him. She believed what he was saying, that he was sincere in seeking a connection with her, not just a quick one-nighter. But she couldn't be less interested.

She frowned down into her drink, disturbed by the realization that even though she didn't view her fling with Marc Lewis as having a future, she couldn't even contemplate dinner with another man while Marc was in her orbit.

Her head came up as she made her decision. "You seem like a nice guy, Kirk, and you've been really honest with me, so I'm

going to be equally honest back. You're a good-looking man, an
I guarantee that you will not have trouble getting some luck
woman to go out to dinner with you. But I'm afraid that woma
won't be me."

"Can I ask why?" Somehow, he managed to make it a friendl
request and not a sulky demand.

"I'm just not looking for a relationship right now," she sai
She could see him withdraw as he interpreted her words as a fo
mulaic rebuff. It prompted her to a moment of revealing honest
"I've been sick recently. And it's made me rethink a lot of thing
I'm kind of catching up on some parts of life that I've misse
out on," she said.

He was silent for a moment, then he nodded. The muscles
his thighs tensed as he prepared to stand, and she found herse
thinking again that he was a very good-looking man.

"Well, it was nice meeting you, Anna," he said. He pulled
business card from his pocket and held it out to her. "If ever yo
change your mind, give me a call."

She smiled and took his card, mostly because it was th
graceful thing to do. He nodded once more, then exited the ba
heading back to the awards dinner, she guessed.

She stared at the small square of card in her hand. Kir
Bowman, account manager, it said. She knew that Leah or Jule
would give their left arm to meet a guy like him. Sincere, attra
tive, built, good job, charming.

But he wasn't Marc Lewis. The thought made her take a b
gulp of her cocktail. As the coffee-tinged alcohol made its wa
down her throat and into her belly, she grappled with all the co
fusing thoughts and feelings warring inside her. She tried
work out if she would have gone out with Kirk Bowman befo
she'd met Marc. It worried her that the answer was probably ye

Quickly her rational self jumped in. It didn't mean anythin
Of course she wasn't going to go out with someone while sh

was sleeping with someone else. She might have loosened up a bit on the sexual front, but she wasn't about to turn into a serial one-night-stand aficionado. And there was no denying that she and Marc had a potent sexual chemistry. All he had to do was look at her and she wanted him. As undeniably attractive as Kirk Bowman was, he had done nothing for her whatsoever.

As though her thoughts had conjured him, her phone suddenly rang inside her evening bag and she saw from the caller ID that it was Marc. Her tummy tensed, and she squeezed her thighs together. Thank God. Thank God he needed her as much as she needed him.

She was smiling faintly as she took the call, feeling very much like the cat that had got the cream.

"Hi."

"Hi. Where are you?" he asked. The deep tones of his voice thrilled her.

"At the awards dinner still," she said.

"When can you leave?" he asked. She recognized the faint rasp of desire in his voice; she was learning to read him now.

"I'm in the bar now, on my own," she said.

"I'll come pick you up," he said instantly.

Anna glanced back toward the foyer, taking in the marble and chandeliers and grand staircase. A wicked idea nudged its way into her mind.

"I've got a better idea. Why don't I get a room?" she said.

There was a moment of hesitation on the other end of the line. She knew exactly what his face would look like: his eyes smoky, his expression intent, focused.

"Yes," was all he said, and then she was listening to dead air.

MARC DIDN'T BOTHER shucking his work suit—he just scooped up his keys and made for the car, feeling like a superhero on a mission. He smiled to himself. He *was* on a mission: to experience pleasure as often and as intensely as possible with Anna Jackson.

He'd planned on having a shower when he got home from his work dinner, going over some papers in bed, then having a relatively early night. But once he was alone the hunger that had been bubbling beneath the surface all evening reared its head. He wanted her. And he was so far gone with wanting her that he couldn't stop himself from calling her cell phone, even though it was well after eleven.

He darted smoothly in and out of the late-night traffic on his way back into the city. The expressway was relatively clear, and he made good time, his thoughts with Anna all the way. He wondered what she was wearing. She always looked fantastic, so sexy. His erection strained against the fabric of his pants. He imagined her in the black lace panties she'd been wearing last night, her butt cheeks curving sweetly below the lace. And maybe she'd be wearing her see-through mesh bra, the one that showed her nipples so enticingly. Checking his rearview mirror and the speedometer, he realized he was speeding. Speeding to get to Anna. No surprises there.

He pulled into the forecourt of the hotel in just under ten minutes. A feat worthy of Anna herself, he decided. He tossed the Jag's keys to the valet, gave him his name, then headed for the reception desk like a heat-seeking missile.

They were expecting him, and he was given a pass card and directions to one of the upper-level suites with alacrity. He tapped his fingers against the railing in the elevator as it whisked him efficiently to the twentieth floor. Thank God for suit jackets—they hid a multitude of sins.

The door to the suite opened with a quiet hush. He walked into a sitting area carpeted with ankle-deep white plush-pile. The furniture was elegant and expensive, the lighting low. He barely glanced at any of it. Tossing his pass card onto a nearby table, he wrenched off his tie and tossed it onto the couch as he stalked toward the bedroom.

She was sitting on a chair beside the bed, a glass of champagne in her hand. She was wearing the black dress he'd first seen her in at the opera house, and he groaned deep in his chest.

"Man, I love that dress," he said.

"You remember it?" she asked, surprised.

"Hell, yeah," he said. He hadn't told her yet how he'd seen her changing in the car park. He grinned. Maybe they could do a little reenactment sometime.

"How do you like it now?" she asked, lifting one leg over the arm of the chair. The black fabric fell back from the slope of her thighs, pooling around her waist. She wasn't wearing any underwear, and his eyes honed in on the neat thatch of curls at the apex of her spread thighs. She was already glistening for him. Which was only fair, because he was so hard he was in danger of bursting a vessel.

"It's the sexiest damn dress in the whole world," he said. "Now take it off."

AFTERWARD, she reveled in the warm weight of his body across hers. He choked on a snort of laughter, and she poked him with a finger.

"What?" she asked, ready to share the joke.

"I was planning on an early night and a cold shower," he revealed.

She laughed self-consciously. "Me, too."

They held eyes for a beat, sharing each other's amusement.

"You have amazing eyes," he said, ducking his head to kiss the corner of her left eye.

"Thanks," she said, trying to hide her surprise. She didn't expect—or need—those kinds of compliments from him.

He rolled off her, smoothing a hand down her body as he did so. She shivered, and realized that she wanted him again already. The glint in his eye said he felt the same—round two was just around the corner.

Suddenly a knock sounded at the door. They stared at each other

"Did you order room service?" she asked after a moment.

Marc winced. "Yeah. I forgot, sorry. Just some champagne and a club sandwich," he explained ruefully.

Another knock sounded. "Room service," a muffled voice announced this time.

Anna wriggled under the sheet and pulled it all the way up so that just her eyes were peeping over the top. "He who order opens…." she said mischievously.

He swore under his breath and tweaked her nipple through the sheet before pushing himself up off the bed.

Snatching a towel from the bathroom, he started wrapping it around his waist as he reached for the door handle. Anna stifled a giggle as she realized he'd grabbed the bath mat. The towel only just met around his waist, leaving a huge patch of ass and thigh exposed. He stared down at himself, annoyed—but it was too late, he'd already opened the door. Anna's eyebrows shot up and she bit her lip to stop from laughing out loud as the room service waiter walked in.

"Evening, ma'am, sir," the man said, eyes carefully straight forward. Standing to one side, Marc held her eye, his expression daring her to say anything about how ridiculous he looked.

In a matter of seconds, the tray had been placed on the dresser, and the waiter was reversing from the room, still resolutely poker-faced.

"Thanks," Marc said drily.

Once the door was closed, Anna let out a huge guffaw of laughter and threw her head back against the pillows.

"You find that amusing, do you?" Marc asked, a smile curving his own mouth.

"Oh, yes. Very," she said.

"Hmm. Well, since I did all the hard work to earn this club sandwich, I think I might just keep it to myself," he said, propping himself against the dresser and lifting the cover on the plate. "Mmm, it smells delicious, too."

Anna sat up, the sheet pooling at her waist. "Are there fries?" she asked hopefully.

"Oh, yes. Lots," he said, popping one into his mouth, his eyes dropping to her breasts.

Knowing he wanted her to plead with him, Anna didn't say anything, just gave him her best sad-puppy-dog look.

"Very effective. Bet that won you a few court cases," he said as he popped some more fries into his mouth, deliberately torturing her.

"As a matter of fact, I have it on good authority that I had a reputation for being formidable in the courtroom," she said archly.

"Formidable." He cocked his head to one side as though he was considering the issue. "Nope, can't see it."

"If I come all the way over there, do I get half the sandwich?" she asked, ignoring his gibe.

"Why don't you try it and see?" he suggested. Anna smiled slowly, then rolled leisurely onto all fours. Doing her best cat impression, she stalked her way across the bed, breasts jiggling, butt wiggling high in the air. She quirked an eyebrow as the bath mat around his waist transformed into a big top in the time it took her to reach the end of the bed.

"Touché," he said.

Sitting cross-legged on the end of the bed, she helped herself to half the sandwich.

"I didn't realize how hungry I was," Marc said as he demolished his half in just a few bites.

"Didn't you eat at your business dinner?" she asked, surprised.

He pulled a face. "Too nervous," he said ruefully.

She stared at him. "I can't imagine you being nervous about anything," she said. He always seemed so confident, so in charge.

"Okay, nervous wasn't the best word for it. I just meant it was a tense meeting. Lots of back and forth and bullshit." He shrugged. "Getting that new data platform could make a big difference for the business."

But she knew he'd meant what he'd said the first time—he *had* been nervous.

"Work means a lot to you, doesn't it?" she asked quietly.

His dark gaze was stern as he glanced up at her. "Hundreds of people and their families rely on me to pay their mortgages and put food in their mouths. Yeah, I take it pretty seriously," he said.

The way he said it, it was almost as though he was talking about his own family, and his employees were his children. She remembered what he'd said about his mother having to work a lot. And how he hadn't mentioned his father at all.

There was a grim set to his mouth, and she wondered what he was thinking. She wanted to ask, to soothe the creases from his forehead, to rub his shoulders and sympathize with him about his tough day.

She shook herself. It wasn't her place to bring him his pipe and slippers and tell him the pot roast was almost done. They were here for sex, nothing more. If she was in any danger of forgetting that, the fact that they were having this conversation naked, sitting on a large bed, was a pretty potent reminder. There wasn't room—or the inclination—for anything more. Not for either of them.

MARC FELT SELF-CONSCIOUS all of a sudden. He hadn't meant to say all those things about the meeting and the business and the responsibility he felt toward his employees. Anna was studying him, her eyes thoughtful, and he was a little shocked to realize that he was almost waiting for her to ask him something more, to probe his feelings, tease him out a little. He wanted to talk to her, wanted to share his day with her.

Quickly his guarded, rational self kicked in. Of course he

wanted to download to someone. It had been a tense meeting, a real pressure cooker. And Anna was a smart lady, he knew she'd understand. That was all it was—he was just keen to let off steam.

Deliberately shifting the mood, he popped the champagne cork. She eyed him for a moment, almost as though she was going to say something, to name what it was they were both doing. Then she smiled faintly and passed her glass across for him to refill. As she sat back on the bed, she took a mouthful of champagne and eyed him appreciatively.

"French. Only the best for Mr. Lewis," she said, keeping it light.

"Of course," he said, taking a sip of his own champagne then leaning across her body to place the glass on the bedside table. Taking advantage of the fact that his body was angled across hers, she spanked his bare butt, hard.

He almost spat out the champagne. "That's going to cost you," he said darkly.

"Hope so," she said, rolling out from under him and darting into the bathroom. He stood to follow her, but his eye was caught by a business card resting beside her evening bag on the beside table. Kirk Bowman, account manager. Who the hell was Kirk Bowman?

Card in hand, testosterone charged, he stalked her to the bathroom.

She was bent over the two-person tub, her butt high in the air as she adjusted the taps. He could see the pink folds between her legs, and his penis stiffened further.

"Who's Kirk Bowman?" he said, holding the card up as though it was evidence.

She glanced over her shoulder, a frown wrinkling her brow. It cleared when she saw he was holding the business card.

"He was down in the bar," she said, squeezing bath gel into the water. "He wanted to take me out for dinner."

"And?"

"And what?" she asked, swishing the gel around in the water to disperse it.

"And are you going?" he asked.

She looked over her shoulder at him again, perplexed.

"Not that it's any of your business, but no," she said a little coolly.

Marc felt a twist of jealousy and anger. The idea of Anna being with another man while she was with him was anathema to him. Everything in him rejected it.

"Maybe we should clear something up. This thing between us might be only temporary, but while it lasts, it's exclusive. You got that?" he heard himself say.

She straightened, one hand finding a hip. Said hip jutted to one side in the age-old posture of a woman about to give as good as she got.

Suddenly he caught his reflection in the mirror behind her. His face was twisted into a dark scowl, and he was standing there naked, with a boner, and another man's business card in his hand.

He looked like a dick.

Before she could open her mouth, he held up both hands. "Forget I said anything. I don't know what got into me," he said gruffly.

Her expression softened, and she crossed the room to his side. Her breasts swayed with the movement, and he eyed their pink tips avidly. Smiling slightly, she plucked the business card from his hand and walked to the toilet. Tearing the card into small pieces, she dropped them in and closed the lid, then hit the flush button.

Then she turned to face him. "For the record—I'm a one-man-at-a-time kind of a woman, okay?"

He nodded, and she walked to him and grabbed his erection. "Now, you planning on doing anything with this?" she asked saucily.

He shook his head at her audacity. "That's a spanking, and a damned good lesson in manners I owe you," he said.

"Yeah?" She sauntered away from him, stepping daintily into the bath and lying down beneath the sudsy bubbles. Picking up a bar of soap, she began rubbing it over her breasts suggestively.

"Now you're really asking for it," he said, moving toward the tub.

And for the next two hours, he proceeded to show her exactly what he meant.

HE WOKE to the alarm. He reached across to flick it off and realized he was alone. Again. He frowned. Was it just him, or did Anna have an aversion to sleepovers? He hadn't seen a sunrise with her yet. He wondered if it meant anything. Then he wondered why he was even thinking about it at all. What did it matter? They were having sex for as long as both of them wanted it to last. A very adult meeting of minds and bodies. No fuss, no muss. Whether she stayed the night or not shouldn't mean diddly.

Rolling out of bed, he walked through to the bathroom and winced at the huge pile of wet towels mounded in the bathtub. Probably they should have taken their horseplay back into the bedroom last night. But then, that was why people paid big money to stay in five-star hotels—someone else got to clean up after their excesses.

Twisting the shower on, he stepped under the jets and reached for the soap. Fifteen minutes later, he was dressed in his rumpled suit and on his way down to reception to pick up the bill. Another surprise awaited him there, too—Anna had paid for the room. She'd even picked up his valet parking tab.

He didn't consider himself a chauvinist or a traditional man in any sense. But he was the millionaire in this equation, and Anna was the self-employed ex-lawyer limo driver. Granted, her limo was a Merc, and she had a very nice flat in Rose Bay...but still.

Irritatingly, there was nothing he could do about it. He

handed over his key receipt to the valet, and waited for the Jag to be brought up. The valet clearly thought all his Christmases had come at once when Marc tipped him a fifty as he handed the car keys over. At least that was one thing Anna couldn't beat him to.

It was just shy of seven, and traffic was still light. It occurred to him as he drove that he didn't remember setting the alarm last night before he fell asleep. Anna must have done it for him. Nice. Of course, it would have been even nicer if she'd been there when he woke up. They could have enjoyed a bit of morning glory, started the day off right.

Turning into his street, Marc shunted the thought aside. It was none of his business if Anna didn't want to stay the night with him. He'd got what he wanted out of the deal, hadn't he?

He punched the coffee machine on as he breezed through the kitchen on his way upstairs, sparing a passing glance for the boxes still stacked in the spare bedroom. He really needed to get around to sorting the house out. When he'd moved in four months ago, he'd furnished the essentials and left the rest for later. There were two living areas still empty, as well as the pool house, the five guest bedrooms and the dining room. Idly he toyed with the idea of asking Anna to come shopping with him. He liked what she'd done with her place; she obviously had a good eye.

He was picking a shirt out of his closet as he pondered the idea, and his eyes narrowed as he registered what he was doing. He cursed, and threw the shirt onto the bed, adding a navy pin-stripe suit to it, and a red-toned tie. He wasn't going furniture shopping with Anna Jackson. What was he, crazy all of a sudden? The rules of their involvement were pretty damned clear—no commitment, no strings, no future.

It was amazing what a few doses of sensational sex could do to a man. Shaking his head, he walked through to the study to check his schedule for the day. He stared at the glowing readout on his laptop with hard eyes as he read the diary entry over again: 3:00 p.m., meeting with Tara and lawyer to discuss settlement.

He couldn't believe he'd forgotten it. The meeting had been scheduled over two months ago to allow for a mutually agreed cooling-off period. At the time, he had felt certain that nothing would alter the rancor he felt at Tara's betrayal and the date had loomed large on the horizon. Now he'd practically forgotten the bloody thing entirely.

His jaw muscles tensed as he considered why he'd been oblivious to the impending appointment. *Anna.* He'd been so busy obsessing about Anna that he'd lost track of everything else. Being brutally honest with himself, he admitted that he'd blown off work every night this week to get home in time to sleep with her again. He'd even deliberately curtailed last night's dinner—all the while pretending to himself that it was so he could get a good night's sleep.

So much for no strings.

Walking back into the bedroom, Marc began to pull on his suit. This was the wake-up call he needed, he realized. He'd almost forgotten what he'd lost the last time he trusted a woman. It wasn't going to happen again.

9

THE LIGHT WAS FADING from the sky as Anna stepped out of her car. The push button on Marc's intercom glowed golden in the dusky night, and she smiled to herself, remembering that first time when she came to see him. She'd been so nervous, so uncertain. A world away from how she felt now. She pressed the intercom button, waiting for the familiar sound of Marc's footsteps as he came to let her in.

The thin string handle on the carrier bag she was carrying dug uncomfortably into her hand, and she bent her knees to rest it on the ground while she waited. She mentally reviewed the bag's contents: delicious gourmet extra-virgin olive oil; a selection of marinated olives; a decadently oozing round of brie; a warm, spicy bottle of her favorite Australian red; and a selection of other luxurious goodies, including Swiss chocolate and Brazilian coffee.

For a second an arrow of doubt raced through her belly. Had she overdone it? After all, she and Marc didn't exactly have a give-each-other-gifts kind of relationship. But, she argued against her more cautious self, this was food. Food they would eat together. Granted, she'd selected things that she knew he loved—his favorite Greek olives, coffee he'd raved about, cheese he admitted as being his one true vice. But it wasn't really a gift. Was it?

She stared doubtfully down into the bag. Maybe she should leave it in the trunk? A car drove past, its headlights illuminating her briefly, and she suddenly registered that she'd been waiting oo long. Where was Marc? Had he forgotten that he'd told her to come to his place once she'd finished work? They'd discussed it in the hazy time after making long, slow love in the hotel last night. She remembered it very clearly—but perhaps he didn't?

She tried one last time, and again the silence stretched, unbroken, for too long. She'd given up and was turning away when the intercom at last buzzed to life.

"I'm on the terrace," Marc's disembodied voice said. "Round the side of the house."

The door clicked open, and Anna blinked. He'd always come and let her in before, not leaving it up to technology to greet her. Grabbing her bag of goodies, she pushed the gate all the way open and stepped through, ensuring it closed properly behind her. Garden lights flanked a path that led around the side of the house. She followed it, inhaling the lush, heavy scent of tropical flowers. It was hard to see properly in the dying light, but she sensed that the garden was very beautiful. He must have a gardener. For the life of her she couldn't imagine him holding secateurs or a trowel.

She was still smiling faintly at this image as she rounded the house and walked onto the terraced patio at the rear of his property. She'd only ever been in a small part of his home—the bedroom, mostly—but now she gasped as she took in the full impact of his spectacular view. Three graded terraces swept down from the house to the edge of the harbor—the first completely flagged with sandstone like the path, the second covered with a thick, vibrant green turf and a series of ornamental trees, and the final and lowest level boasting a pool. The sun was sinking on the horizon, setting off his insanely amazing view of the Sydney Harbour Bridge. Ferries and smaller boats cut their way across the harbor, leaving white-spumed trails in their wakes, and the overall effect was of overwhelming wealth and privilege. For the first time in her fling with Marc she was acutely conscious of the disparity between their lives. She was comfort-

able, content with her apartment and beautiful car and low-ke
career. But he was in another stratosphere. She knew he owne
three cars—the Jag, a four-wheel drive of some sort and a vintag
Ferrari that he only drove occasionally. And she knew that he ha
a building with his name on it in north Sydney. But this view.
this view was the ultimate status symbol.

The sound of someone swimming told her where she woul
find him, and the tension banding her shoulders relaxed a notcl
He'd been in the pool—that was why he'd buzzed her in. Nothin
more meaningful than sheer convenience. Placing the carrie
bag just inside the French doors that opened onto the terrace, sh
went down the broad, deep steps until she was on the lowest leve
He was slicing up the pool, his strong arms cutting through th
water like scythes. She enjoyed the play of the dying sun on hi
tanned arms and back, marveling at his strength and speed. H
gave no indication that he knew she was there, and after a whil
she turned to the view, mesmerized by the color show the su
was providing as it retired for the day.

The lack of splashing told her when he'd stopped swimmin
and she turned in time to see him step from the water, his broad
shouldered body glistening with moisture. He wore midthigh
length board shorts, and his dark hair was slicked sleekly to hi
skull, highlighting the harsh planes of his face and the chisele
lines of his mouth. It made him seem harder, implacable, almo
intimidating as he approached her.

"Some view," she said drily.

He didn't match her smile, his dark eyes sweeping down he
body as he stood dripping in front of her.

"Let's go inside," he said.

The old hunger was in his eyes, but something was different
She frowned as she preceded him up the stairs, terribly aware o
him following close behind her, his tall, near-naked body sti
damp from the pool. He'd simply slicked the excess moistur

from his arms and legs before following her up the stairs, but he stopped to collect a towel from a nearby sun lounger when they arrived at the house. The silence stretched between them, and for some reason Anna felt a tangle of nervous knots forming in her belly. She'd never been tongue-tied with him before, never been at a loss for something to discuss with him. He had a keen, analytical mind, and a sharp sense of humor. She knew he appreciated her take on things, and that he enjoyed her brand of humor. But tonight she got the distinct impression that he wasn't in the mood for talk.

"Um, how was work?" she finally asked as he led her into the house.

He shrugged one broad shoulder as he headed toward the staircase.

"Work was work. As it always is," he said dismissively.

Okay, he was definitely not in the mood for talking. Anna hesitated at the bottom of the stairs as he started up them.

"Look, if tonight's a bad time for you, if you want me to go…" she said, offering him the opportunity to renege on their arrangement, very carefully not acknowledging the hurt she felt at his cool, hard demeanor. They were lovers, nothing more. If he wanted an evening to himself, he was more than entitled. She just needed to know, that was all.

He paused halfway up the stairs, staring down at her. She felt his dark gaze roam up and down her body, then at last it seemed to zero in on her mouth.

"I don't want you to go," he said baldly. He turned and continued his ascent, and she stood staring at his receding back for a few beats before following him. It felt like a mistake, staying when he was so clearly in a dark place. But her body needed him. With one glance he'd managed to strip her bare, and she was already anticipating his hands on her skin. She had to have him.

He was waiting for her when she entered his bedroom. Her

heart skipped a beat as he stepped closer. She wondered if it would always be like this, if he would always be able to arouse her so quickly, so readily, with just a look or a gesture. As he lowered his head, dark eyes glinting with desire, she realized that when the hunger ended, so, too, would their fling. That was the deal, really, wasn't it?

His lips were cool from the pool, and the thin fabric of her shift dress was swiftly soaked through as he hauled her up against his damp body. His kisses were different tonight, all control or finesse gone as he ravaged her mouth, his hands demanding and impatient on her body. She didn't care, she just wanted him close, some part of her exhilarating in his savagery. She made a small, needy sound as his hands slid up onto her breasts, and the next thing she knew she was being tumbled back onto the bed and he was pushing her skirt up. He tugged her panties off impatiently, and she loved the urgency in him. She felt the coolness of his skin against hers as he kneed her legs apart, and she spread her legs in welcome as the familiar weight of him settled between her thighs. He made an animal sound of approval as his seeking hand found her wet folds, and she bit her lip, anticipating the usual bittersweet torture of his caresses.

But no sooner had he touched her than his hands were gone, and there was a quick pause for him to protect them before the thick heat of him was sliding inside her, buried deep, his hips flexing as he withdrew to plunge into her again. His body was tight with tension as he pounded himself into her, and even as part of her reveled in his raw need and hunger, another part of her registered that his face above hers was fixed and hard, his eyes tightly closed as he rode her. There was a resigned intensity to his expression—as though he was trying to lose himself in her.

But despite herself, despite her growing doubt and unease, she couldn't stop her body from responding. The familiar tension was coiling tighter and tighter inside her, and she wrapped her thighs around his hips and gave herself up to his mindless domination. Her orgasm tore a cry from her throat even as he shuddered his climax into her. While she was still shivering with aftershocks, he withdrew from her in one smooth, fast move, and then he was gone. She heard the shower come on, and she stared at the ceiling, trying to work out what had just happened between them.

Her dress was rucked up around her waist, and she sat up, tugging it down, then reached for her underwear where he'd discarded it. She was sitting on the edge of the bed, waiting, when Marc emerged from the en suite bathroom, a towel slung around his waist. He pushed his hair back from his forehead when he saw her, and she caught a glimpse of something cold and lonely in his eyes. He really didn't want her there, she realized.

"Listen, I'll just go," she said, springing to her feet.

"It's fine. If you want to stay," he said, shrugging, his dark gaze roaming over her body.

He meant if she wanted more sex. Absurd, ridiculous tears pricked at the back of her eyes. He was like a stranger. The funny, warm, considerate man she'd laughed and made love with over the past week had disappeared behind a cold, implacable facade. And she didn't want to have sex with this new Marc, even if he could bring her to a screaming climax like the one she'd experienced not five minutes ago.

Shaking her head, she turned for the door.

"Anna, wait," he said.

She paused, watching as he crossed to his bedside table, yanking the drawer open to extract his wallet. She watched with growing confusion as he pulled four hundred dollars from between the supple leather folds.

"For the hotel room," he said, offering the money.

She shook her head instinctively. "It's fine," she said.

"I insist," he said, twitching the hand with the money imperiously, indicating that she should take it.

Suddenly she remembered how arrogant she'd found him when they first met.

"I covered it. The room was my idea," she said coolly.

"At least let me pay my half," he insisted.

"Why?" she asked abruptly, feeling pushed around and not liking it one little bit.

"Does it matter?" he asked, exasperated. "Just take the money, Anna."

"Why?" she demanded.

"Because I don't want to feel obligated," he bit out.

It felt like a slap, and she had to work very hard at not letting her shock and hurt show on her face. Thank God she'd once been a lawyer.

"Fine," she said very coolly, plucking two hundred dollars from his hand. "Now we're even."

Turning on her heel, she exited. She had nothing else to say to him. Or, more accurately, she was very afraid that if she stayed she might not be able to stop herself from demanding what had changed, why he was being like this. She didn't have the right to ask such things, she knew.

But there was one thing that resounded clearly inside her as she let herself out the gate and slid into the sanctuary of her car.

It was over. Of that there could be no doubt. From the moment he'd buzzed her in the gate to the moment he'd held that money out to her, the whole evening had been one big salutary lesson: *it was time to end the fling.* Because he should not have had the power to hurt her. She should not have felt the threatening sting of tears when it became clear that he didn't want her there. Somewhere along the way, lust had turned to liking, even to respect and admiration. And she'd stepped over the line.

A solitary tear ran down her cheek, but she scrubbed it away fiercely. She would not cry over Marc Lewis. He had been her lover, a walking hard-on that she'd enjoyed for a week or so. That was it. They barely knew each other. He didn't have the power to hurt her.

She knew it wasn't the whole truth. But it would get her through the night. And the next night, and all the nights afterward when she craved Marc's hands on her body.

It was over. It had to be.

As soon as she was gone he swore, then started down the stairs after her. But the sound of the front door clicking shut had already sounded by the time he'd reached the halfway landing, and he stopped in his tracks. What was he going to say to her? Apart from, "Sorry, I was angry with my soon-to-be ex-wife and I took it out on you?" That was a conversation neither of them would welcome or relish.

He'd just taken something uniquely pleasurable and simple and made it very complicated, he realized. And in doing so had probably ruined it. There had been a finality in Anna's last words, in the determined swing of her hips as she made for the door.

And perhaps that was the way he wanted it, if he was being honest with himself. Seeing Tara today had brought back an avalanche of memories and emotions that he'd been positive he'd put paid to. They were half memories, faded emotions, true, but they'd been enough to remind him of why he didn't want to get involved again. Sitting opposite Tara, staring into her gray eyes, he'd searched in vain for the woman he'd once loved. But the woman staring back at him bore little resemblance to the girl he'd met and married when he was twenty-five. This woman was slimmer, more composed. Her mouth was held more tightly, her neck more stiffly. She dressed more conservatively. She laughed less often.

And she looked sadder. This last thought struck him as he sat on the balcony outside his bedroom nursing a whiskey and staring out at the ink-dark water of the harbor. He wondered if she was still with John, if their relationship had survived the exposure of their affair and the breakup of her marriage. He could find out, if he wanted to. Alison would probably know; she made it her business to keep tabs on Tara. But he didn't care. That was a strange realization—the ball of anger that he'd nursed toward the other man had seemed as insoluble as concrete at one time. Now it had gone.

The business side of the divorce had been a breeze. Tara was being surprisingly fair-minded. She didn't even want half, which she'd have been more than entitled to given the span of their marriage. She'd kept their old house, a more modest dwelling in Balmain, and she'd asked for the deed to the beach property. That had caused a pang, but in the interests of expediency he'd agreed. She kept her shares in the business, and he had the option of buying her out in twelve months' time should he choose to do so. And that was it. No children or pets to carve up. Just assets and lost dreams and hopes.

All in all, not the grueling session it could have been. Very civilized, in fact. No accusations thrown, no tearful insults or character assassinations. He'd even stood up from the table feeling vaguely satisfied with the entire proceedings. And then they'd stepped into the elevator at the same time on their way out of the building.

At first Tara had just kept her eyes straight ahead, hands wrapped around the straps of her handbag as she held it in front of her like a shield. He realized as they plunged toward the ground that she was laboring under some strong emotion, and sure enough, before the doors opened on the ground floor she turned to him, eyes burning, to spit out what was on her mind.

"Do you know what I think is the saddest thing about our marriage, Marc?" she said. "Not once have you ever asked me why."

"I would have thought the answer to that was fairly obvious," he responded coolly.

"Would you? Tell me, then—why do you think I had an affair?"

Just remembering the challenge in her words made him angry all over again.

"You're the one who slept with another man for more than a year, Tara. It's a little late to be playing the self-righteous martyr now, don't you think?"

"You think I should have been content with what I had, don't you? You think the nice car and the nice house and the good prospects should have been enough." She'd stared hard at him then. "Ask yourself this, Marc. Were you happy? Were all the nice things enough to make it all worthwhile for you?"

"I guess we'll never know, will we, since you thought so little of the ten years we'd spent together that you screwed our accountant behind my back every chance you got," he'd said tersely.

That had shut her up, but he couldn't silence her words as easily now as they echoed around his head. Had he been happy? He tried to think back to the time before he'd discovered Tara's betrayal. It seemed so long ago that the memories were the mental equivalent of sepia photographs.

Shaking his head, he tossed back the last of the whiskey. The liquor burned a trail down his throat, and he stood and leaned against the railing, bringing his mind back to his present problem. Anna.

He'd pushed her away tonight. He should have told her not to come over, but he'd wanted her, needed her. Then, as soon as he'd slaked his need he'd been overcome with resentment at the power she had over him. He'd thought about her all day. He couldn't get enough of her luscious body. And he couldn't resist her.

So it was a good thing that their fling was over. Tara had just reminded him of why it was important to ensure he was the one calling the shots, and where Anna was concerned, he was out of control. It was tough admitting that to himself, but it was better to face an unpalatable truth than ignore it. His desire for her had shown no signs of burning out. And he'd begun to think about more than just her body. He'd started to care.

So. It was for the best. Refusing to believe anything else, Marc went inside to pour himself another whiskey.

It was over.

THE PHONE WAS RINGING as Anna let herself back into her apartment. For a second she allowed herself to hope it was Marc, despite her newly formed resolution. But she knew better. He could have stopped her as she left his house. Or called her on her mobile phone as she drove away. No, it wouldn't be him.

"Thank God you're home. I need to talk." It was Danny, sounding wound up and confused.

"What's wrong?"

"I'll tell you in five minutes. I'm on my way to your place."

Anna put the phone down and took a deep breath. Crossing to the bathroom, she turned the tap on and wet her hands, then ran her damp fingers over her face and into her hair. It helped, marginally.

Danny's knock sounded on her door almost immediately, and she went to let him in. He strode past her, hair askew, shirt crumpled, face screwed up in confusion.

"I just don't get it," he said by way of greeting.

She shut the door. "Something up?" she asked ironically.

"Why would someone deliberately go out of their way to turn someone on, then just leave them high and dry? What kind of sick, twisted act is that?" Danny demanded.

"Why am I getting the feeling that last night didn't go so well? What happened with Ben?" Anna asked.

"Nothing. Zilch. Nada," Danny said, exasperation oozing from every pore.

Anna frowned, remembering how keen Ben had seemed last night.

"What, after all that flirting he just up and left? Not even a kiss?" she asked, incredulous.

"Oh, no, we kissed. And it was pretty bloody amazing, too. That man has strong lips. Great lips."

Danny was shaking his head, eyes unfocused and far-off as he remembered.

"Well, that's not nothing," she said, confused.

Danny made an exasperated noise. "You don't kiss someone like that unless you're going to do something about it. And Ben was not interested in follow-through. He wants a *relationship*." Danny spat the word out like it was poisoned.

Despite the darkness of her own evening, Anna found herself stifling a smile. She had a vivid, high-definition image in her mind of the shocked, stunned expression on her brother's face as Ben turned him down. Danny was a good-looking man. And gay guys weren't generally known for their self-restraint. She'd bet a month's wages that it had been a long time since Danny had a knock-back.

"Thanks for feeling my pain," Danny said drily as he registered her amusement.

"What did you say to him?" she asked when she trusted herself to speak without laughing.

"I tried to talk him around, but he wouldn't stay. I mean, come on—like it's going to kill him to have a night of hot sex." There was a serious note of bewilderment in her brother's voice.

"Did he say anything else?"

"Yeah, on the way out the door as he left me with a gigantic boner. He said he really likes me. A lot. But that he's looking for a relationship, and he knows that I'm not a relationship type guy. He said he'd like to be friends. Friends!"

"Well, that's nice, isn't it? I mean, he likes you, clearly," Anna said cautiously, not really understanding why her brother was so worked up. Surely he wasn't just piqued at Ben's rejection?

"It's bull, that's what it is. You don't kiss someone like that if you're not going to follow through," Danny complained sourly.

"Maybe he just got carried away?" she suggested.

"Maybe he's just a little cock-tease," Danny said. "Friends! Can you believe it? I don't need more friends!"

"You don't exactly need more lovers, either, Danny," Anna observed.

Danny swore, then swiftly apologized. "Sorry. I don't know, this guy's just got me all worked up, and I don't know why. I mean, what's wrong with a bit of harmless casual sex? Especially when the chemistry is right?"

"I guess Ben just doesn't see it the way you do. Some people need emotional involvement with their sex," she said. *And some people find emotional involvement with their sex, despite their best intentions,* she added mentally.

"Then he shouldn't have kissed me," her brother said sulkily.

Anna wasn't quite sure what Danny wanted her to say. Ben had pretty much taken the decision out of his hands, after all. Unless…

"Ben seems like a nice guy," she suggested warily. "Smart, cute. Hot."

"Thanks. I hadn't noticed any of the above," Danny said snippily.

"Well, maybe you should go out with him a few times, see how things go," she suggested.

"What? Try and wear him down, you mean?" Danny asked, his expression thoughtful as he toyed with the idea.

"No, Danny! I meant maybe you could actually consider seeing someone for more than one or two bouts of casual sex. Having a relationship, dare I say the dreaded *R* word," she said, exasperated.

Danny laughed outright. "I don't think so, Anna Banana. In case you haven't noticed, I am not a relationship kind of guy."

"Still, if you've never tried it…"

"Anna, trust me—I know this about myself. I like living alone. I like my apartment the way it is. I like suiting myself. My life is great. I get all the sex I want when I want it—what would I need a boyfriend for?"

There was a kind of willful ignorance to her brother's declaration, and she wondered if she should call him on it. Was it possible that he truly didn't crave emotional intimacy with someone he loved? That he got what he needed from a combination of his close-knit friends and his flings?

It all felt painfully close to her own truths, and she had no answers to offer him.

"Maybe he's just the one that got away, then," she offered philosophically.

Danny grunted frustratedly. "People who can kiss like that should not be allowed out without a written warning," he said.

"You'll get over it. You've still got your little black book," she reminded him.

"Mmm," Danny said, and she got the distinct sense he was reluctant to replace Ben with one of his regular lovers.

He stayed for another hour, and she let out a sigh of relief as she closed the door on him. She loved him dearly, but tonight she needed to be on her own. Still, she found herself musing on Danny's problem as she climbed into bed. Was it possible that he'd never really had any kind of relationship? He was twenty-eight, after all. Surely there must have been some guy along the way, someone he'd wanted a stronger, more permanent connection with?

Not knowing these things was a hangover from their more distanced, arm's-length relationship prior to her diagnosis. She wondered how many other things she didn't know about him. Or her father and other friends, for that matter. Keeping herself all bound up nice and tight had kept her at a distance from her friends and family, too, she now saw. Something else to add to her list of things to change in her life.

Thinking about Danny and her family only kept her from thinking about herself and Marc for a few minutes. Then she registered the faint scent of his aftershave on her sheets, and she remembered all the times they'd made love on the bed, and on the rug in the living room. And that time on the kitchen counter.... It's over, she told herself sternly. And not before time, if the distinctly mopey tone of her thoughts were anything to go by.

Determined, she bounded out of bed and dragged off the sheets. Stuffing them into her laundry hamper, she pulled crisp, clean sheets from her linen cupboard and made the bed in short order. The fresh linen felt cool against her skin—and didn't smell of Marc, more importantly.

Despite her best efforts, he was still the last thing she thought about before she fell asleep, however. Disturbingly, it was the haunted look in his eyes that stayed with her as she drifted off. It was just a fling, she told herself resolutely. And it's over.

THE NEXT FEW DAYS seemed to crawl by. Anna had tried to go cold turkey on her desire for him before, but this was different. This time it wasn't just the sex she thought about. Although she thought about that a lot, too. So much so that she was beginning to wonder if maybe she had a problem.

A lot of the time, however, she just thought about things that Marc had said. Or his laugh. The glint he got in his eye when he was about to tease her. Or the smell of his aftershave and the way his hair curled over his shirt collar.

She wanted to call him. But he hadn't called her. It was over. They both knew it. Their fling had been flung, had run its course. It had gotten messy, suddenly and quickly. It was time to cut her losses and move on.

If only someone would put out a manual on how to do that, she'd be just fine.

After two tortured days, she dusted off her holiday brochures in desperation. She needed something to distract her, something to look forward to. Stabbing a finger blindly at the brochures, she went online and booked herself a week in tropical Bali, departing in just two days' time. She chose a deluxe ocean view room at the Sofitel Seminyak, and she promised herself a shopping expedition for new bathing suits and other resort wear.

All of which chewed up about an hour. Leaving her thoughts free to roam back to the topic du jour, Marc Lewis.

If anything, her obsessive thoughts only proved how right her decision was, she told herself. Despite Danny's rules, she'd let her guard slip and had started to get involved with Marc. Every time she saw a dark green Jag in traffic and her stomach lurched, every time she saw a tall, dark-haired man on the city streets and her pulse picked up, she reminded herself that she'd broken her own rules and gotten involved, and so it had had to end. She'd made the right decision. The smart decision. Absolutely.

Which was why it was so ridiculously unfair that she should find herself unable to breathe when she arrived home from work on Thursday night to find Marc's Jaguar parked out front of her apartment. She seriously considered driving on, but he'd seen her and she didn't want him to think she had any reason to avoid him.

And, deep down inside, maybe she didn't want to avoid him. What did that mean?

Her heart was pounding in her ears as she got out of the car. Not even glancing his way, she pulled off her cap and threw it onto the passenger seat, then ran her hand through her hair. Not that she cared if it looked wonky. It was just habit, that was all. She was not for even a second worried about whether her lipstick had worn off, or if any of her perfume had survived the day.

She could see him getting out of his car in her peripheral vision. She'd forgotten how tall he was. How dangerously attractive. How much she craved his touch.

Wrapping her fingers around her house keys, Anna dug her

nails into the palm of her hand. Anything to keep her focused and strong. It was over. It had become too dangerous, and it was over.

She forced a neutral expression onto her face as she approached him—inevitable, because he was standing by the entrance to the apartment block.

Her legs slowed of their own accord when she was just a few feet away, even though she knew she should just breeze right past him. That would be the sensible thing to do, right? The noninvolved thing.

They stared at each other for a loaded moment. Then he spoke. "I'm sorry. I was a shit. It won't happen again," he said, voice low and sincere.

His eyes were dark and intense as they held hers. Something inside her shifted, melted. It shouldn't be this easy. She needed to hold true to her decision. Because…because… He stepped forward, and she just stood there, unmoving, as his aftershave swamped her.

"I've missed you," he said, pressing his lips to hers in a gentle, searching kiss. He peppered kisses across her cheekbone, then nuzzled her ear. Someone made a faint, strangled noise, and she realized it was her, and that she was turning her head to give him access to her neck. Infinitely gentle and tender, he nipped and kissed his way down to her collarbone.

Just as her insides were turning to liquid, he stepped away.

"Go and get changed. I'm taking you out for dinner," he said.

She stared at him stupidly, her brain fogged with lust. "You don't want to come up?" she asked.

"Not yet," he said. The smile he flashed her was faintly tortured, and she saw he wanted her as much as she wanted him. But he wanted to prove something to her, too.

She found herself smiling. "Give me five minutes," she promised.

She didn't allow herself to think about what it was she was

bing as she raced through the shower and dragged on a dress.
here was no reason why they couldn't resume things where
ey'd left off, was there? As long as he understood that she
emanded his respect. Right? And as long as she remembered
e rules. If she was very careful, if she guarded against letting
ings get beyond what they had already, she could have this.
ouldn't she?

He took her to Café Sydney, high in the old Customs Building
bove Circular Quay. They had an intimate table on the balcony,
nd she felt cosseted and seduced by the candlelight and the dark
ood and the excellent service.

"I want to explain," Marc said as the waiter removed the
shes after their main course.

She sat up a little straighter, holding up a hand to stay his words.

"You don't have to say anything. I don't need details. That
as the deal, wasn't it? I just need to know it won't happen
gain," she said.

"I want to tell you. You deserve an explanation," Marc said
mply.

His dark eyes were warm as he scanned her face, and she felt
e rush of desire between her legs as his gaze dropped to her
easts hungrily. She would listen, because she needed him. But
didn't mean anything.

"I'd had a meeting that afternoon with Tara, my ex-wife.
he…had an affair. I thought I was over the anger. But I guess I
asn't," he said slowly.

"I understand. I should have gone home when I sensed some-
ing was up. But…I didn't," she said, unable to admit that she'd
en unable to forgo her nightly fix.

"I found the things you brought," Marc said.

Anna felt herself flush. "Just some things for the cupboard.
nce you always seem to be the one who cooks."

"Because I'm the one who can," he teased, eyes flashing.

They were silent for a moment, then he reached for her hand. His thumb smoothed circles around her palm, and she shivered at the shafts of desire that went rocketing through her body. She'd missed him so much. Her body craved him.

"I'm sorry if I hurt you, Anna," he said.

It was too much. She didn't understand this new game they were playing. Sex was one thing. Fish and chips on her run another. But she didn't need him taking her out to fancy restaurants. And she definitely didn't need him staring into her eyes like this. This was about sex. It had always been about sex.

"Let's go home," she whispered, desperate to return to the rhythm she knew.

His eyes smoked over, and he nodded once. "Yes."

His car shot through the streets, and she admired the burled walnut dash and soft leather seats.

"Not quite a Mercedes, but nice," she judged cheekily, keeping things light, doing everything she could to shift things back to what they'd once had.

He shot her a slow smile, knowing she was goading him. At her apartment, she led him up the stairs and straight into the bedroom. The feel of his body against hers was the sweetest torture in the world. She'd missed his touch so much. She was almost sobbing by the time she'd dragged his shirt from his shoulders. They fell onto the bed and came together frantically, bodies straining for closeness, their faces tight. Afterward, she felt a hazy contentment. She told herself it was the absence of need.

He traced circles across her back, his breath warm on her nape. Occasionally he pressed kisses there, and she smiled to herself. Soon they would make love again.

Her eyes drifted closed, then sprang open again as she remembered something.

Her body must have stiffened, because he put a hand on her hip.

"What's wrong?"

Anna let out a little laugh, then shook her head. "Nothing. I ust remembered—I'm going to Bali the day after tomorrow."

She could feel him tense, knew what he was thinking. They'd ust gone a week without each other. It had been unbearable. But here was nothing they could do about it. Unless...

She turned to him, impulsive, letting her desire lead her. "You ould come with me," she said.

He stared down at her for a beat, and she suddenly felt very, very foolish. She'd just stepped over the line again, hadn't she?

Then he smiled. "Give me the details. I'll get my assistant on t tomorrow," he said.

She found herself smiling back at him. He was coming to Bali vith her. They could make love whenever they felt like it. It vould be the holiday of a lifetime.

She sighed as he ducked his head and took her nipple into his nouth. Desire ripped through her, and her hips rocked instinctively.

"Yes," she moaned.

A week in Bali with Marc. Right at this minute, she couldn't hink of anything she wanted more.

10

A WEEK IN BALI with Marc. Had she been insane last night? Anna woke to the perfectly formed realization that she had just made a very big mistake. The pillow next to her still bore the indentation of Marc's head where he had lain beside her talking and laughing last night. The sheets still smelled of his aftershave. And she had just agreed to spend a whole week in his company.

They were supposed to be having a fling. It was about sex. Wasn't it? So why had she felt so relieved when she saw him on her doorstep last night? Why had she turned to goo when he'd taken her out for dinner and said sorry? And why had she lost her head and invited him on vacation with her? She could imagine Danny's face when she told him—she'd broken two of the three golden rules of having a fling without even blinking.

What was she doing? She asked herself the question over and over. Was she trying to have a relationship-by-stealth with Marc? She shook her head at the very idea. She didn't want to be tied down. But she didn't want to be without him, either. She told herself it was simply because he'd awakened her, found some new, exciting, sexy woman inside the old Anna and set her free. She was addicted to his lovemaking, that was all.

Somehow, it all rang a little false, however, and she found herself creating interesting and believable excuses for why she'd changed her mind about the invitation. But even though she reached for the phone to call Marc more than once, something stopped her every time. She was so confused, so messed up, that she gave up valuable swimsuit-shopping time to stop by Danny's office and seek counsel.

A chirpy young assistant showed her to her brother's office, and she saw immediately that he was with someone. Ben, to be specific. They were seated at the table, mock-ups for a print advertising campaign laid out in front of them. Their heads were bent toward each other, Danny's brown hair offset nicely by Ben's golden blond. Their expressions were very intent, very professional, but Anna couldn't help noticing the way Ben reached out to touch her brother's arm to draw his attention to something. And the way her brother's thigh was pressed up alongside Ben's, even though there was plenty of room for both of them to have their own space.

It was abundantly clear to her that Ben was really into her brother. The awards ceremony had been enough to deduce that. Added to Danny's report of what Ben had said to him afterward, Anna didn't think she was too far off base in guessing that Ben might even have a crush on her brother. And her brother wasn't immune to him, either, if she was any judge. Hence his agitation at being rejected. Hence the way he was sitting right now. Studying them unnoticed for a few seconds, she got the distinct impression there was a battle going on: on one side, her brother, bent on seduction; on the other, Ben, with a far more committed, long-term game plan in mind.

Interesting.

As loath as she was to break up her brother's love-in, she needed help, so she tapped lightly on his open door. Both men's heads shot up, and she was amused to see they shared the same look of chagrin at being interrupted.

"Sorry," she said. She smiled a welcome at Ben. "Hey."

"Hey, Anna. Good to see you," he said.

She smiled again and turned her attention to Danny. "I need five minutes."

He must have read the desperation in her eyes. "Vixen crisis?"

"Vixen disaster," she clarified.

Danny's eyebrows shot up and he turned to Ben. "Can we do this later? After two?"

"Sure, not a problem. See you around, Anna," Ben said as he exited.

Anna tried not to be amused by the way her brother followed Ben hungrily with his eyes.

"Careful, you're drooling," she said as he closed his office door to give them some privacy.

Danny groaned and scrubbed his face with his hands. "I swear, he's going to push me into an early grave. We played racquetball last night, and he wore these teeny-tiny little shorts. And he has these legs...I can't even talk about it," Danny said, shaking his head in disbelief.

"You guys played racquetball?" Anna asked, surprised.

"Sure. Why not? Got to do something to stay in shape." Danny shrugged, supercasual.

"I thought you didn't need any more friends?"

Danny shrugged again, but when she just raised an eyebrow he rolled his eyes and caved in. "Okay, you got me. I'm working on him. If it kills me, I am getting him into my bed."

"Hmm. Has it occurred to you that perhaps Ben might be working on you, too?"

Danny frowned. "What do you mean?"

"He likes you, Danny. I think he wants to have a relationship with you."

Danny fidgeted uncomfortably. "He wants to sleep with me. He just has to wrap it up for himself so it's acceptable. I'll help him get over that, don't worry."

Anna opened her mouth to comment further, but then it sudenly occurred to her that perhaps the same thing could be said f her brother—he was wrapping up his growing relationship ith Ben as a seduction, when in fact he was genuinely growing care for the other man. Maybe the only way for her brother to ce the idea of a potential relationship was to sneak up on it. Or, ore accurately, for the relationship to sneak up on him.

"So, what's up? What have you done now?" Danny asked, rowing himself back into his chair.

"Why do you think I've done something wrong?"

"You've got that frightened rabbit look in your eye. Come on, it it out."

"I invited him on holiday to Bali with me," she admitted meekly.

Danny whistled. "Nice. Staying the night, and making plans." e enumerated the rules she'd broken on the fingers of one hand. Next you'll be lying in each others arms naming the kids and orking out which schools they'll go to."

Anna stiffened, a panicky feeling invading her stomach. "I now I made a mistake. I just need help to undo it. Please."

He blinked. "I don't see how you can. You can't uninvite omeone. Didn't Mom teach you anything about manners?"

Anna sighed. "Why do I always have to make things so messy?"

Danny studied her for a beat. "Why'd you ask him?"

"I wasn't thinking. It just popped out of my mouth."

"You must have wanted him to come or you wouldn't have sked."

"I honestly didn't give it too much thought."

"Hmm."

"What's that supposed to mean?"

"Well… You sure you're not falling for this guy?"

Her denial was instant. "No. I'm attracted to him, that's all. nd he's a nice guy, I like being with him. But it's just about sex, ally. I mean, we have really, really, really good sex," she said, most convincing herself.

"Yeah, all right, I get the message," Danny said, frustratio
showing in his voice. "Your love life is stellar. Have a little cor
sideration for those of us in the cheap seats."

"Sorry."

"You know, it's not the end of the world if it does turn int
something more," Danny said. "Plenty of flings have turned int
relationships in the history of the world."

Anna stared at him. This was not what she wanted to hea
"Marc Lewis and I are having a fling, period. There is no rela
tionship, future or present. Neither of us want that, I assure yo
I have plans. He has an ex-wife to deal with. This is definitel
just a fling."

"Whoa, back off there, Cujo. I was just saying that sometime
you need to be flexible. These things aren't always black an
white, are they?"

"For us they are."

"Okay. It's your life." Danny shrugged.

"Thanks," she muttered. "Look, I'd better go buy a swimsuit

"Go red. You look good in red," Danny said.

"Okay. And good luck with the racquetball."

That wiped the smile off his face. Healthy to remind him sh
wasn't the only one navigating her way through a complicate
personal life at the moment.

"Thanks," Danny said drily, and she kissed him goodbye.

"I'll bring you back a knockoff Rolex or something," sh
promised.

"Only if it's bad-taste chunky and it breaks in a few days
Danny joked.

She glanced back over her shoulder as she exited, and Dann
was crossing the hallway to Ben's office. She wasn't sure wh
she was backing to win—Ben, or her brother. She had a sudde
whimsical thought—maybe they both could win. Then she shoo

er head, thinking of her own situation. Someone always ended
p losing in these situations. The trick was getting out before
elings ran too deep.

ARC SETTLED BACK into the well-padded seat and stretched out
is legs. Beside him, Anna was still trying out all the gadgets that
ame with being in the first-class cabin.

"I still can't believe you upgraded my ticket," she said as she
ddled with the seat controls.

She was like a kid with a new toy, and he felt an unexpected
irge of pleasure at seeing her enjoyment. In truth, he'd upgraded
er because he was rich enough to command the comforts of
fe—but her enjoyment was a nice bonus.

It had been hell getting out of his tight business schedule on
ich short notice, but he'd done it. He was looking forward to
aving a break. And after the past week of self-denial and absti-
ence, a week away with Anna was just what the doctor ordered.

He'd regretted his boorish behavior as soon as she was gone
at night, but it wasn't until the day after he'd insulted her and
ent her packing that he'd realized how much he craved her.
hat alone was enough to convince him he'd made the right
ecision. But he'd underestimated his desire for her. And it
asn't just her body he wanted. He missed her jokes. The way
ie had of arching an eyebrow at him, calling him on his bullshit.
nd the way she was happy to cherry-pick the things she was
ood at in life and let the rest go to hell—like being great behind
ie wheel but useless in the kitchen.

He liked her. That was what it was. She had become, dare he say
, a friend. And he'd hurt her. That had put the whole situation in a
fferent light. And when he'd found the bag of gourmet foodstuffs
ie'd brought around, he'd felt like the world's biggest arsehole.

Admitting to himself that he missed her was hard. But he did
. Once he'd surrendered to the realization, it hadn't seemed

quite so bad. There was no reason for them not to take up the relationship from where they'd left off, after all. If he could w her back, apologize, there was every chance they could continu seeing each other, no strings attached. It suited her. It certain! suited him. What did he have to lose?

He glanced across at Anna as she accepted a glass of chan pagne from the stewardess. She'd said yes. She was in his li again. She caught his eye, smiled slightly and settled back in h seat, flicking through the in-flight magazine, for all the world a though she didn't have a care in the world.

She was wound up about something, though. She was hidin it well, but he could feel the tension thrumming through h body. He considered asking what was wrong, but then he re minded himself of their deal. They were both here for fun. If sh wanted to talk about anything, she'd bring it up. She was straight-up kind of woman, and neither of them wanted to burde the other with unnecessary baggage.

The plane began to taxi, and she put the magazine down.

"I'm so sleepy now," she confessed. " I shouldn't have ha all that champagne in the lounge."

"Then sleep," he advised.

"But then I'll miss out on all this luxury," she said, eyein the cabin.

Her bottom lip pouted sexily, and he eyed it for a long bea How long was this flight again? Six hours? He forced his eyes— and his mind—away.

"I'll wake you if anything really decadent happens," he prom ised.

She wasn't entirely convinced, and she made a valiant effort stay awake, but within an hour her head had drifted onto his should and she was breathing steadily. He looked down at her, admirin the way her eyelashes fanned darkly against her creamy ski

Smiling faintly, he spread her blanket over her knees, just in case she got cold. Then he stayed very still, so he wouldn't wake her.

Even she had had her fill of first-class travel by the time they landed in Bali's Denpasar airport.

It was dusk, and the air was dense with humidity as they exited the airport terminal. Marc looked around with interest as their driver led them through row upon row of parked cars until he at last found his limo. Even after just a few minutes of humidity, the air-conditioning inside came as a welcome relief.

"Oh, dear," Anna said, pulling her T-shirt away from her skin. "I hope it's not going to be too hot for me."

Marc tore his eyes away from the dark shadow of cleavage that her plucking movements revealed. If he had his way, this would be the hottest week of Anna's life.

Their driver raced out of the airport, cutting and weaving through the city streets on his way to the tourist areas of Kuta, Legian and Seminyak. The streets were thick with other taxis ferrying recent arrivals like themselves, and in and amongst them all was a constantly changing tide of motorcyclists.

Kuta was a frenetic hub of activity, the streets filled with people walking between clubs and restaurants, but as they moved into the quieter, less developed area of Seminyak there was more green, less commerce, and suddenly they were barreling down a seemingly deserted rural road, nothing but the occasional stone-tumbled house or rice paddy on either side of them.

He heard Anna gasp with delight as she caught sight of their hotel, and he craned his neck to see as the taxi swept up the front drive. It was certainly impressive, the huge reception area shaped like an open-sided pagoda. Sandstone pillars, screens of carved wood and seemingly acres and acres of natural stone floor stretched across the foyer. An exotically dressed porter greeted them and took their bags, and they were escorted politely to a guest relations officer to check in.

"I have a little confession to make," Marc said as the guest officer fished out their reservation.

Anna frowned, then a rueful expression came into her eyes as she saw the writing across the top of their forms.

"You booked us a private villa?" she said.

"I should have asked, I know, but my secretary was doing everything on the hop..."

Anna shook her head, waving a hand to stop his lame explanation. "Just be honest—you're used to being spoiled. Nothing but the best for Mr. Lewis."

It was true, he realized. "You're right. I am spoiled."

"And a bit arrogant."

He ducked his head in acknowledgment. "True."

That teased a smile out of her. "And too charming for your own good," she admonished.

"Well, as for that, it's not for me to judge whether I'm charming or not...." he said with mock modesty.

She shot him a saucy look, and suddenly he was aware of how long it had been since he'd had her. She seemed to read his need, because she turned back and signed the register with alacrity.

A porter appeared to see them to their room, and they passed down broad stone stairs out into the night, following a cobblestoned pathway lit with miniature pagoda lanterns around to the private villa area of the resort. The porter led them in through the gate which secured the walled garden of their villa and into a beautifully landscaped courtyard. They crossed over a small stone bridge to get to the entrance of the villa itself, and then they entered a roomy, airy, very modern yet distinctly Balinese living area.

"I leave you," the porter said politely. "Bedroom is upstairs. Please explore."

Bowing, he shook his head at the tip Marc offered, and slipped out of the villa. Anna dumped her purse and took off to explore. Smiling at her enthusiasm, Marc crossed to the wall of windows at the back of the villa. There was another exquisite courtyard outside, complete with a private spa, a lap pool, an open sided shade pagoda with curtains for lazing away the days and a couple of luxurious-looking sun lounges. He rolled his shoulders, trying to remember how long it had been since he'd had a holiday. A long time. In fact, he couldn't remember the last time he and Tara had taken time out to just be with each other.

Unbidden and definitely unwanted, Tara's words came back to haunt him. *You never asked why, Marc.*

"Marc! Get up here and check out the bathroom. I think I've died and gone to heaven!" Anna was standing at the top of the stairs, already half stripped, her eyes wide and excited.

"I don't give a stuff about the bathroom and you know it," he growled, heading up the stairs after her. She just smirked at his intent expression and disappeared. He followed the sound of running water to find her stark naked, staring greedily at a huge spa bath, complete with a row of luxury bath products lined up beside it.

"Last one in gets the tap end," she said, but he grabbed her before she could step in, hands hungry on her breasts and hips and butt as he pulled her close.

They kissed deeply, languorously, both tired from the plane trip, but needing each other nonetheless. He broke away briefly to shed his clothes, and then they slid into the water together. Ten minutes and lots of soapy, slippery hand work later, they slithered out again and fell onto a pile of towels, unwilling to be apart for even the length of time it would take to find the bedroom. Anna arched up toward him as he entered her, as always so sweet and tight, and he rubbed his five-o'clock shadow across her sensitive nipples.

"Oh, yes," she moaned, and he gave himself up to the task of satisfying his need for her.

Afterward, they ordered room service and slid into fluffy

hotel dressing gowns so they wouldn't scare the waiter when he arrived. They snacked on satay skewers and the ubiquitous room-service club sandwich, swapping bites and laughing a little guiltily over the mess they'd made of the bathroom.

Then jet lag and plain old exhaustion caught up with them, and they were standing side by side in the bathroom preparing to brush their teeth.

"Of course you've got an electric toothbrush," Anna scoffed as she squeezed toothpaste onto her more conventional brush.

"Recommended by dentists everywhere, as a matter of fact," Marc said archly.

"Hmm. You'd buy an electric ear cleaner if they invented it, wouldn't you?"

"Got one," he said, deadpan. She eyed him for a moment, then obviously decided he was having her on.

"I bet you're a good poker player," she said, speech muffled as she began brushing her teeth.

He just raised an eyebrow mysteriously, switching his brush on and concentrating for a moment on the mundane act of dental hygiene. His mind wandered, as it often did when he was brushing his teeth, and he got something of a shock when he came back to the here and now and caught sight of their reflections in the mirror. He and Anna, both of them with floppy, towel-dried hair after their antics in the spa, clad in twin bulky white dressing gowns, their mouths foaming with toothpaste.

It was a ridiculously domestic scene. A comfortable, familiar scene. And disturbingly intimate as a result. He rinsed and spat out his toothpaste, cleaned off his brush and smiled vaguely at Anna before exiting into the bedroom.

He stared hard at the carpet. He'd committed to spending a whole week with a woman he was supposed to be just sleeping with until he got her out of his system. He pictured her face in the mirror again, her skin shiny clean, her cheeks bulging like a chipmunk's as she brushed her teeth, her eyes unfocused as she thought her own bathroom thoughts.

She'd looked adorable. Utterly adorable. And he wasn't in the market to adore anyone. Was he?

He exhaled quickly, fighting off a surge of panic. He didn't want to feel this way about Anna. He didn't want to feel this way about anyone. Hell. Why had he agreed to come on this holiday? What had he been thinking?

Anna walked into the bedroom, shedding her robe as she walked. Her breasts jiggled invitingly, their rosy tips drawing his eye. Okay, that was one good reason for coming to Bali. But it still left a hell of a lot of hours in between for them to fill up.

"I am *soooo* tired," Anna sighed as she threw herself onto the giant bed. Yawning hugely, she pulled the sheet up over herself, then reached across and switched off the light on her side of the bed. She glanced across at him where he stood frozen halfway between the bed and the doorway, just barely containing his panic.

"You coming to bed?" she asked, a frown pleating her brow.

"Sure," he said. He shed his own gown, tossing it on the chair at the end of the bed. Then he slid between the sheets, reaching quickly for the light on his side of the bed.

And for the first time ever, he found himself in bed with Anna Jackson with sex the farthest thing from his mind. Hell. Hell. Hell. What had he done?

"Good night," she sighed, and he heard the rustle of linen as she made herself more comfortable.

By contrast, he lay there like a log, stiff with tension, listening to the sound of her increasingly steady breathing.

What was he doing here? How on earth had he allowed himself to slide into what was beginning to feel dangerously like a relationship?

Brain whirring, he assessed his options. Today was Saturday. He could wait till Monday, then manufacture a work emergency.

That way he could indulge himself in a bit of R & R, and then bail after two, maybe three days. He felt the tension ease from his body as he considered this plan from all sides and found a lot to like about it. After all, Anna had been going to come on this holiday alone, anyway. He'd just be giving her the best of both worlds.

Instantly the tension was back as he imagined Anna on holiday alone. What if he left to go back to Australia and some cruising Lothario decided to try his hand? The thought of someone else in Anna's bed made him grind his teeth. Then he reminded himself of the discussion they'd had in the hotel. She'd said she was a one-man woman. And he believed her. He trusted her.

Again, the tension eased from his body and it was his last thought as he drifted off to sleep: he trusted Anna.

SHE WOKE TO FIND a hard male body curled against her back, one hand flung around her waist. The body felt warm and firm and hairy in all the right places and she snuggled into it, wiggling her bottom to encourage a more perfect spooning action. Instantly she felt the nudge of Marc's erection against the curve of her butt. She wiggled some more, and the erection hardened further. She bit her lip, remembering what he'd done with his soapy hands in the bath last night. She could feel herself slickening with desire, and she gave a little sigh of satisfaction as Marc nudged her leg forward so he could slide himself inside her from behind. His hand was firm on her hip as he rocked his pelvis, his erection hot and hard and slippery as it moved in and out, in and out.

"Marc," she panted as he shifted gear, his movements becoming more urgent as desire tightened inside them both. She moved with him, rolling onto her knees so that he could take her more readily, each thrust perfection. His hand slid over her hip between her legs, and she felt the rasp of his hairy chest on her back as he reached for her clitoris. It was swollen with need, and he thumbed it skillfully. Within seconds she was crying out, arching back, welcoming his final deep thrusts as he came, also.

They collapsed onto the sheets, both out of breath. She stared at the ceiling, basking in her recent release and a healthy dose of relief. She'd been worried about the whole staying-the-night thing. Silly, really. Except it had been one of the things that Danny had told her to avoid, and she'd religiously stuck to it. Until now. But this was good. Hell, she'd just woken up to instant, sensational sex. What was there to worry about?

"Well. Good morning," Marc said drily after a few moments of comfortable silence.

Anna couldn't help it; she got the giggles. "What's so funny?" he demanded, but she could only shake her head and laugh some more. It was all going to be okay. They were going to have a great holiday.

He shook his head, then calmly arranged her so that she was facing away from him again and he could curve into her back, just as they'd been when they woke up. His arm slid around her waist, and he nuzzled the nape of her neck.

"Go back to sleep so I can wake you up again," he said, his voice already drowsy.

Anna smiled into her pillow, loving the feel of his body pressed so closely to hers. It wasn't a sex thing, she realized. It was more than sex.

Her eyes sprang open instantly. More than sex. *More than sex?* There was no *more than sex* with Marc. Sex was it. It was the beginning, the middle and the end. There was nothing else. That was the deal they'd made. More importantly, that was what they both wanted. He'd only hinted at his reasons for wanting to remain unattached, but she knew it had something to do with his marriage. The man was barely separated—of course he wasn't interested in a relationship. And she didn't want one. She needed to be free. It was very important to her that she not get involved.

She'd just been looking for passion, that was all. She didn't wan
commitment. Or…love.

Did she?

She waited until he was fast asleep again before easing away
from him. She used the downstairs shower so she wouldn't wake
him, and pulled on her new red one-piece swimsuit. It was only
6:00 a.m., but there was no way she could sleep, body clock aside
Lying in Marc's arms was far too disturbing to her equilibrium.

She quietly explored the downstairs layout, discovering a
second bedroom, a study complete with computer setup, and a
fully equipped kitchen as well as the downstairs bathroom. She
couldn't imagine either of them mustering the energy to cook
while they were here, and she figured that was just as well. The
more time they spent in crowds doing touristy things the better.
The whole villa was spacious, with high ceilings, clean lines and
lots of simple yet classically designed Balinese timber furniture.
Stone and wood, she was fast discovering, seemed to be the hall-
marks of Balinese interior design.

Villa explored, she tied a sarong around her waist and stepped
out into the early Bali morning. The first thing she noticed was
the heavy cloak of humidity settling on her, and then she smelled
the incense burning on the morning air. Exotic and beautiful, she
thought as she let herself out the gate. She almost stumbled
over something on the doorstep, and she frowned down at what
looked like a small box made out of woven banana leaf fronds,
filled with flowers, rice and even a broken cracker and some
sticks of incense. Her expression cleared as she remembered her
travel agent explaining that the island's population was mainly
Hindu and that there were devout women who did nothing all
day except prepare and distribute offerings to the gods. This
must be what she'd been talking about. As Anna wandered
around the hotel's lushly landscaped grounds she saw dozens of
the offerings—in stairwells, doorways, where paths met one

another. She also saw dozens and dozens of lizards, tiny green and yellow geckos no longer than her smallest finger, their eyes bright black pinpricks that stared at her cautiously when she stopped to examine them. She'd never been a big fan of reptiles, but she decided that she liked these—as long as they kept their distance.

The panicky feeling in her chest had subsided by the time she returned to their villa. It was impossible to stay tense when the very air itself seemed to embrace her with fragrant warmth. The delicate frangipani blossoms, the incense, the swish of palm trees moving in the breeze—it was all hypnotic and incredibly restful, and she'd found a new lightheartedness as she let herself in through the gate. She was in Bali with Marc, for good or bad. They had a week together. She refused to spend the time second-guessing herself and worrying. She knew what she wanted, and what he wanted. It was silly to even worry about anything else. If there was a problem, if things were shifting, they could just deal with it when they returned to Sydney. How much could things change in just a few days, anyway? There was still plenty of time to pull out before either of them got too involved.

He was coming downstairs in his board shorts, chest bare, as she entered. He raised his eyebrows at her. "Been for a walk?"

"Mmm. It's so beautiful. The hotel grounds are beyond description. They even have lotus blossoms on a lake."

"Great. I'm starving," he said, grabbing the room service menu with single-minded intentness.

"There's a pavilion down near the pool with a breakfast buffet. I think it's included in our room charge," she said.

He looked up from the menu, eyes shining. "Cooked breakfast as well as continental?" he asked hopefully.

Bemused, she shrugged. "I guess. I didn't ask…."

"Let's go." Stopping to grab a T-shirt, Marc pushed her ahead of him out of the villa.

"There's no rush. I'm sure there's plenty for everyone," she assured him as he hustled her through the gate.

"I love hotel breakfasts. Especially the buffet kind. So many choices. It's great."

He set a clipping pace, his long stride eating up the cobblestones as she gave directions to the pool.

"Oh, yes," he said reverentially as they surveyed the buffet. Cold cereals, hot cereals, fruit, cheeses, deli items, a selection of traditional Indonesian foods including nasi goreng and a huge range of breads, muffins and pastries was arrayed before them.

"And you can order your cooked breakfast from the menu on your table," the helpful waiter supplied in perfect English.

Anna stifled a smile as Marc rubbed his hands together. "Okay, where to begin?"

He went back a total of four times, as well as putting away an enormous cooked breakfast of hash browns, bacon and poached eggs on toast. Anna watched with amazement. It was just like the old joke where an impossible number of clowns pile out of a Mini at the circus.

Finally he sat back and patted his belly. "No more room," he announced with pride.

"No kidding," she said, eyeing his midsection with trepidation.

"I love hotel breakfasts," he said again, flashing her a winning smile.

"No kidding," she said, but she found himself grinning back at him. This was a side to him she hadn't seen before. Indulgent. Fun. Endearing. Who would have thought that a multimillionaire like Marc Lewis would be obsessed with hotel breakfast buffets?

When crunch time came, he found it hard to leave the buffet, however. Highly amused, she pointed out that he could launch an assault on it again tomorrow morning and at last he conceded that they could go laze by the pool.

Surrounded by sandstone, it was crystal-clear and perfect,

with a number of frangipani trees arching their branches over the aquamarine water. Padded lounges were scattered around the edges, and three open-sided shade pagodas, larger versions of the one in their villa, marched down one side of the pool.

"*Ohhh,* the water is perfect," Anna said as she stepped into the shallow end.

Marc was busy eyeing up the shade pagodas. "I think we want to get ourselves one of those," he said, appreciation in his tone.

She wrinkled her nose at him. "Nothing but the best," she teased.

He glanced down at her, amused. "I am an arrogant bastard, aren't I?"

She couldn't help herself. She leaned close and snaked a hand affectionately around his waist, then nuzzled his neck. "In a very nice way," she agreed.

His laugh rumbled through his chest, and she watched him saunter across to check out the pagoda, admiring the animal grace of his walk. It didn't escape her notice that the other women around the pool also followed him with their eyes. He was that kind of man.

She had sunk into the water up to her chin by the time he came back looking very pleased with himself.

"Done," he said smugly, and she splashed him playfully. She watched as the pool boy he indicated crossed to place two large towels in the pagoda, pulling the curtains shut to indicate it was taken.

"Wow. Today Bali, tomorrow the world," she mocked lightly.

He grinned, then splashed her mightily as he dove in beside her. They swam lazily for twenty minutes, then made their way, dripping, to the pagoda to grab their towels. Anna finished drying herself off first and crawled onto the pagoda's cushioned base, spreading her towel out. Marc followed suit, fussily arranging his so that there were no wrinkles to annoy him. She hid a smile, amazed at all the little idiosyncratic things a person could find out about someone while on holiday. As Marc prepared to roll over onto his back, she noticed he'd collected a dried leaf on his foot.

Wanting to be helpful, she leaned across to brush it off, then paused, frowning.

"Oh," she said, frowning.

He froze. "What?"

"Well, I thought you had a leaf stuck to your foot. But it's a frog," she explained, fascinated by the dried flat, leaflike frog carcass stuck to his instep.

"What?" he asked, face paling.

"Yep, it's a frog. A dead, dried-up old frog," she confirmed.

He moved like lightning, rolling to the edge of the pagoda, dangling his leg off it and shaking it furiously. "Has it gone? Has it gone?" he demanded, hamming it up shamelessly.

Very much amused, she moved forward to check. "Nope."

He swiveled on his back, waving his foot in her face now. "Get it off!" he insisted, his eyes wide with mock panic.

Laughing now, Anna flicked the dried frog with her fingernail and it fluttered to the ground. Marc collapsed back onto the mattress, one hand pressed to his forehead dramatically.

He was so funny. Whimsical even. And she would never have known any of this if they hadn't come to Bali together. And right at that moment, right then, as he was pretending to be scared of a tiny, dried-up frog, his handsome face pulled into an expression of boyish fear, she fell down the last stretch of the slippery slope from lust to liking to love. For good or ill, she loved Marc Lewis.

11

SOMETHING HAD CHANGED. He wasn't sure when it happened. But it had definitely happened. After that first panicky night, he'd been determined to be cautious, careful. He'd even gone so far as to inquire about an earlier flight back, using the Internet connection in the villa's study. But he hadn't gone.

He could put some of his decision down to the fact that Bali was beautiful, a true tropical paradise. Its people were welcoming and warm, and even if the streets were filled with opportunistic hawkers, it was all part of the experience. The hotel was perfect, and their villa an oasis.

But most of his reasons for staying were down to Anna. He'd nailed it that first night as he watched her brush her teeth. She was adorable. And he was beginning to suspect that he wanted to adore her.

It should have sent him into a freaked-out, get-me-the-hell-out-of-here spin. But it didn't. It kept him exactly where he was—by her side, enjoying his first holiday in years.

Their first day they spent by the pool, lounging and swimming and reading trashy novels they borrowed from the hotel's "library"—a collection of books other guests had left behind. They had lunch there, sitting cross-legged in their pagoda, then they dozed, the curtains drawn around them for privacy. He'd wanted her then, but even drugged with lust he'd been able to see that making love within five meters of the hotel swimming pool was probably pushing it. They'd gone back to the villa and lazed the afternoon away pleasuring each other.

On Monday, they ventured out into the busy streets and encountered their first hawkers. He was sure he would remember the look of consternation on Anna's face forever as she tried to find a polite way of easing away from the persistent street vendors. She'd been anguished, torn between giving them short shrift and understanding that this was the way they made their living.

It was impossible not to feel incredibly privileged as they moved along the popular Rasa Legian shopping district. Australian dollars bought an enormous amount in Bali, and Anna was constantly shaking her head over the disparity.

By the time they returned to their hotel, they'd been footsore, dusty and starving. Anna was the one who spotted the vouchers that had been delivered while they were out. As honored guests, they were being gifted with two complimentary Balinese massages. She looked up from the vouchers with the light of anticipation in her eyes.

"Let's go this afternoon," she said.

They navigated their way to the hotel's spa complex, and sipped curiously at cups of incredibly sweet ginger tea while they waited for their masseurs. A very demure young Balinese girl led them to a changing room, and handed them two plastic packs and a dressing gown each before leaving them in privacy.

"What are these?" Anna asked, examining the plastic pack. Her expression cleared as she opened it to reveal a pair of shapeless, sexless disposable underpants.

"No! They do not expect us to wear these!" she asked, a wide, incredulous grin on her face.

"I think they do," he said, indicating a sign on the wall explaining that they were for reasons of hygiene and safety.

Giggling uncontrollably, Anna pulled hers on. "Oh yes, these are going to be all the rage on Bondi beach next year," she said, striking a mock sexy pose.

She was in absolute fits by the time he'd puiied his on, and in the end he had to tie the robe of her gown for her and push her ahead of him out of the changing room.

"It's just that you're so…and they're so…" she tried to explain as she wiped the tears from her eyes.

"I get it," he assured her, very much amused.

They were led into a large, attractive room with twin massage beds, and welcomed by their masseurs—in Balinese tradition, he had a male masseur, Anna a female. He drowsed his way through the first half hour of the treatment, enjoying the slick, practiced movements of his masseur's hands. Halfway through, he reluctantly roused himself enough to roll onto his back. Any and all relaxation evaporated, however, as he saw that Anna was doing the same thing—and her masseuse was not covering her breasts with a modesty towel. He frowned, not liking the idea that his masseur was able to look at Anna any time he liked. Okay, the guy probably saw hundreds of tourists a year. But this was Anna. He didn't want another man looking at her, even if it was incidentally.

She was very quiet afterward as they thanked their masseurs and began making their way back to the villa, their skin fragrant and still slippery with scented oils.

"Good massage?" he asked, wondering at her silence.

"I think so. Yes, I guess," she said thoughtfully.

"What kind of answer is that?"

"Well…maybe you didn't notice, since your eyes were mostly closed," she said. "But when she got me to roll onto my back, she didn't cover me up."

"Oh, I noticed," he growled. She shot him an amused look.

"At first I was a bit self-conscious, but it's like being at the doctor's, right?"

"No, but carry on," he said. She punched him playfully on the arm.

"Stop it. Anyway, the long and the short of it is that she felt me up," she finished in a rush.

"What?" he asked, stopping in his tracks.

Anna nodded. "Yeah. That's what I thought. She was massaging my stomach, and her hands were kind of moving up, and I was thinking, no, surely not. But then she just did it—she massaged my breasts."

Her eyes were sparkling with amusement at herself. "Goodbye relaxation, let me tell you!" she joked. "I swear I almost ran from the room!"

They pushed through the gate and into the villa, Marc trying to get the image of Anna having her breasts massaged out of his head. He couldn't work out if he found it erotic or disturbing.

"I need a shower," she announced as she slicked a hand up her arm. "I'm as slippery as a greased pig."

"But a lot sexier," he murmured, all rational thought dissolving as he eyed her glistening breasts and torso as she stripped off her clothes. Moving close, he slid a hand across her skin.

"Mmm," she said, eyes closing seductively. Within minutes they were naked, sliding erotically against one another, their skins smooth and oiled, their movements languorous. She smelled of cloves and vanilla and frangipani, and they made love slowly, infinitely attentive to one another's needs, mouths and hands and fingers probing, teasing, touching. They came together, his face pressed into her neck, inhaling the smell that was uniquely Anna.

Now it was Wednesday. They were halfway through their holiday, and he couldn't think of a time when he'd enjoyed himself more. He'd booked a table at a popular local restaurant for dinner. Gado Gado was just two minutes walk up the beach, and it came highly recommended. As he ran gel through his hair carelessly, he realized he was looking forward to spoiling Anna some more. She was so open to everything, so ready to engage. He found her…captivating.

She entered the bathroom behind him, and his eyes darkened as he saw what she was wearing. It was a Bali purchase, a thin halter-neck dress in white broderie anglaise, its bodice fitted, with a flared skirt that ended midcalf. Her skin was an inviting latte color after three days of careful exposure, the contrast very sexy with her blond hair and toffee brown eyes. She looked beautiful. And very desirable.

"Maybe we should stay in for dinner," he said as he turned to face her.

She smiled, stepping close to put her arms around his waist.

"What did you have in mind? Room service?" she asked.

"And you for dessert." Her pupils dilated, and he heard the breath hitch in her throat. She was so damned responsive. No wonder he couldn't get enough of her.

No wonder he was thinking about her all the time.

But it didn't explain why he was pushing her away now, patting her on the backside when she turned inquiring eyes to him. He wanted to take her out, show her a nice time. Pamper her. Show her he cared.

Which, he was beginning to realize, he did. More and more so every day.

It scared the hell out of him. But not enough to make him run. He'd never been a stupid man, and he knew a good thing when he was on to it. Perhaps he'd always known with Anna, from that first moment when their eyes locked in the rearview mirror of her car. She was special.

He just had to decide what he was going to do about it, and how far he was prepared to go to keep her in his life. At the moment he had nothing to offer her. Yes, he was getting a divorce, but he had no illusions about himself—Tara had screwed with his head. He needed to sort himself out before he could tell Anna any of the things that were on his mind.

Patience, he told himself. *She's not going anywhere. Get it right this time.*

MARC'S HAND WAS WARM and firm in hers as he led her across the sand to a fairy-light-adorned restaurant that was next to the hotel. They were both wearing flip-flops, and they stopped to shake off the sand before entering the high-ceiling, thatch-roofed restaurant. Like so many Balinese buildings, one side was completely open to the elements, extending the floor plan of the restaurant out onto a deck that fronted directly onto the beach.

It was all so beautiful, so perfect. And Marc was so funny, so handsome, so sexy. And so very, very lovable, as it turned out. She'd learned so much about him over the past few days. As he relaxed, winding down from his demanding lifestyle, she saw more of his humor, his gentleness, his wittiness. She felt her heart squeeze in her chest as he held her seat out for her, his dark eyes gentle on her. He'd secured them a table at the very front of the deck, offering them an unobstructed view of the inky dark rolling surf. Around them, people talked and laughed quietly, but tonight it felt as though the two of them were in a private bubble, a world of their own.

She'd been fighting her growing feelings for days now, trying so hard to convince herself that she was simply infatuated with Marc, obsessed with his body, even. But she was in love, and tonight she was sick of fighting it. *Just have tonight,* she told herself. *Tomorrow you can regret it.*

The menu was very European. Marc had salmon; she had chicken. The heat made tackling desserts impossible, but they lingered anyway, finishing their bottle of wine.

"Have I told you how beautiful you look tonight?" Marc asked after a comfortable pause in the conversation.

She smiled. "Yes. But feel free to say it again."

"You look very sexy with a tan, Anna." His glance ran over her, and she marveled at the fact that he could turn her on with just a look.

"You don't look so bad yourself, Mr. Lewis," she said, studying him appreciatively. His olive skin had darkened to a decadent mahogany, making him look exotic and dangerous and infinitely attractive.

"Thanks for inviting me to share your holiday. I've had a great time," Marc said, raising his glass and holding her eye.

"Ditto. I'm not quite sure what I would have done on my own," she said.

"I think there are a few guys by the pool who would have helped you out," he said drily.

She cocked her head. "Jealous?" she teased.

"You know I am."

There was a very serious, very intent look in his eye. She should look away, she knew. But she'd given herself permission to have tonight, hadn't she?

But he surprised her with his next comment.

"You know, I haven't been on a holiday for years," he said, relaxing back into his chair.

"Really. I would have thought that you and your wife…?" Anna asked before she could stop herself.

He looked out at the ocean. "No. Tara and I put a lot of things off to build up the business," he said. "It seemed important at the time."

It was the first time he'd ever said her name. Tara. Anna was both angry with the woman on Marc's behalf, and grateful to her for being stupid enough to throw him away. Otherwise, where would Anna be?

"I grew up pretty poor," Marc explained, obviously seeing the questions in her eyes. "My father…well, he wasn't around a lot.

He fancied himself as a bit of a musician, but mostly he drifted with the harvest seasons, picking his way around Australia."

"So that's why your mom was always working?" she asked, remembering what he'd said that first night together at his place.

"Yeah. He hardly ever sent money. He was a shit, actually. There were other women. And he gambled…." Marc shrugged, his face hardening at the memory.

"I bet your mom is proud of you," she said, wanting to ease the haunted look from his eyes.

"Yeah. She's got a place up on the coast. She likes the warmer weather," he said, smiling fondly. "She hasn't had to work for a while now." He said it with a quiet pride—not bragging, just owning his achievements.

"My mother died when I was thirteen," Anna said. She almost put her hands up to cover her mouth—she hadn't intended to say that, not at all.

Marc's hand found hers. "That must have been hard, Anna. I'm sorry."

She shrugged a shoulder, but she realized she wanted to tell him. *So stupid,* a little voice said inside her. *So dangerous.* But she ignored it.

"She had breast cancer. She lost both her breasts, but it was too late. She died at home, and we all looked after her. But mostly it was me—Danny was too small, and Dad was just so cut up…." She realized she'd misted up.

"You must have been a tough little kid," he said.

"Not as tough as you, I bet," she said, desperate to lighten the mood.

He reached out and rubbed a thumb across her cheek. "Let's go back to the room," he said.

She nodded, and he broke contact to signal for the bill.

They walked through the soft, dry sand down toward the water, and Marc rolled his trouser legs up so they could wade their way back to the stretch of beach in front of the hotel. Not talking, they slowly made their way back onto the hotel grounds, back to their villa.

She let Marc lead her outside to their private pool courtyard, and she let him undress her, his touch gentle, almost reverent as he slid her dress from her body. She watched as he undressed, and then he drew her into the water. It was pleasantly tepid against her naked skin, and she felt the silky slide of it as it embraced all of her.

He pulled her close, buoyancy sending her bobbing against him, and she wrapped her legs around his waist. They kissed. Deep, soul-searing kisses.

"You're so beautiful," he said as he looked down into her face.

She felt beautiful, too. Beautiful and desirable and so in love that it hurt.

He moved toward the shallow steps behind them until her back was resting against the smooth tiled surface. He ducked his head and suckled on her nipples, and she threw her head back and felt the sharp tug of desire between her thighs. She could feel his hardness pressing against her belly already, and she shifted minutely so that he could slide into her.

He moved inside her, the sensation exquisite. She watched his face intently, loving the heat and passion in it. Then he stilled, a frown forming.

"We shouldn't," he said, and she knew he was talking about protection.

"It's okay," she assured him as he began to withdraw. "I know my cycle. We're safe."

He hesitated still, and she tightened herself around him. He groaned, and then he was moving inside her again, long, slow, voluptuous slides, the water lapping at their bodies, their soft sighs echoing across the water. His hands came up to cup her face, and his gaze was dark and intent as he stared down into her eyes.

"Anna," he said, and she knew it was impossible for him not to see that she loved him. But she wouldn't ruin it, she couldn't. So she stared back, her heart in her eyes, trying to deny the intensity and sincerity in his gaze even as she reveled in it. They came together, gazes locked, truths revealed.

As soon as her passion ebbed, Anna felt the reality of her situation creeping in. Keeping her face carefully neutral, she feigned a shiver and slid from his embrace.

"I'll get you a towel," he said, and she admired the grace of his body as he rose from the water. He was magnificent, with long, clean, muscular limbs, a flat belly and broad, strong shoulders. He strode into the house, careless of leaving a wet trail, the arrogance of a successful man in every step. He came back in his robe, with hers in hand, and she stepped from the water into its enveloping embrace. She smiled faintly at him, afraid that if she didn't find some way to protect herself, she'd be crying all over him in about thirty seconds flat.

"I'm going to go up to bed," she muttered as he tied the cord on her gown snugly.

"Sure," he said, and she realized with dismay that he was going to come with her.

Still wrapped in the gown, she slid into bed, and she felt the mattress dip as he got in beside her. Instinctively she curled away from him, even though she knew it would invite his embrace. A form of self-torture, she thought as his body pressed against hers, his arm coming possessively around her and his mouth finding the nape of her neck.

She squeezed her eyes shut tight, rocked with emotion. Sliding her hand over his arm, she held him tightly, fiercely. She loved him. And this was the most she could ever have of him. A tear slid down her nose and onto her pillow, and she bit her lip. She would not, could not expose herself to him like this.

After a brief battle with herself, she regained control of her motions. She could hear his breathing deepening behind her, and she smiled stupidly to herself. He could sleep through anything. God, she loved him.

Which was going to make it very hard to do what she had to do.

HE WASN'T IN THE BED when she woke the next morning, and she sighed with relief. She needed some time to get her head together, come up with a game plan.

Remembering the intent, gentle look in his eyes last night, Anna dug her nails into her palms. Because she couldn't deny it any longer, even just to herself. He had made love to her last night. It hadn't been just sex, the simple slaking of a need. It had been two people worshipping each other with their bodies. Beautiful and perfect.

They cared for one another. If Marc didn't love her, he was well on the way.

And she had nothing to offer him.

That was the horrible, honest truth she'd been hiding from herself. It was why she'd been so intent on not getting involved, why the very thought of falling in love, of committing to a relationship made bile burn in her throat.

Of its own accord, her hand found the discreet scar beneath her breast.

She was thirty-two years old. Her mother had died at thirty-five.

She felt as though she was staring into the deepest, darkest abyss in all the world as she faced her oldest fear head-on. She didn't want to die. Not the way her mother had. But, more than anything, she didn't want to hurt Marc. There was no guarantee that her cancer wouldn't come back. It was the knowledge that had been driving her for months now, pushing her to change her job, to find the fun in life, to live more, to experience things. She was living on borrowed time, and she had to make the most of it.

She could hear Marc moving around downstairs. She wanted

nothing more than to run down into his arms and pour out all her hopes and fears. To ask him to reassure her, to promise that things would be okay. But he couldn't promise her that, and she had no right to even ask him to. This was her battle. The kindest most generous thing she could do was extract him from the equation before their feelings deepened further.

She could still remember the heart-wrenching sound of her father sobbing at her mother's funeral. A part of him had died when she did, and Anna would never knowingly put another human being through that pain and loss. Not when she loved him and she could prevent it by being cruel to be kind now.

Resolve hardened her jaw. She threw back the covers and strode into the bathroom. Ten minutes later, she'd made a phone call and was dressed in swimsuit and shorts and padding down the stairs.

He was lying by the pool, a newspaper crumpled on his chest. A half-eaten croissant was testament to the fact that he'd already raided the temptations of the breakfast buffet. He opened an eye as she approached.

He looked absolutely gorgeous, relaxed and fit and sexy. Her stomach clenched, and she forced a smile.

"Right, what are your plans for the day?" she asked him brightly.

He frowned. "Same as usual. Did you have something else in mind?"

She shrugged, digging her hands into the back pockets of her shorts so she wouldn't grab him and hang on for dear life.

"I'm going parasailing," she said. "Then there's a guy who teaches introductory scuba and takes you out to a nearby coral reef."

"Right. That all sounds very…energetic," he said.

"And tomorrow I was thinking of maybe doing a bungee jump. There's a brochure for a tour operator who takes you up north, and you jump off a bridge."

"Bungee. Right." Marc folded the newspaper and swung his

egs over the side of the sun lounge so that he was sitting upright. "What's going on, Anna?"

"Nothing. I'd just planned on doing this stuff, and time's getting away from us.... So..."

He eyed her steadily.

"Is this because of last night?" he asked directly.

She kept her tone light, her eyes veiled. "Of course not. Last night was amazing. You can do me in the pool any time," she said breezily. "I just want to have some fun, that's all."

His eyes narrowed, and he was silent for a long moment. Finally he stood. "Fine, let's go then."

She stared at him in dismay. "I thought you'd probably just want to hang here, relax," she said.

"You thought wrong," he said.

She could see he wouldn't be moved. And even while it wasn't quite what she'd planned, it was better than sitting around staring into each other's eyes. She had to keep him at a distance. Start putting back the barriers between them. For his sake and hers.

WATCHING ANNA GET strapped into the bungee harness, Marc felt a large, fierce hand clutch his heart and squeeze hard. His gaze shot to the platform where another tourist with a death wish was stepping tremulously to the edge. With a smothered howl, the young guy leaped off, and Marc watched him plunge fifty meters toward the ground before the bungee cord halted his fall.

He turned back to Anna, determined. "This is stupid. Don't do it," he said.

She frowned, shook her head. "It'll be fine. They've been doing this for years."

"Anna, one of the guys at the hotel said a woman ruptured her bowel doing this last year."

She just shrugged. "I'll be fine."

He regarded her broodingly. She'd been like this since yes-

terday morning. On the surface she was the same old Anna, bu
something vital had been withdrawn from public display. She'
thrown herself into the scuba and parasailing, insisting on doin
the most extreme version of each activity, pushing their guide
to made it faster, harder, scarier.

In bed, she was intense, driven, wild—incredibly sexually sat
isfying, but the woman he'd made love to in the villa's privat
pool was AWOL. And he wanted her back.

"I don't understand why you're doing this," he said, angry nov

"It's on my list," she said. "I want to do it."

"What list? What are you talking about?" But she just shoo
her head again. The guide was preparing to lead her toward th
jump-off point, and Marc grabbed her arm.

"Anna—please, don't do it. For me?"

She stared at him a moment, and he saw something dark an
scared in her eyes. Then she seemed to shake it off.

"Relax. I'll be fine," she said.

He set his jaw as she shuffled toward the jump-off poin
furious with her and himself for letting this happen.

She glanced across at him once before she moved to the ver
edge of the platform, offering him a thumbs-up. That wa
supposed to reassure him, he assumed. He turned his back de
liberately, but he couldn't not watch.

Knuckles white as he gripped the balustrade of the viewin
area, Marc felt his heart stop as she leaped out into space.

"Jesus," he hissed under his breath as she plunged down int
the ravine.

If ever he'd needed a revelatory moment, this was it. He love
Anna. Yes, he was a mess, but he'd been half in love with her fo
weeks and just because he hadn't said it out loud to her didn'
make it any less true. He should have said it that night in the pool
The words had been in his mind. But the shadow of Tara's infi
delity and the failure of his marriage still hung over him. *Yo*

never asked why, Marc. He needed to know why his marriage had died. He needed to understand before he could offer a future to Anna. But he should have said something. She deserved it. He'd wasted enough time. He made a silent promise to himself that the second he was alone with her he'd tell her how he felt.

His gut clenched with fear as she neared the bottom of the drop, and his gaze switched to the bungee cord. If it should fail… But she was already bouncing back up, her cry of triumph and exhilaration bouncing off the canyon walls. His pulse settled, and he realized she was safe. Just a matter of waiting for her to be winched back up now.

She was rosy-cheeked and starry-eyed with excitement when she was released from the safety harness. She bounded to him and threw her arms around his neck, kissing him passionately.

"That was the most amazing bloody thing in the world!" she said, then she started dragging him away.

He followed her willingly, unsure of what they were doing until she dragged him off the path back to the car park and into the jungle.

"Anna," he said. "Where are you going?"

She tugged on his hand, pulling him farther into the dense foliage.

"I want to do it, here, right now," she said as they stepped into a clearing.

"What…?" Marc asked even as she ripped her top over her head, her breasts jiggling as she tugged off her bra.

"I want you to screw me. Now," she said, reaching for his belt buckle.

For a second he allowed his desire to guide him, his erection already growing in his boxers, but there was a frantic desperation to Anna and he sensed that something was very wrong.

"Anna, stop," he said as she grappled with the closure on his pants.

She shot him a frustrated look and reached inside his boxer to grab his erection. Determined to get to the bottom of this, he stepped backward and grabbed her hands.

"No. Not until you talk to me."

She froze. "I don't want to talk," she said.

"Tough. You've been running around like a teenager with a death wish for the past two days. I want to know what's going on."

She flushed, then went very pale. Then her chin came up. "I'm having fun. That's what this is supposed to be about, isn't it? This holiday, us? Fun?"

She reached for his crotch again, but again he stilled her.

"This isn't just fun anymore and we both know it. Anna, I love you," he said, trying to pull her close.

But she dug her heels in, eyes wide as she held herself away from him.

"No, you don't. It's just the sex. That's all. It'll pass," she said. It sounded like something she'd said to herself a hundred times.

"No, it's not. I love you. I want to share my life with you. I don't want to go back to separate beds and stupid rules about no strings, no future."

She stared at him, then she crossed her arms over her chest and turned away. Fishing her bra from the forest floor, she slid it on and fastened the clasp with shaking hands. He watched her frowning. What was going on? He knew she felt something for him.

She turned back to him once she had her tank top back on.

"I'm sorry, Marc, but it's over," she said. It was the last thing he'd expected.

"What?"

"I don't want a relationship. I explained that to you right at the start. Sorry, but that's just the way it is."

"I didn't want one, either, but we're great together, Anna," he said, not quite believing this. "I know you feel something for me. This has been about a lot more than sex for a long time."

"Maybe," she conceded. "Which is why it's best to end things now. You're a good-looking, successful guy, Marc—you'll meet someone else. Believe me, I have nothing to offer you."

"That's bull, and you know it!"

She threw a hand in the air, and he saw that she was close to tears. He reached for her. "Anna…"

"Just leave it, Marc. I want to go back to the hotel."

Pushing him away, she headed back toward the road. Frowning, hurt and confused, Marc stared after her. What the hell was going on?

ANNA STARTED PACKING the moment she got back to the villa. Marc lingered downstairs, and when he at last joined her in the bedroom he surveyed her half-filled suitcase with disbelieving eyes.

"There's a flight out this evening. I'm going to see if I can get a seat."

She couldn't look at him. She felt as though she was going to be sick, all her feelings were pushed down so hard inside her. She flinched when he crossed the room and slammed her case shut.

"You're not going anywhere until we talk. Tell me what this is about, Anna."

"It's over, Marc. We agreed, when one of us wanted out, that was it. I want out," she said. It would have been more convincing if her voice hadn't quavered, but she'd said it.

He reached out, pulling her to him. Catching her chin, he forced her head up so she was looking him in the eye.

"Now say it. Tell me you don't love me and I'll let you go."

She swallowed unshed tears and steeled herself to hold his eye. "I don't love you."

"Liar."

But he let her go. Hands shaking, she jammed the rest of her clothes into her case, then began checking the wardrobe and drawers for anything she may have left behind. He stood watch-

ing her for a while, then he turned on his heel and left. She heard
the slam of the front door as he left the villa, and sank onto the
edge of the bed.

Sobs shook her body. It was the hardest thing she'd ever done.
Harder than nursing her mother those last few weeks. Harder than
sitting opposite her doctor and hearing the bad news about her
own diagnosis.

Hauling in a deep breath, she wiped her arm across her eyes.
She had to keep moving, get this over and done with. It was best
for both of them. One day, Marc would thank her, she knew.

THE SKY IN SYDNEY SEEMED brighter, wider when Marc returned
home. A car was waiting at the airport, and he handed his case
to the driver and slid into the backseat.

Impossible not to think of Anna when he saw the driver get
into the front, his chauffeur's cap perched on his head. Brooding,
Marc stared out the window as they pulled away from the curb.

She'd been gone when he got back to the villa. He'd been
tempted to follow her, but pride held him at the hotel. He'd seen
out the remaining two days of their holiday, given her some
breathing room. But he wasn't giving up. They were meant for
each other. He knew it in his bones, and he was not going to rest
until he'd gotten to the bottom of her rejection.

If she truly didn't love him, if there was some root cause that
would stop them being together, then he would walk away. But
he hadn't achieved the status of millionaire by thirty by giving
up on things he wanted.

There were other issues to sort out before he tackled Anna
again, however. Pulling his mobile phone from his carry-on bag,
he hit the speed dial for his old home in Balmain. As luck would
have it, John answered the call.

"Is Tara there?" he asked. Surprisingly, he felt only a mild
twinge at the thought of the other man occupying his former home.

There was a long silence, then Tara picked up the line. "Marc. How can I help you?" She was wary, cautious.

"I need to talk. Can I come over?" he asked bluntly.

"I don't think that's a good idea," she said hesitantly. "John's here."

"I don't give a toss about John. I need to ask you something."

She said yes, and half an hour later he was exiting the car in front of the gracious double-fronted Victorian terrace that he had once shared with Tara. It felt like a lifetime ago.

She opened the door before he could knock, showing him into the front living room.

"You look very tan. Have you been on holiday?" she asked politely.

"Bali," he said briefly.

"I see. Can I get you a coffee? Or something else to drink?" he asked, hands clenched tightly in front of her.

"Relax, Tara, I'm not here to beat my chest."

Her shoulders dropped a margin and she studied him closely. "Then why are you here, Marc?"

"You said I never asked. But I want to know now. Why did you have an affair? Why did our marriage fall apart?"

She sat opposite him, her eyes sad. "Marc, we never saw each other. It was inevitable, even if I hadn't had an affair. You were obsessed with the business. So driven. And before you say that I was happy to reap the benefits of your hard work, I know that. I let it happen, too. But there are more important things. Love. Companionship. Passion. But the only thing you seemed interested in was being the provider, the big money earner."

He stared at her, feeling his defenses bristling. "That was my job. I was the husband last time I looked."

"But it wasn't a life sentence, Marc. I was always happy to share the burden. But you wouldn't let me work. And you wouldn't even talk about starting a family until you had all your ducks in a row—the business earning a certain amount, the right house, the right cars. I realized one day that it was never going to be enough for you."

"That wasn't true. I was ready to try for kids," he said, but the words sounded hollow even to his own ears.

"With who? Me, the stranger you occasionally brushed past in the hallway?" Tara wiped a tear off her cheek. "I was lonely, Marc. And I should have had the courage to get out of our marriage before I started anything with John. But I wasn't brave enough. I knew how much it meant to you that our marriage was a success. I didn't want to hurt you."

"Nice job." But there was no sting in his words.

"Yeah, I know," she said.

There was a long silence as he processed what she'd said and realized that it was mostly accurate. He *had* been an absentee husband. He *had* been obsessed with ensuring their security. And it seemed that his obsession had cost him his marriage.

"I know that being different from your father is very important to you. When we were married, I always knew that I never had to worry about you being unfaithful, because you were so determined to be better than him, a good provider and a loyal husband. The saddest thing of all is that in trying to be everything that your father wasn't, you pushed me away. You might as well have been off with some other woman, or doing a stint picking grapes or harvesting apples," she said.

"Believe me now, they're two very different things. You should talk to my mother sometime," he said, unable to let Tara paint it all her way.

"No. You're right. I'm sorry," she conceded. "But the fact remains that you simply weren't there most of the time. I was lonely."

Marc's hands were locked together, and he was fighting the urge to deny all the things Tara was piling on him. She had played a part in the dissolution of their marriage, too. But he also knew she was right. Deep in his heart he knew it was true.

It was an ugly irony that in dedicating himself to being the "perfect" husband, the ultimate provider, he had destroyed any chance his marriage had had. He'd thought that being faithful to Tara and ensuring their security was enough. But he hadn't been present, he knew that in his gut. He'd been busy elsewhere. And his wife had forged her own life despite him.

He looked up to find Tara watching him. "I'm sorry. I'm sorry if I made you unhappy," he said, and he meant it.

Another tear rolled down her cheek. "We made each other unhappy, Marc. If I had had the courage of my convictions, if I'd spoken up when you first started slipping away from me, we might have had a chance. But I wasn't brave enough. I've never been very courageous, I'm afraid. But I'm getting there. I've had to."

Another long silence stretched between them.

"Can I ask you something?" Tara asked tentatively.

"Of course."

"It's personal," she warned. "Have you met someone else? Is that why you're here?"

"Yes."

Tara smiled. "I'm glad. And I'm glad you came to talk. You'll make someone else a great husband, you know. Just as I'm going to make John a great wife. Maybe our marriage was the mistake we both had to make before we could find ourselves."

Marc shifted in his seat. "It wasn't all bad," he defended lightly. "I distinctly remember some good times."

"So do I." She just smiled at him, and he realized that he couldn't find a shred of resentment or anger toward her.

His marriage was truly over. And he was ready to move on. With Anna, if he could just work out what was driving her.

He stood, offering Tara his hand. "Thanks. You've been...extremely helpful."

Tara ignored his hand and embraced him, her cheek cool against his. "Look after yourself, Marc. And good luck. She's a lucky woman."

He only hoped that he could convince Anna to share the same opinion.

12

IT WAS AMAZING how a person could still function when it felt as though her heart had been ripped out of her chest and stomped on. It had been four days since Anna had come home from Bali on her own. Her tan was fading. But every day the ache in her chest grew more painful. She'd done the right thing, though. She'd said it to herself so many times now that it had become a mantra. And she believed it, she really did. But it didn't make the pain go away.

Standing in front of the bathroom mirror, she decided she looked awful. Her skin seemed waxy despite her tan, her eyes dead. She told herself it was because she couldn't sleep. But she knew it was because she was grieving. For so many things. The loss of her childhood when she'd nursed her mother through the final weeks of her illness. For the loss of the woman she could have been, if she hadn't had the specter of death hovering over her world. For Marc, for the love they'd shared. For those few amazing weeks of joy, pleasure and pain.

Sighing, she pulled open the vanity cabinet and dragged out her makeup bag. Blusher and a heavy hand with some sparkly eye shadow made her look presentable. She tried a smile. Academy Award–winning.

"God, you look terrible," Danny said the moment he opened the door. "What did they do to you in Bali?"

"Thanks a lot," she said, shoving her gift at him and moving past him into his open-plan warehouse apartment.

Movement caught her eye and she turned to see Ben getting up from the sofa.

"Ben," she said, surprised. Her brother had invited her over for dinner, and she'd assumed it would just be the two of them. Had been looking forward to it, actually. She needed very badly to unburden herself right now, even just a little. Even just to tell him things were over with Marc felt as though it would be a release.

"Hi," Ben said. "How was Bali?"

She realized he looked nervous. What was going on here? She turned to Danny, and caught him mid complicated eyebrow semaphore with Ben.

"Have I interrupted something?" she asked, glancing back and forth between the two of them.

"No," Ben said at exactly the same time that her brother said, "Yes."

"Okay," she said. She switched her attention to Danny. "Do you want to reschedule? We can do this another time."

"You haven't interrupted anything," Danny clarified. "It's just that Ben thinks we should wait a little longer before we start publicizing. But you know me—boots and all."

Anna frowned as her brother crossed to stand beside the other man, putting his arm around him. She smiled as realization dawned.

"*Ohhhh,*" she said, nodding knowingly. "You guys got together at last, yeah?"

"Yep. Ben's moving in with me," Danny said. She couldn't help but notice the slightly defiant note to his voice. It was so typically Danny to go from one extreme to another like this. Only he could switch from being the poster boy for partying to suddenly becoming Mr. Committed in the space it took her to go to Bali and ruin her life.

"That's great," she said, and she meant it. Okay, a year ago she would have been freaking on the inside, worried her brother was moving too quickly. But she knew better now. Life was for living. If he and Ben had a chance at happiness, they should go for it.

"We know it's early days," Ben said, obviously worried about what she thought. "But we both feel strongly. When you know, you know. You know?"

"I know," Anna said, aware there was a sad note in her voice. Oh, how she knew.

"Great, well, that's one down. Just Dad to go," Danny said, moving away from Ben and heading for the kitchen.

"What?" Anna said, shocked. "You're going to tell Dad?"

Danny took the lid off a steaming pot on the stove. "We're having carbs. Pasta, in fact. I know they're a no-no after six but Ben loves pasta." He shot the other man an indulgent look.

Anna batted off his distraction. "Danny. You can't just drop something like that and expect me not to react. You've decided to come out to Dad?"

"I'm twenty-eight. I'm sick of pretending to be something I'm not. Ben and I told the people at work yesterday, you today, and that just leaves you-know-who."

Danny's tone was light, but his hands were shaking as he put the lid back on the pot.

"I think it's great," she said gently. "You know I've wanted you to do this for ages."

"There hasn't been a good enough reason before." Danny shrugged. Ben came and stood beside him, sliding his hand into Danny's back pocket. Clearly they were still in the "inseparable" stage of their relationship.

"Dad loves you, Danny. He would never reject you," Anna said. It was a discussion they'd had a million times, but Danny had always argued that what their father didn't know wouldn't hurt him. Anna knew that deep down he was afraid that he would lose their father's love when he told him who he really was.

Looking at them standing there, hips leaning against each

other, affection evident in every glance they exchanged, she realized that her brother had at last found something to help him make the step into being proud of his sexuality. Love was pretty powerful stuff.

Before she started getting sappy, she reached into her bag and pulled out the bottle of champagne she'd brought to go with dinner.

"Well, now we've got a proper reason for opening this," she said.

Ben busied himself getting flutes from the cupboard, and Anna dumped her bag on the kitchen counter.

"So how did it go with the hot stud? Or is that why you look so exhausted?" Danny asked as he flicked on another burner on the stove and poured olive oil into a frying pan.

"It was fine. Great. But we decided it was probably best to end it. You know," Anna said. She thought she did a creditable job of sounding casual, but Danny stopped what he was doing and stared at her.

"Once more, with a little more feeling this time," he suggested drily.

She shrugged, darting a glance at Ben as he poured the champagne. "It's over. I really don't want to talk about it."

Danny looked as though he was about to argue the point, but Ben tactfully started asking about Bali, and conversation soon fell to comparing Asian holiday destinations. They were carrying their bowls of pasta across to the table when Danny spotted the brochure in her bag.

"Hey, what's this?" he asked, sliding the glossy pages free.

"What? Oh, yeah. I'm buying a motorbike," she explained as she pulled out a chair.

Danny frowned. "This is a Ducati, Anna. Do you have any idea how fast these things go? And how much they cost?"

"Sure. Why do you think I want one?" she said, smiling at Ben as he passed her the parmesan cheese and pepper mill.

Danny sat down at the table and pushed the brochure toward her.

"Twenty thousand dollars for a bike? Where are you going to get that kind of money?"

"Danny," Anna said, shooting Ben an embarrassed look.

"Sorry, but this is important," Danny said, his gaze remaining fixed on her.

Finally she sighed, lifting a shoulder impatiently. "I have investments. I pulled in a pretty nice income when I was a lawyer, you know."

"Enough that you can afford to blow twenty grand on a bike when you've just started up a small business?"

She rolled her eyes, stabbing her fork into her food. "Can we please change the record? It's a beautiful bike, and I've always wanted to learn to ride. I don't see the issue."

"I did the creative for the road authority's awareness campaign on motorbikes last year. Do you have any idea how many motorcyclists are killed annually?"

"You can get killed crossing the road, Danny. Or die slowly in a hospital bed. I'm happy to take my chances."

Danny stared at her for a long beat. "Please don't get a bike. They're dangerous. They're stupid."

She just stared back at him.

"At least promise me you'll sleep on it a few weeks before you take the plunge," he finally conceded.

"Fine. I'll sleep on it. Happy?"

"No. Something's going on, but I'm not going to try to drag it out of you if you don't want to talk. That's never worked with you."

She felt a pang at the hurt in Danny's voice. It was true, she was reverting to Old Anna tactics, not telling him what was really going on in her world. But it was too hard to talk about right now. Too raw. Maybe, in a few weeks, a month maybe, she would be able to explain.

"So, have you thought about how you're going to tell Dad?" she asked, deliberately changing the subject.

Danny shrugged a shoulder. "Just invite him over here like this, I guess," he said. "Introduce him to Ben, get it over with."

"Mmm," she said thoughtfully, privately appalled. It would be tantamount to slapping their father in the face with a dead fish.

"What?"

"Nothing. I just thought it might be easier if you did it on Dad's turf. And without Ben there. Sorry, Ben, but I think Dad might find it a bit confronting, first off the bat. He'll be fine with it, but if you're there he'll feel he has to put on an act…."

"And that's a bad thing?" Danny joked. She could see he felt sick about it, though.

"I think you should listen to her," Ben said quietly. "And, like I said before, you don't have to do this yet."

"Yeah, I do. I don't want to slink around pretending that we don't exist. We're better than that," Danny said, and Anna had to look away from the love and passion in her brother's eyes. If ever she'd had any doubts, that look killed them.

She put her hand on Danny's arm. "Do you want me to come with you? Even if I just wait out in the car?"

She could see he was tempted, but Danny shook his head. "I'm a big boy. I should do this on my own."

"Well, the offer's there if you need it. And think about what I said about doing it somewhere Dad is comfortable."

"Sure, thanks."

She didn't push any further. Who was she to be offering anyone advice, anyway? She'd made such a mess of her own life. God, she wanted Marc so much that she felt hollow inside. Hollow and desperate.

"Anna. Are you okay?" Danny asked suddenly.

She realized she'd been staring at the table, and that her eyes were full of tears.

"No. But I will be," she assured him.

If only she believed it. If only she didn't crave Marc with every breath she took. Why did doing the right thing have to hurt so much?

MARC HUNG UP the phone, frustrated as all get-out. He'd left half a dozen messages on Anna's machine and mobile, he'd sent flowers, he'd sat out front at her apartment like a two-bit stalker—but it had been nearly a week since Bali and he still hadn't been able to catch her. And he got the distinct feeling things would continue that way if she had her chops.

He ran a hand over his face. How did you get through to someone who was determined to avoid you? And was he an idiot to even keep trying? Maybe he was just reading things into the time he'd spent with Anna. Just because he'd fallen head over heels in love with her—despite all his reasons not to—didn't mean she felt the same. She'd called him arrogant more than once. Wasn't it the height of arrogance to assume she felt the same as he did?

But no matter what he said to himself, it didn't stop the way he felt. Maybe it wasn't rational. But he felt it in his gut, in his bones—that night in the pool, he'd looked into her eyes and her heart had been there. They had touched souls, not just body parts.

He was pacing in his study, the same few squares of space that he'd been walking ever since he got back from Bali. As he turned on his heel, his eye slid over a shot of himself and Alison. It had been taken a few years ago at his sister's birthday—

That was it! Galvanized, Marc sprang for the keyboard on his laptop, clicking his tongue impatiently as the screen dragged itself back from sleep mode. Anna had a brother. Danny. She'd mentioned him several times. He even vaguely knew what the guy looked like. Fingers stabbing at the keyboard, he called up the online white pages and typed in Daniel Jackson. Three pages of listings came up and he stared at the screen in disgust. How to narrow it down? Screwing up his face, he tried to remember if Anna had ever mentioned where her brother lived, or what he did for a living. His expression cleared as their night at the hotel came back to him. She'd joked about Danny winning an award for a print advertising campaign. And she'd laughed over the fact that he'd caught a taxi to her place to collect her, even though his apartment was in Surry Hills, just five minutes from the hotel where the awards had been held.

Tongue between his teeth, Marc typed the suburb into the search field to refine his selection. Then let out a big gust of air—there was one Daniel Jackson in Surry Hills, but "for privacy reasons" he'd requested a silent number.

Marc swore, then grabbed the phone. He was dialing his personal assistant's number when he realized it was nearly eleven. Slowly he put the phone down. He was a demanding boss, but not that demanding. He would have to wait until tomorrow, but it should be an easy matter of finding out from the awards organizers where Danny Jackson worked. And then he would have a conduit to Anna.

Staring out the window at the dark night sky, Marc let himself remember what it felt like to kiss her, to be inside her, to hold her in his arms. He had to take a shot. He didn't have a choice.

DANNY'S HAND FELT DAMP as Anna slid hers into it and gave him a squeeze.

"Okay, big breath, in we go," she said as they walked up the garden path to their father's house.

Danny had called her the day after their dinner to take her up on her offer to come with him.

"It might make me the world's biggest pussy, but, hey, I'm gay. I'm supposed to be a big wuss," he'd said.

Anna didn't think he was a wuss at all. She thought he was

incredibly brave. There was no doubt that this would be the most difficult conversation of Danny's life.

"Hey! I didn't know you were coming to the movies with us, sweetie," their Dad said as he opened the front door and saw them both standing there. "Fantastic, the more the merrier."

It was a Thursday night, Danny and her father's regularly scheduled movie night. He had his jacket in hand, and he stepped toward them, starting to pull the door closed behind him, ready to head off to the cinema complex.

Danny shot Anna a panicked look. "Um, Dad. Do you think we could step inside for a moment?" she improvised.

"Sure. You need to powder your nose or something?"

Anna smiled, not wanting to worry her father unnecessarily. If she told him she wanted to talk to him, she knew what conclusion he'd jump to. He'd think it was about her being sick again, and she didn't want to put him through that unnecessarily. And this was Danny's news, not hers. She was just here to hold his hand, literally and figuratively.

"Yeah," she said. She could feel Danny's tension as he followed her into the house. They stood awkwardly in the tidy living room, everything around them neat as a pin. Anna shot her eyes to Danny, and he grimaced nervously. Slowly their father seemed to realize that something was up.

But before he could voice his concern, Danny turned to him. "Dad, there's something I need to tell you," he said. His voice quavered uncertainly, and Anna swallowed, anxiety tightening her own belly.

In the car on the way over, Danny had joked that he'd come up with a foolproof way of breaking the news: *Hey, Dad, I'm dying. Just kidding—I'm only gay.*

They'd laughed about it, because they'd needed to release the tension. But the truth was that there was no foolproof way.

"Listen," Danny started again. "You know how all these years you keep asking me when I'm going to settle down with one girl and stop playing the field?"

Their father frowned. "Yeah?" Then his face cleared. "Danny—you're not going to tell me you've got some girl pregnant?" he asked.

Anna bit her lip. Danny looked anguished.

"No. I haven't got a girl pregnant. The thing is, Dad. All these years... I'm not really into girls, if you know what I mean."

There was a profound silence in the room. Their father looked baffled for a beat. Anna reached out to touch his forearm.

"Are you saying...are you saying you're gay, Danny?" he finally asked.

Danny sucked in a big breath. "Yes. That's what I'm saying. I'm gay."

The words seemed to resonate in the small space. Their father lifted a hand, then dropped it as though he wasn't quite sure what to do with it.

"For how long?" he finally asked. "How long have you known?"

"Since high school, Dad. Since I was about fifteen."

Their father nodded, then turned to Anna, his face carefully blank. "And you've known all along?"

"Pretty much," she said.

"Well." He just stood there for a few more beats, and then he turned on his heel and exited the room.

Anna gasped, her hand going to Danny's arm as his shoulders sagged.

"Shit!" Danny said. "Shit! That was just great. Gosh, I wonder why I've put off doing that for so many years?"

He was crying, and he dashed the tears away angrily. Anna tried to pull him into her arms. "He was just shocked. He'll come around."

"Will he? What's a bet there won't be any more cosy movie nights. My friend Phil's father never touched him again once he came out, you know. Afraid it was catching, I guess."

Danny was working himself up into a state. Anna grabbed both his arms and gave him a shake. "Stop it! I'm going to go talk to him. He's shocked. Give him a chance. You've been playing a part with him for years, Danny. Of course he's going to need to adjust. Be fair."

She wasn't sure if he heard her, but she left him and stepped into the hallway. Her father's bedroom door was closed, and she tapped on it lightly.

"Dad? Can I come in?"

There was no answer, but she heard a muffled sound and realized that her father was crying. Without hesitation she pushed the door open. He was huddled on the edge of the bed, sobbing into his hands.

"Dad!" she said. She hadn't seen him this distressed for years. Not since her mother died.

Sitting beside him, she slid her arm around his shoulders. "It doesn't change anything. Danny's still the same person he's always been. He still loves you," she said tentatively.

Her father made an inarticulate sound, then lifted his tear-streaked face.

"All these years with you kids. I've tried to make up for your mother not being around, to be mother and father. But I've obviously failed. All these years, and Danny was too scared to tell me the truth!"

Anna stared at him. "You're not upset that he's gay?" she clarified.

Her father bristled. "What sort of a bigot do you think I am? Danny's my son. I'll always love him, no matter what."

She almost laughed with relief. Her father was hurt that Danny hadn't told him earlier! He wasn't about to repudiate him for being gay.

"Dad, Danny is out there in the living room right now thinking that you can't handle the fact that he's gay," she explained carefully. "I think it would be great if you went out there and told him what you just told me."

"But that's just stupid," her dad said.

"There's a reason he's held on to this for so long, Dad. He's been so scared of what you would think."

"When have I ever said a thing against gays? Tell me?"

"It's not you. It's everyone else. The kids at school when he was growing up. People on the streets sometimes. I've been with Danny and his friends when people have hung out car windows and screamed abuse at them. Hell, I've even been called a fag hag."

"That's disgusting. You're far too attractive to be a fag hag."

Anna choked back a laugh as her father surged to his feet.

"Danny!" he called out imperatively as he left the room.

She stayed where she was. This next bit they could do without her. Her eye fell on the ornate photo frame beside the bed. It was a photograph of her parents on their wedding day. She picked it up, smiling down at their youthful faces. They'd both been so young, just twenty and twenty-two. But, as her father had explained more than once over the years, they'd been in love, and nothing was going to stop them.

She could see it in their faces, too, as they stared adoringly at each other. Her fingers clenched around the frame. Her father had never stopped loving her mother. She knew how it felt now, to love someone that much.

Standing, she put the frame back on the bedside table. It had to get easier. It just had to.

MARC TAPPED HIS FINGERS on his steering wheel, eyes glued to the entrance to the apartment block across the road. A grim smile twisted his lips. In the space of a few days, he'd been reduced to this—sitting out the front of Anna's brother's apartment, waiting like some desperate teen suitor. If he wasn't so determined to win Anna around, it'd be funny.

He sat up straighter as a black Mercedes pulled up at the front of the building. His pulsed quickened—it was Anna! He'd hoped to talk to her brother, but she was actually here, right now. Movements jerky, he shoved the car door open and shot out of the car. But he'd barely taken a step across the road before she was pulling away, leaving her brother to step into the building.

Marc hesitated, staring after the receding lights of her car. God, it was good just to see her, even just a glimpse. He shook his head at his own thoughts. Man, did he have it bad or what? Maybe the desperate-teen analogy hadn't been too far off after all.

Squaring his shoulders, he headed across the road. He knew what apartment number her brother lived in now, where he worked, what car he drove. It had only taken twenty-four hours to find out the essentials. He took the steps to the second floor and counted off the doors until he found apartment two-twenty. Determined, he knocked briskly.

Danny opened the door, and he could see another man standing in the background, a bottle of wine and a corkscrew in hand. He knew from what Anna had said that her brother was gay, so he didn't bat an eyelid.

"Danny, you don't know me, but I need your help—"

"I know you," Danny said, cutting him off midflow. "You're Marc Lewis."

"Anna's spoken about me?" he asked, hope surging.

"Not lately, no," Danny said, a distinctly cool note entering his voice. "You must have stuffed up pretty badly."

Marc realized this was his chance, here and now.

"I love her. And I think she loves me. But she broke it off, and she won't return my calls," he said, aware there was raw need in his voice, but not having the time or energy to be embarrassed about it. There were bigger, more important fish to fry.

"Ah," Danny said as though he'd just found the vital piece of a puzzle. "I see." He turned to the blond guy with the wine bottle, obviously gauging his opinion. When he turned back, he stepped away from the door.

"Perhaps you'd better come in," he said. "I'm not promising anything, mind, but Anna's been pretty miserable lately."

Marc ducked his head in acknowledgment. Passing inside, he prepared to put his case forward—someone had to help him get through to Anna.

ANNA TUGGED the two pieces of leather hard, and finally squeezed the stud through the hole. Sighing, she let her tummy out. There was a distinct possibility that she'd bought her leather bike pants a size too small. She sank onto her haunches, then stood back up again. The brand-new leather was supple but squeaky, and she decided that it would give enough so that she wouldn't have to do battle with the zipper every time.

Reaching for her leather gauntlets and her bike helmet, she started toward the door. She'd had her learner bike permit for two days, and this would be only her third ride on her spanking new Ducati S2R 1000. She'd yet to find out what it could really do, to really open it out and hammer it, but already she was reveling in the sense of freedom the bike gave her. The powerful throb of the motor between her legs, the adrenaline rush of being so exposed, so vulnerable—she really knew she was alive when she was riding.

A nice change from the rest of her life, that was for sure. When she was riding was the only time she didn't think about Marc. It was possible that would wear off as she became more accustomed to the demands of the bike. And then she'd simply have to find something else to push the limits. Whatever it took. That was the name of the game she was playing.

Opening the front door, she pulled up short as she saw Danny there, hand raised ready to knock.

"Hi," she said, suppressing a guilty little shiver when she saw his expression darken.

"What are you doing? Are those bike leathers?" Danny demanded instantly.

She sighed. "Yes. Before you ask, I bought the Ducati. Quick, get the hissy fit over and done with."

"This is because of Marc Lewis, isn't it? You fell in love with him and now you're freaking out, aren't you? Talk to me, Anna," Danny demanded.

"This is about my life, nothing else. Getting the most out of every last minute."

"You won't have many more last minutes if you keep going on like this. I've seen Marc. He told me about the bungee jumping. And the parasailing and the scuba diving and God knows what else you've been up to. Are you trying to die, Anna? Is that it?"

"What do you mean, you've seen Marc?" she asked, paling.

"He came to see me. He was desperate. He told me what happened in Bali."

That explained why the phone calls had stopped. A part of her felt a little thrill that he was being so persistent. But it was pointless.

"I told him to come over. I think you should talk to him," Danny said.

"Just because you're Mr. Out and Proud doesn't suddenly make you an expert on relationships, Danny! I don't want to see him."

"Fine, then I'll just send him on up and you can tell him that yourself," Danny said.

Anna choked. "He's here? Now?" Her pulse jumped crazily. God, she wanted to see him so much. Even just hear the sound of his voice.

"Waiting in his car downstairs. You need to talk to him, Anna," Danny said.

Furious tears welled up in her eyes as she glared at him. "You are my brother, and I am telling you that I don't want this," she said.

"It's for your own good. You've been stewing on your own

for too long," Danny said, and she watched with growing panic as he turned and headed down the stairs to get Marc.

For a moment she just stood there, filled with fear, then she spun around and strode toward the back door.

MARC GOT OUT of his car as Danny exited Anna's apartment block.

"Man, she is so damn stubborn!" Danny said, shaking his head. "Good luck—she's in one hell of a mood."

"I never thought it was going to be easy. Nothing with Anna ever has been," Marc said wryly, an absurd hope in his heart. At least now he had a chance. He would sit her down and talk to her until the cows came home if he had to, but she was going to admit she loved him or give him a damned good reason why they couldn't be together.

He had a gut feel about what that reason might be now that Danny had told him about Anna's cancer scare. Danny had been guilt-stricken over betraying his sister's confidence when he realized Marc didn't know about her lumpectomy. He'd just assumed Anna would have told him such an important thing. But she hadn't. In fact, she'd deliberately lied about how she got her scar. Which was why Marc knew it was important, pivotal even.

Clapping Danny gratefully on the back, Marc turned toward the building. He was going in.

He'd barely taken a step forward when the sound of a motorcycle being revved to life echoed down the apartment block's driveway.

"Shit!" Danny said, breaking into a run.

"What's going on?" Marc demanded, instinctively following the other man.

"Anna's bought herself this monster of a motorbike. A bloody Ducati!" Danny explained, just as a motorbike shot past them and out into the street.

Marc caught Anna's eye briefly as she braked and did a right-hand turn, her technique still a little dicey. He took in the prominent L plate on the rear of the bike and felt a clutch of fear in his belly.

"Anna!" he called, but she shook her head and gunned the throttle. The bike took off just as he lunged forward, and he ran out into the middle of the road, watching her accelerate to the corner of the street where it intersected with the main road.

"Goddamn it!" he cursed, every muscle tense with impotent anger.

Danny came to stand beside him. "She's the most stubborn woman on the planet," he said, almost admiringly.

His eyes still on Anna where she waited at the end of the street, indicator on to signal a left-hand turn, Marc opened his mouth to respond—just as Anna accelerated out into the main intersection. Almost immediately the heart-stopping sound of screeching tires cut through the air, closely followed by the distinct sound of a car hitting something solid.

"Jesus. No!" Marc swore, muscles bunching as he bolted forward. Danny wasn't far behind him as he pounded his way to the end of the street. Marc's lungs felt as though they were going to burst, he was so filled with panic.

Anna had to be okay, she had to.

He rocketed out into the main intersection where a number of cars had pulled up, hazard lights blinking. A middle-aged woman was standing outside her car, hands pressed to her face.

"I didn't see her! I was just turning into my driveway and I didn't see her!" The woman was crying.

Anna was lying on her side against the curb, the bike pinning her body to the ground. Two young guys were working to haul the bike off her as an older woman talked briskly into her mobile phone, calling an ambulance. Anna's body was motionless, Marc saw, and a surge of nausea burned his throat.

"Get out of the way," he hollered brusquely, shoving the shocked young men out of the way and bracing himself to lift the bike. With a surge of adrenaline-fueled power, he wrestled it off her, dropping it to one side and instantly crouching by Anna's still form.

"Anna! Anna, please," he said as he bent over her. She was lying on her left side, her helmeted head in profile to him. Fingers shaking, he slid his hand beneath her chin strap carefully, worried about a spinal injury. To his everlasting relief, he felt a strong and steady pulse beneath his fingers.

"Please tell me she's alive," Danny said, and he realized the other man was crouching beside him, his face creased with fear.

"She's alive."

The sound of an ambulance siren had never been so welcoming. Crouching lower still, Marc lifted the visor on Anna's helmet, needing to see her face. Her eyes were closed, and he could see a dark bruise already forming over her left eye.

"She must have smacked her head against the curb," he guessed.

Then firm hands were on his arm, and two paramedics were taking his place by Anna's side.

He and Danny stood to one side as they slid a spinal collar on and moved Anna onto a spinal board. Throughout, she remained unconscious and Marc almost cracked his teeth, his jaw was clenched so tightly.

At last they were lifting her into the ambulance, Danny climbing in to accompany her to the hospital.

"I'll see you there," Marc promised, already turning to head back to his car.

Anna was alive. And she had to stay that way because he knew without a doubt that he couldn't live without her.

ANNA WOKE with the disorienting sensation of moving while prone. As full consciousness returned, she remembered what had happened. She'd been focused on Marc, thinking about how much she wanted him, then the car had appeared out of nowhere. She'd had a split second before it hit her, and his face had filled her mind.

She tried to move her head, registering the dull ache of a bruise on her face, and the fact that her neck was wrapped in a soft spinal collar.

"She's awake," someone said, and Danny's face appeared above her.

His eyes were damp as he reached for her hand. "Hi," was all he said, and she felt a rush of guilt as she saw how much she'd scared him.

"I'm sorry. I'm so sorry," she said.

Danny shook his head. "Shut up. You're alive. Who cares about anything else?"

But Anna suddenly realized how close she'd come to dying and started trembling with the shock of it.

"It was so stupid. So stupid. What was I thinking?" she muttered over and over.

"Good question," Danny said. "But it can wait."

The ambulance slowed, then there was a jerk as it halted completely.

"Possible concussion, good pupil reaction, no sign of internal bleeding or broken bones," one of the ambulance attendants was reciting to the nurse who helped them pull her gurney from the ambulance.

She'd been so lucky. Not even a broken bone! She stiffened suddenly, remembering the most important thing of all.

"Marc!" she said, trying to sit up. "Where's Marc?"

Marc had been there. Marc had seen everything. He must have been horrified. She could only imagine how she would feel in a similar situation.

The nurse looked to Danny, who shook his head. "Marc's o
his way, Anna," Danny said.

It wasn't what she wanted to hear. Because suddenly sh
knew she'd made a terrible, terrible mistake. The worst mistak
of her life. And she needed to tell him. She needed to ask hir
for a second chance.

"Miss, you need to stay calm," the nurse was saying, her eye
on the blood pressure cuff on Anna's arm. "I'm sure your frien
will be here very soon."

Anna subsided back onto the gurney and they wheeled he
through a short corridor and into a cubicle. She could barely hol
back the tears as she waited for them to have done with he
checking her pupil responses, cutting her expensive new leather
off to check for broken bones. All she cared about was Marc.

She barely listened to the doctor as he explained to Danny th:
they were happy with her overall condition, given the circun
stances, but they would like to keep her in overnight to monit
her concussion. She kept her eyes glued to the small crack of th
outside world visible between the curtains, hoping to see Marc'
tall form there.

Finally, she saw a dark blur of movement, and he was stridin
into the cubicle as though he owned it, dark eyes crisp and a
sessing as he took in the doctor to one side, the pressure cuff sti
attached to her arm, Danny holding her hand.

"Marc," was all she could manage, and she sat up with a jer
and threw herself into his arms.

Despite the throbbing pain of her bruised face, it was lik
coming home, pure bliss. The smell of him, the feel of him, th
essence of him. How she loved him.

She realized she was telling him just that, over and over. "
love you, I love you, I love you." Peppering kisses across his fac
hands grabbing at him. After a few seconds he caught her fac
gently and held her still.

"Easy, Anna. It's okay," he soothed. Vaguely she was aware that Danny and the doctor were making themselves scarce, but he really didn't care who was there.

"I'm so sorry. I thought I was making it better, but I was making it worse. I didn't know," she babbled.

Marc pressed a finger to her lips, infinitely tender. "I know about the cancer, Anna. I understand. I think I do, anyway."

"I didn't want you to be like my father. I didn't want to die leaving so much behind," she said, tears starting in her eyes.

"It's not going to happen, Anna. We'll make sure you have regular checkups. We'll buy organic, for Pete's sake. We'll do whatever it takes. But we won't do it without each other," he said.

There was a great deal of determination and love in his tone and a serious expression in his eyes. Anna closed hers for a moment, scared to think how much she'd almost lost. If it hadn't been for the Ducati...

"Thank God for that bike!" she said reverentially.

"Are you kidding me? I'm going to have the thing melted down to nothing, or crushed or whatever they do. Destroyed utterly. I never want to feel like that again in my life."

"But I would never have realized how stupid I was being. I thought I was being sensible. Smart. But when that car was sliding toward me the only thing I could think about was how much I loved you, and how much I was going to miss out on." She reached up a hand to touch his face lovingly. "I'm so sorry. I'm so sorry for being too scared to believe in a future, for not even trying for a future for us."

"It doesn't matter," he said simply.

Looking into his eyes, she knew he meant it. And that he loved her, body and soul. No matter what their separate intentions, no matter how hard either of them had tried to play the game and keep it to just sex, they'd wound up in the same place.

Marc pressed a kiss to her palm, then held it to his chest.

"I love you, Anna," he said, ducking his head to kiss her.

And even though she was bruised and battered, with a drafty, inadequate hospital gown barely maintaining her dignity, Anna felt the familiar shift of desire deep inside as their tongues met and their lips caressed each other.

"Mmm," she said against his mouth, and she felt him smile.

"Don't go getting any ideas. You've got a head injury, and we're in an emergency ward," he warned her as she strained closer.

"So? I love you, too, by the way," she said, kissing him again.

This time when they pulled apart there was a faint flush on his cheekbones, and he hooked a finger in the gaping neckline of her gown and snuck a peek at her breasts.

He made a strangled noise, but he stepped away.

"Later," he promised her.

"But—" she objected.

"No buts. We've got forever," he said.

And she realized he was right.

SUMMER OF SECRETS

**The series comes to its
stunning conclusion this June with**

SATISFYING
LONERGAN'S HONOR

(Silhouette Desire #1730)

by *USA TODAY* bestselling author
MAUREEN CHILD

Their attraction had been wild...
and too long denied. Now they were
face-to-face once more. Would the secrets
of their past pull them apart again?

On sale this June from Silhouette Desire.

*Available wherever books are sold,
including most bookstores, supermarkets,
discount stores and drugstores.*